EXTREME
FACTION

D1615820

Also by Trevor Scott

EXTREME FACTION

Trevor Scott

Salvo Press
Corpus Christi, Texas

EXTREME FACTION

Copyright © 2011 by Trevor Scott

Salvo Press
Corpus Christi, Texas
www.salvopress.com

Library of Congress Control Number: 2011923640

ISBN: 978-1-60977-022-8

Cover iStock Photos by Sadık Güleç and SCM Studios

Printed in the United States of America

Visit the author at: www.trevorscott.com

Acknowledgments

To the twenty million people of Kurdistan in Iraq, Iran, Turkey and scattered about the Earth, I hope you find freedom and autonomy soon. I by no means wanted to imply with this book that Kurds are terrorists. I have the utmost respect for the Kurdish people everywhere. You are a proud people with a great history and a bright future. To the people of Odessa, Ukraine, please forgive me for placing streets where they shouldn't be. As always, I salute my Air Force, Army, Navy and Marine Corps colleagues past and present—millions of dedicated men and women who have kept this nation free. To the land of the moose and wolves and the Greater Mesabi Men's Book Club, may the beer and the testosterone continue to flow.

PROLOGUE

IRAQI KURDISTAN
March 1988

A cool breeze swept down out of the mountains. The man dressed in the local attire of a sheep herder, his beard thick and dark, sat down against the trunk of a pine. He brought his closed left fist from his side to his lap and slowly opened his fingers. Sitting there, still in shock, was a black beetle, the name of which he had no clue. Suddenly, legs started moving, tickling his palm, as the bug made its way up his index finger and sat helplessly, its antennae scanning the air for an escape route.

Without any further hesitation, the man popped the bug into his mouth, crunched down once and swallowed. Surprised, he hunched his shoulders and started searching among the rocks, needles and leaves for relatives or distant cousins.

Then with the soft, cool air came a sound that he knew well. Jets. More than one. Quickly he pulled a pair of camouflaged folding binoculars from inside his shirt, to his eyes, and began to focus.

Within seconds, two Mirage F1s, side-by-side, swooped down between the mountains, barely above the ragged tree-tops, and crossed right in front of him. He had just a flash to focus the optics as the two jets whizzed by him.

Drop tanks? No. They were on the outer pylons. Some type of bomb.

He only wished he had caught the tail markings, something more than the Iraqi Air Force symbol. Some clue to where they had come from.

In less than a minute, he heard a percussion. Nothing loud like a two thousand pounder. An air burst? That made no sense. The jets would have still been in Iraq. Unless... Then he saw the jets off in the distance, above the mountains, drifting slowly back toward the west like knights having vanquished dragons.

Gathering his backpack, he jumped to his feet and began running along the ridge, pushing back the tree limbs in his way and slipping among the rocky embankment. When he came to a high precipice overlooking the valley below, he stopped suddenly, breathing heavily, and brought the binoculars to his eyes. He expected to see plumes of smoke, buildings burning, maybe even tanks or artillery or some other metal contraption twisted and mangled beyond recognition. But he saw none of that. There was nothing. Only the village.

He checked his map and compass, verifying he wasn't entirely crazy from his diet of bugs and worms for the last few days, but he was right. He could see that the village was in Iraq, although close enough to the border of Iran to almost forgive such a mistake, but only if the pilots too had been sleep deprived like him. This wasn't a mistake.

A shocking revelation swept through his body when he

realized how stupid he had been. An air burst without damage. Proof of why he was there. The Iraqis were using chemicals or biological agents on their own people.

He thought of running as fast he could, but knew he could never outrun what had come from those bombs. Only the air could save him. He grasped a handful of dirt and threw it into the air and watched the particles float off the cliff toward the village. The air would clear toward Iran, he realized. But he would have to wait. How long? Thinking back on his training, he wasn't entirely sure. Perhaps nobody really knew that answer.

After he had made up his mind to ascend the mountain to the village, his plans were changed by repeated air strikes. The second wave had been older MIG 23s, and then the Swiss Pilatus aircraft, turboprops buzzing like a saw through the air. More airbursts followed by cluster bombs.

He watched the sun set on the village that night, and then the next day he slowly worked his way down out of the mountains to a dirt road leading toward the village.

It did not take long for his fears to be realized. First there was the flock of sheep, some twenty or so, lying alongside the road, bloated like someone had pumped them full of air. In the ditch next to them, his arms wrapped around a dog, was the herder, his mouth contorted and his eyes missing. His skin was blotched with pustules.

He wanted to be anywhere but there. He could simply turn around and make his way north across the border into Turkey, the way he had come. Find a phone and contact Incirlik to have an air force helicopter pick him up. But for some reason he knew he had not seen the worst of it.

He had to move forward, if for no other reason than to witness the horror that lay ahead.

When he reached the village, there would be no escape now. Corpses lay strewn about the street, piled like firewood against ancient stone walls. Moans of pain echoed through the alleys.

He drifted among those still living, some with horrible open sores on their face, hands and arms. It was not as if he knew what he had to do, as he knew what he had to see and hear and feel. With all his knowledge and training, he was still helpless. He could do nothing. And perhaps that was the greatest horror of all.

That evening, as he stumbled out of town, he came across the young woman. She was perhaps fifteen, with long black hair, passionate eyes that had been crying for a long time, and a blank stare looking off to nowhere.

She had been to the village, she said. Everyone was dead in her family but her. And only because she had been sent to the neighboring village to buy a goat for her father. Now she could not even find the goat. She searched about the area, her eyes shifting wildly. The goat was gone.

He took her into his arms and held her. Then the two of them shuffled out of the village, never turning back, never trying to think what had happened there. To think would drive to insanity, for insanity is what it was.

1

ODESSA, UKRAINE
Now

A red glow lingered across the Black Sea harbor, as the dark Volga sedan pulled up to the curb at the base of the Potemkin Steps. The driver cut the lights, but kept the engine running.

In the passenger seat, Jake Adams started to open the door.

"Just a minute," the driver said, reaching for the glove box. He retrieved a bundle, a rag wrapped around something and held in place with a rubber band. "Here. You might need this. Odessa is a dangerous place now."

Jake took the package from Tully O'Neill, the Odessa station chief for the new CIA. "I see the Agency spares no expense with packaging," Jake said.

The driver let out a breath of air as he lit one cigarette from another.

As Jake unwrapped the package, he found what he had asked for earlier in the day, a 9mm automatic. "A Makarov?" Jake said. "Jesus Christ, are you trying to get me killed?"

Tully hunched his shoulders and puffed on his cigarette, bringing the tip to a bright orange. "Short notice," he said. "Took it off a dead Russian last month."

"How'd he get that way?"

The Odessa station chief smiled, letting out a stream of smoke in the process. "His magnetic personality attracted a shitload of lead."

Jake inspected the gun, pulled out the magazine from the butt and ran his thumb over the top round. "Standard Soviet-era 9mm jacketed." He shook his head. "I'll be lucky if the fuckers don't blow up in my face."

Shrugging, Tully continued his assault on his cigarette.

Jake strapped the gun under his sweater and then swung his leather jacket over that. He went for the door handle again.

"Keep an eye on Tvchenko," Tully said. It was more of an order than a request. "I'll bet my left nut he still has ties to the GRU."

"I don't know about that." From what Jake had heard, Russian military intelligence had truly become the oxymoron civilians joked about.

"Trust me." Tully smiled like a politician about to screw his constituents. "The Cold War might be over, but there are some who'd rather go back to the good old days."

"He's denounced chemical and biological weapons publicly..." Jake stopped himself in mid-thought, knowing that he didn't believe his own words.

"Yeah, I heard the two of you got along like a couple of comrades," Tully said. "Bought his vodka-induced drivel when he told you the Russians forced him to come up with the most deadly fuckin' weapons known to man. The kind that make you wish you'd been nuked all to hell."

Nobody had to tell Jake about that. He was constantly haunted by the memory.

"People change."

"Don't count on it." Tully checked his watch. "You better get going. Your employers might be expecting a little protection. After all, that's what they hired you for." He let out a slight laugh and then continued, "Call me after dinner and I'll pick you up and debrief."

Jake got out and shut the door on a cloud of smoke. Almost immediately the Volga pulled away from the curb, its lights flicking on, and then lost its way around the harbor road.

Glancing around, Jake started up the long flight of stairs. When he reached the top of the Potemkin Steps, he hesitated for a moment and swiveled his head about, studying both directions of the quiet street.

Suddenly, two blocks up the road, a dark Mercedes sedan pulled away from the curb, turned its lights on after twenty meters, and cruised toward him slowly.

He tensed his left biceps against the gun butt under his jacket, almost reached for it, and then thought better of it as the sleek sedan passed by. No concern there.

Letting go with a cleansing breath, he glanced back down the stairs he had just climbed.

Satisfied he had not been followed, he stepped lightly along the cobblestone sidewalk, the cushioned soles of his hiking tennis shoes barely audible over his own heart beat.

Jake Adams knew he was being excessively cautious. It was a habit he had learned first in Air Force intelligence during his counter terrorism briefings. Never pattern yourself. Never travel to work the same way each day. Later, when he worked for the old CIA, he had refined those skills. Backtrack unexpectedly. Use windows for mirrors. It was all coming back to him in the darkened streets of Odessa. Some things he could never forget.

As he got closer to the Maranavka Hotel, one of the oldest and best preserved in Odessa, he noticed others dressed in their finest suits, dropping off expensive cars with the valet, and then regally strolling through the grand entrance like movie stars at a premiere. He, on the other hand, wore casual khakis, a gray sweater, and a black leather jacket. He assured himself that the blood red tie, although barely visible, was dressy enough for any occasion.

He continued toward the hotel door.

It had been one of the most beautiful spring days the city had seen in years. The agricultural conference at the university had kept all the attendees inside, locked in meetings on how to reduce crop loss to insects, and how new strains of wheat were far more resistant to harsh winters. Luckily, Jake had avoided that.

Flashing a name tag at the two armed doormen, Jake wandered inside.

The first day of the three-day conference was over, and most in attendance had looked forward to a dinner party where much of the real business would take place. He knew the scientist he had met years ago would be there to give a speech, and he was looking forward to talking with the man again to see for himself the transformation he had heard about. Had the man really changed that much?

Hesitating in the entrance of the expansive ballroom, Jake scanned the room. The place was over a century old, with mirrors on both sides that reminded him of the

Palace of Versailles, giving the room a false impression of great width. The domed ceiling was high, its carved white wood trimmed with gold.

Noticing his colleagues across the room at the bar, Jake smiled at MacCarty and Swanson as he approached them.

"I see you two have started without me," Jake said, picking up a glass of champagne from a tray on the bar. Technically he was working, but one glass wouldn't hurt.

MacCarty and Swanson were from Bio-tech Chemical Company of Portland, Oregon. During the day they had split up into various lecture halls, pitching their most recent insecticides and fertilizers. Bio-tech president, Maxwell MacCarty, and his assistant, Bill Swanson, the vice president of research and development, had wanted for years to push for lucrative new markets in Eastern Europe and the former Soviet countries. They already had an extensive share of the U.S. market, had penetrated the tough Western European countries, and had started making a move in Southeast Asia. But the Ukraine, the bread basket of Eastern Europe, was a wide open market and MacCarty knew it.

And that was one reason MacCarty had hired Jake just a week prior to his departure for the agricultural conference in Odessa. Jake had built his security business in Portland into a respectable, exclusive entity of one. His reputation had grown significantly in the three short years since going private. Working alone had its advantages, not having to depend on someone else's mistakes, but he did miss the camaraderie of his past.

The dinner party was just beginning. Guests were still streaming in. There were company representatives from all the major industrialized nations: Germany, France,

Italy, Japan, England, as well as from countries like Spain, Israel, Russia, Belorus. All of the companies had one thing in common. They wanted to sell their products to anyone who would buy them, and perhaps exchange ideas that could be useful in their home countries.

In his late thirties, Jake had already lived an interesting life. Had seen more of the world than a dozen others would ever see. He had a strong face that always needed a shave. His longer, dark hair, looked like it had come directly from a stiff breeze and he had combed it back hastily with his fingers, which was never far from the truth. Dressed as he was in leather and cotton, he looked more like a hunting guide than the company executive he was pretending to be.

His employers resembled the comedy duo Abbott and Costello. MacCarty was the tall, slim one with just enough brains to keep the short and socially inept Swanson from making a total ass of himself.

MacCarty, dressed impeccably in a three-piece Italian suit, set his glass on the bar. "Did you meet up with any old friends?"

Jake shook his head. "Afraid not. They've all been transferred." Jake had told them that he had worked for a while at the Odessa consulate. He had actually passed through many times during the destruction and withdrawal of chemical and biological weapons from the Ukraine, after attending a quick course at the defense language school in Monterey. At the time, he was a captain with Air Force intelligence, and an expert in chemical and biological weapons. His degree in geopolitics and his master's in international relations had given him a broad picture of the world. That was one of the reasons the CIA had originally recruited him, and even a better reason to quit. He wasn't great at following orders blindly. Those were things for ignorant young soldiers to do. And God knew the world had always needed those.

Swanson was a short, balding man with a tubular midsection. His exercise regimen consisted of turning the steering wheel vigorously as he searched for the closest parking spot to a burger joint, while maintaining control of his jelly donut.

"You missed the last meeting today, Jake," Swanson said. "It was an interesting talk by the former chief of the Agriculture Research Institute in Kiev. They've discovered a chemical that kills bugs on the spot and then infects the larvae as well. It makes them sterile."

"Too bad we couldn't do that selectively for humans," Jake said, smiling. He had come to a rather abrupt agreement with Swanson early on. They had agreed not to love each other.

Not answering, Swanson picked up another glass of champagne and sucked most of it down in one gulp. Then he raised his bushy brows as he noticed an attractive woman crossing the open dance floor.

Jake turned to see what was so interesting. The woman was tall and dark in a sleek, black dress cut low in the front and back. Her black hair, thick and curly, flowed over her shoulders with each step. When she reached a table of four men, they all rose to greet her, shaking her hand and then kissing the back of it.

"Now that's a woman!" Swanson declared.

"I agree," MacCarty said.

Jake couldn't believe his eyes. He had met Chavva at a state function over a year ago in Istanbul. She was the arm ornament of an Israeli diplomat at the time. He remembered her mostly for her wide, exotic eyes, even though she had no real faults. She was almost too perfect. Jake had flown to Istanbul from Rome looking for the daughter of a wealthy Seattle businessman. An Italian playboy needed a toy for a few weeks, and the young American woman was like a Barbie Doll to him. Jake found the young woman at the party and dragged her kicking and screaming to the airport. He hated those jobs, but the businessman had paid him well and the girl had been only seventeen. Chavva, on the other hand, was all woman. They had met just before he found the girl, set a date, and then couldn't keep it. Damn babysitting.

Without explanation, Jake walked over to the woman. He stood off to her side as she talked with the men from an Israeli company. Her eyes were focused on an older man, an Omar Sharif in his later years. The man, like MacCarty, was dressed in a fine Italian suit that accentuated his broad shoulders and still-firm body. The Rolex watch and the four rings with multiple diamonds were nice touches.

Jake didn't understand everything being said, but pieced together the standard chit chat about the weather and Odessa landmarks. When Chavva was done speaking with the man, she turned and immediately recognized Jake. She excused herself and walked over to him.

The Israeli businessman watched her carefully over the top of a wine glass, like a father or lover would.

"Hello, Chavva," Jake said. "It's nice to see a familiar face."

She smiled. "I thought you said you'd give me a call." Her English flowed with a sultry, thick accent.

"As you recall, I left in a hurry," Jake explained.

She fixed her eyes on him, as if looking for a lie. "Do you always drag young girls off into the night screaming?"

"She was seventeen, the daughter of a friend who thought chastity was more than some cute preppie name." He smiled at her and gazed into her wondrous eyes. He didn't remember them being so large and round. So intense. So dark.

"Do you work here?" she asked.

Jake took a sip of champagne and then shook his head. "No. I work for a company that produces fertilizer and pesticides."

She glared at him with disbelief.

"They needed someone who knew the area," he said. "They're thinking of opening a plant near Kiev."

"I see. I'm certain you know a great deal about fertilizer." She smiled and sipped her wine.

"Exactly."

"Give me a call," Chavva said. "I'm staying at *the* Odessa Hotel."

She turned and walked back to the table of men.

Jake watched her smoothly swaying hips before returning to MacCarty and Swanson.

"Do you know her?" MacCarty asked.

Looking across the room at her, Jake said, "We've met."

Everyone sat down for dinner. Jake was transfixed by Chavva the whole time. They exchanged glances and smiled. He thought back to his first meeting with her in Istanbul. There had been something strange about that. She had approached him as if she knew him, and he had to admit at the time that she did look familiar. But he had never figured it out.

After dinner, there were a number of speakers, with translators working overtime. Finally, the keynote speaker, Yuri Tvchenko, one of the foremost authorities on biochemical research in the world, came to the podium. Since the Soviet break-up, Tvchenko conducted research and lectured at Kiev University. He had only recently moved to Odessa, working for a private institute. Officially, he had become Ukraine's greatest opponent of chemical and biological weapons. When they had met years ago while Jake worked for Air Force intelligence on one of his trips to the Ukraine, the man had impressed Jake as someone who believed implicitly in the deterrent nature of nuclear, biological and chemical weapons. Jake wondered what had changed the man's mind.

After Tvchenko's talk, the crowd mixed together for more drinks, attempting to do business. MacCarty and Swanson drifted off to the bar, while Jake stood alone at the edge of the ballroom watching the social ballet.

Tvchenko made his way across the ballroom, speaking briefly to admirers, shaking hands, and then, recognizing Jake, he headed directly toward him. Tvchenko was a large man with gray hair and a red face that looked as if a chemical had burned his skin at one time. He wore a cheap wool suit, Bulgarian probably, that seemed to drape over his pendulous body.

When Tvchenko was in the center of the ballroom, he bumped into Chavva and she spilled her drink on his sleeve. He apologized to her, and she wiped his suit with a napkin.

Continuing on, Tvchenko stopped next to Jake, and they shook hands briefly. Something wasn't right with him. He was anxious or nervous or both. Tvchenko tried to open his mouth to speak, but his jaw clenched tightly. Beads of sweat poured from his forehead. He reached up desperately for his neck, where his blood vessels were bursting outward. He gasped for air, grasped his chest, and threw up all over the floor. Then he toppled down into his own vomit and twitched uncontrollably.

In a second he was dead, his eyes bulged open, looking up at Jake in horror. A woman screamed.

Jake quickly checked the man's pulse, but Tvchenko was gone. He backed away a few steps and suddenly felt a pain in his right hand. Rubbing away a tiny dot of blood near his life line, he wondered how it had gotten there.

The next few minutes were a chaotic mess.

2

JOHNSTON ATOLL, NORTH PACIFIC

The plane shook and rattled in turbulence, clouds swirling swiftly across the windscreen. The pilot tightened his grip on the controls and banked and dipped to the southwest.

Baskale had flown through tight mountain passes, across scorching deserts, but never over such a great body of water. And he had no intention of setting down in the ocean. He hated the water, where creatures lurked below, waiting to rip a leg from the helpless idiot who bobbed about. He preferred to face his enemies eye to eye.

Rocking and rolling, one engine sputtering, the old Navy C-1 transport, last used to deliver mail to aircraft carriers before being decommissioned, made more strange sounds than Baskale cared for. Sweat bubbled from his freshly-shaved face, where his thick beard had disguised his rough, jagged jaw just hours ago. His thick, dark hair stuck straight up through the head set, which he monitored constantly for any sign that they had been discovered.

In a moment, the plane broke from the clouds, and Baskale could make out the outline of the tiny island chain below. He had never been there, only studied the maps and charts. There was Johnston. His zealous eyes narrowed toward the barren set of rocky islands, desolate dots of nothingness that a brisk wind from Allah would bury in waves. He could finally see an airstrip. Searching the controls, which were not entirely familiar to him, he prepared himself for a tenuous landing. There would be a heavy cross wind.

All Baskale could smell was the ham. He was sick of it by now. From the moment they had stuffed the smoked ham in the back, hijacked the plane, and flown off in a hurry, he wondered how Americans could even eat the stuff. Give him a good leg of lamb any day. But the odor of pork also brought a pleasurable smile to his weathered face. It was a power he had never felt before.

He glanced over his shoulder at his three men. They all looked like airsick children in colorful costumes, traditional Hawaiian shirts. They had never worked together, but Baskale knew they were as dedicated as him. He could tell by their vigor on Hawaii last night. They had killed without question. They would do anything to make this work. Including die.

Over the radio, the air traffic controller cleared them for landing.

Baskale smiled and then dropped the landing gear and straightened the plane to the runway. The wings flipped up and down with gusts of wind. It took all the strength in both his arms to battle the controls.

Ten miles off the tiny island, the fishing trawler clicked

along at five knots, rolling in the gradual swells. Wind whipped across the bow.

The captain of the boat, Atik Aziz, a short, dark man with intense eyes, lowered the binoculars to his chest and turned to his first mate at the wheel.

"Hold it steady along this reef," Aziz ordered.

Aziz was a wiry Turkish Cypriot who had fought hard against the Greeks until it had become fruitless to do so, and until he had found it more profitable to work for himself. Now he controlled his own destiny, something few men could say for themselves.

"Our timing must be perfect," the captain said, as he shifted to a broad stance to balance himself.

The first mate nodded, not knowing what he was really agreeing to, but not wanting to ask for details either. Sailors who asked too many questions could slip overboard, never to be seen again.

Aziz yelled orders to the two other crew members to lower the fishing nets, his gravely voice reverberating off the wooden decks. How could they appear to be fishing without the nets in the water? He had no respect for this rag-tag crew. He had lost his real men to an Israeli gunboat, and replaced them with these pathetic boys when he could find no others on short notice after this job came up. The long journey had been difficult. They had changed their flag and the nameplate at the stern as some would their underwear. He would have to live with his decision to use these amateurs until the right moment. He glassed the island again. A smile crossed his face as he watched the plane set down.

On the island, the delivery plane from Hawaii had just

landed, and the three crew members and the pilot were off-loading crates of food into a blue truck with U.S. Air Force stenciled on each door. Baskale kept an eye out for security police, but saw none—only an officer and an unarmed aide.

It was Easter morning, and it had become a ritual to fly in fifty fresh hams from a small vendor in Pearl Harbor, who meticulously smoked them, injecting them with a special sauce that had remained a secret, but had each base commander at the Johnston Atoll Chemical Agent Disposal System, begging for more year after year.

Colonel Stan Barker was no exception. He stood outside the operations building in battle fatigues below the airport tower, supervising the entire project with a young airman in blues at his side. Barker was in his second year of command, his last year before heading back to Arizona to retire. He wanted to please the troops, who considered the isolated duty a hell-hole and felt the only reason they were there was because they had pissed someone off down the road. And what better way to please the troops than by appealing to their stomachs. Barker grinned as he took in a whiff of the succulent pork. This year would be better than any other. Even the cooks would get a break, for Barker had ordered all food to be catered. Sweet potatoes, Idaho russets with gravy, and a special pineapple dessert.

Two of the men, their colorful shirts soaked in sweat, stopped loading for a moment after making repeated trips from the plane to the truck.

Colonel Barker stepped forward briskly, his hands on his hips. "You boys have a problem with hard work?" he yelled. "Get your ass in gear. We've got men to feed."

The largest man started toward the colonel, but Baskale

grabbed his arm, holding him back. Baskale whispered into the man's ear, and the man nodded, smiled, and went back to work.

When the men were finished loading the truck, they closed up the back and piled into a Suburban. They would follow the truck to the dining facility and cook for the Army and Air Force troops. Everyone would get a day off this Easter.

At noon the meal was ready. The soldiers and airmen, who had spent the entire morning in a heated game of softball with plenty of beer, piled into the dining facility, hungry.

Colonel Barker, having umpired the game, was in the lead, lauding the aroma of the ham, ubiquitous in the air. He had the men from Hawaii load extra ham on his tray.

"I hope it's as good as last year," the colonel said, winking.

Baskale smiled and continued quickly loading trays. He needed to push people through as fast as possible.

Within the hour, the entire base, nearly a thousand military, civilians and contract workers had eaten the ham. Even the small contingent of security police officers guarding the gates to the chemical weapons storage facility had eaten meals delivered to them.

The four men from Hawaii disappeared temporarily. They would wait patiently for the ham to do its magic.

In a short while everyone was debilitated. Those who were not puking their guts out, had lapsed into comas or died.

Returning to the dining facility, Baskale and his three men armed themselves with submachine guns they had stashed in a crate. They stepped over people lying strewn in contorted piles. Some had made it out the front door, only to collapse on the grass or sidewalk outside. The largest of Baskale's men found the colonel dead in his chair at the head of a table, his face plastered into a plate of mashed potatoes. The man leveled his gun on the colonel and fired a burst into him. Blood exploded from each hit. The man smiled. Baskale pulled at him, and they hurried outside to the Suburban and piled in.

Baskale drove toward the chemical weapons storage site. If there was a body in the road, he would not swerve. Instead, he'd gun the engine and jump the body like a speed bump, his three men laughing each time he did it. The base looked like the villages he had seen bombed in his youth. Twitching bodies. Women hugging their children, looking up to the sky as if asking God why.

He crashed the truck through the metal fence at the storage site and went on to the secured bunkers. After blowing the locks on storage building Alfa, they rushed inside. Baskale smiled when he opened the first container. Inside, there was a cluster bomb with over a hundred four-pound bomblets containing deadly nerve gas. They closed the water-tight container and all four, in unison, hoisted the bomb onto the truck.

By now, the Cypriot registered fishing boat had made its way to shore and was docked at the pier. The captain ordered his men to tie the boat fore and aft. As they waited for the truck, two crew members refueled the boat with diesel, topping off the tanks. This was not a normal fishing trawler. It had a modified engine that could crank out over forty knots in the open seas, with extra fuel tanks where fish would have normally been stored.

The truck rolled to a stop. Baskale jumped out, smiled at Aziz, and explained that everything had gone as planned.

In a matter of minutes, the nerve gas weapon was loaded aboard the boat and they were steaming at full speed to the east.

CIA HEADQUARTERS
Langley, Virginia

The Director of Central Intelligence stormed into the communications room. John S. Malone, a former Navy admiral, demanded respect and got it. He was used to being called away from his family, even during the holidays, but he never liked it.

The new CIA was six months young, and Malone was determined to make it work. The plan to combine all intelligence into one cohesive unit was needed. Yet there were many who wanted the new organization to fail. Some had declared that combining the CIA, the FBI, NSA, DEA, ATF, and all the various military intelligence and law enforcement functions under one roof, was a ludicrous notion. It was too much like the KGB in its heyday, with its multitude of directorates. Those on Capitol Hill who had fought for it, the president among them, had hoped to streamline the bureaucracy. In the end, though, nothing had actually changed, with the exception of building another layer of bureaucracy between the CIA and the executive and legislative branches. The process had been more complex than anyone in the former organizations had ever encountered. Those forward-looking individuals who set it up hoped that the end result would be a network that resembled the most finely designed computer system with unencumbered software. In reality, the additional layer actually made it more difficult for the CIA to get its message to the president.

Malone wanted to be hands on, in the thick of the action. He was a hulk of a man, with a chest like a football offensive lineman. Over the last few months he had grown a bushy mustache, and would twirl the ends in tense moments. He was twisting away at it now. "This better be good, gentlemen," Malone growled.

A nervous analyst handed the director a hard copy of the message received from Johnston Atoll. It was a cryptic message, at best, punched in by a dying Air Force communications controller from the island.

When Malone was finished, he handed the message to his assistant. "It doesn't say how many dead, or the security of the weapons."

The director of operations chimed in. "The Navy diverted the guided missile frigate Long Beach, that was en route to Guam, to the island. They've dispatched their helicopter to the site and should be on the ground by now." The DO, Kurt Jenkins, had been career CIA and one of the only top ranking officials to survive the recent shake-up. He was a slight man with round glasses. He looked more like a nerdy bookkeeper than someone who ran the largest number of clandestine officers and secret operations in the world.

"Do we have communications with anyone there?" Malone asked.

The DO shook his head. "No, sir. It doesn't look good. An Air Force intel officer at our Hickam office had a telephonic with the comm center at Johnston for a few minutes. But he didn't get much. Something about a crew flying in Easter dinner from Pearl Harbor. Ham."

The director twisted at his mustache again. "The entire island was poisoned?"

"It appears so," Jenkins said. "The Air Force is checking into it now."

The secure phone on the console buzzed and the analyst picked up. In a moment, he handed the phone to the director. "Sir, it's the Navy frigate commander."

The director picked up and listened carefully. His expression changed from concern to a gravity not often seen from him. "A medical team is on its way, and the Air Force is flying evac planes that way as we speak. Have your men secure the area. I don't want the press involved. You're in charge there, commander." He handed the phone back to the analyst and turned to the DO. "At least a hundred confirmed dead, with more dying as we speak." He paused for a moment. "And one of the weapons is missing."

"Shit!"

Malone turned away. Someone had one of the most deadly nerve agents ever conceived. Terrorists probably. He had to think fast, be strong. He could not let this happen on his watch. "I'll inform the president," the director finally said. "In the meantime, I want maximum effort on this. I don't care who you have to pull from other operations. Also, I want satellite tracking of every Goddamn ship in the Pacific. It appears that they didn't escape by air. I want each craft vectored and boarded by the Navy or Coast Guard."

"Yes, sir." The DO hurried from the room.

3

NEAR LAKE VAN, TURKISH KURDISTAN

Darkness and thick clouds had turned the barren mountains into a black abyss. The tiny village nestled against the steep mountains had only one dirt road leading to it. It was nearly one a.m. when the truck wound its way up the lonely road.

Mesut Carzani reflected quietly in the passenger seat, shifting his glance periodically to his driver, a strong man a little younger than himself but one who looked much older. They had fought together for decades as Peshmerga guerrillas in northern Iraq. Kill or be killed. There was nothing in between. Striking targets in and around Baghdad, and then fleeing to the mountain havens in Iran and Turkey. Futile efforts, at best, but they were at least men of action.

Carzani's face was a road map of wrinkles, each one leading to a place he had been. He knew the mountains. He knew the people. They trusted him. And he would use that trust to his advantage. They had tried warfare, but there had always been too many factions. Too much second guessing. The Kurds needed a strong leader like him to put Kurdistan on the map as something more than a footnote in history books.

The truck snaked up the last hill and squeaked to a halt at a mottled brick house on an isolated drive above town.

The last to arrive, Carzani had waited down the mountain, watching the others drive by, and ensuring that their position had not been compromised. As the most recent leader of the Partia Karkaris Kurdistan in Turkey, the most extreme faction fighting for Kurdish autonomy and a homeland, Carzani had convinced Kurdish leaders from Iran, Iraq and Syria to meet and discuss a unified effort in their struggle. Others had found homes—the Israelis, the Palestinians, the Armenians. Now, at twenty million strong, it was their turn. The PKK had clashed with Turkish troops in the past, but were trying to keep a low profile until just the right moment. They remained huddled in the mountains, their traditional sanctuary, tending flocks of sheep and goats, and collecting weapons and support from the people. That is what they needed most for their movement. The will of that many people could not be denied or ignored. The world would have to listen.

The small town was completely sympathetic to the cause. The entire area was on alert, with weapons drawn in positions in the woods, on building tops, peering out through darkened open windows. There would be no chances taken this time. There was too much at stake.

Carzani, protected by four armed guards, slid out of the truck and entered the safe house. Two guards remained at the door outside, and two inside.

The sparse room he entered held only an old wooden table with a bench on each side. A stone fireplace, freshly stoked, provided much of the light and all of the warmth.

Sitting at the table, glaring at Carzani as he approached, were the three tribal leaders who would hopefully join forces with Carzani. Each man had a personal body guard behind him, and each rose now to greet the Turkish Kurd with a kiss on both cheeks. All of the three leaders had sent a messenger, initially agreeing to a unified front, subject to the outcome of this meeting.

Carzani took a seat. "I trust your trips went well," the PKK leader said.

There was no response.

"As my message said," Carzani continued. "I have a plan to ensure we are listened to by the international community. When you hear what I have to say, you too will be convinced that a free and autonomous Kurdistan is finally possible."

There was still no response.

Mesut Carzani peered around the room at the security guards. "We must have complete privacy." He shifted his eyes toward the door.

The three other leaders reluctantly waved and nodded for their men to step outside. When the room held only the four leaders, Carzani pulled a map from inside his jacket and spread it out on the table.

"Remember Halabja," Carzani muttered solemnly.

MOSSAD HEADQUARTERS, TEL AVIV

The director of Israeli Intelligence, Mikhael Chagall, entered the secure room in a hardened shelter below ground, and shuffled immediately to his assistant who was standing next to an analyst at a console.

Chagall was a slight man, barely five feet, who had ascended to the top of Mossad by intellectual superiority, without leaving many enemies in his wake. As was tradition in Israel, no one knew the name of the current director, except for high ranking government and military officials. And Chagall preferred it that way. It allowed him to do his job more completely, without the fear of retribution from a brutal media.

"What do you have, Yosef?" the Mossad director asked.

The assistant handed the director a message that had just been deciphered, and the two of them went into an isolated, soundproof room. The message sender was identified by a code, and only the director and his assistant knew the identity. When the director was finished with the message, he immediately shredded it.

"So they are finally meeting," Chagall said. "It means nothing."

His assistant lowered his brows. "They are twenty million strong, Mikhael."

Chagall approached his old friend and placed a tiny wrinkled hand on his shoulder. "We are allies traditionally, Yosef," he muttered. "We will do them no harm. They are not Arabs or even Persians. They are merely lost sheep looking for home."

MI-6, LONDON

"Tvchenko is dead," the chairman of Britain's foreign service said. "That's why we called you in off your holiday."

The chairman, Sir Geoffrey Baines, knew he didn't need to explain himself to his field officers under any circumstances, but it made difficult assignments much more palatable. He sat back in his leather chair, which squeaked with each movement from the robust man, and he studied his officer carefully. He prided himself on being able to read people simply by observing their face. He was rarely wrong.

Baines was a consensus builder. Some, his critics mostly, considered him far too accommodating. Yet, for the past four years he had gotten results. The foreign service was in higher favor with parliament and the public than at any other time since World War II.

Sinclair Tucker had never had a private meeting with the chairman before. At thirty-eight, he was a field officer who had seen action first in Eastern Europe during the waning days of the Cold War, and more recently in the Balkans, where he had just arrived from two days previously for a short Easter vacation, after working six months in Odessa, undercover, as a British businessman. He had been part of a four-man advance team seeking markets for telephone communications equipment. Actually, he had been keeping an eye on Yuri Tvchenko. Tucker knew that the scientist had been seen with foreigners on numerous occasions, and was closing in on what he was currently working on.

"How?" Tucker asked.

"It appears he was poisoned in some way at the conference," the chairman said.

Tucker shook his head. He had wanted to stick around Odessa during the conference, but had been ordered to take leave. His boss thought he had been working too hard. Needed a break. Besides, Tucker was supposed to be working for a communications firm, which had nothing to do with agriculture. He could not simply show up. But Tucker had realized that it would have been a perfect opportunity to make contacts, with all those representatives from various countries together.

"Murdered in front of all those people?" Tucker said.

"Afraid so. We're not sure what this means, but we need you back in the country as soon as possible."

"Of course."

"One more thing," the chairman said. "I understand that you're friends with an American there, Jake Adams, a former CIA officer."

Tucker lowered his gaze. "Jake is there? Yes, sir. Why do you ask?"

"I've gotten word that Adams was with Tvchenko when he died. Stick close to him. Will he work with you?"

Tucker had known Jake Adams for years. They had first met when Jake was an Air Force officer verifying the withdrawal of chemical weapons from the Ukraine. Later, during the Gulf War, they had worked together once again in Turkey. They had spent more than a few nights drinking from Diyarbakir to Istanbul. He had even gone pub crawling with Jake in London once while they were both on leave. What in the hell was Adams doing in Odessa? Would Jake Adams work with him? That depended entirely on Jake. He had always done what he wanted, regardless of the consequences. He knew that Jake had left the Agency more than three years ago, so what was he up to now?

"Jake follows orders when the occasion strikes him right," Tucker said, smiling. "It's not that he's a rogue. It's that he doesn't trust just anyone."

"And what about you?"

"We have some history. If I ask him nicely, I'm sure he'll show us some consideration."

"Good! You're packed, I assume. Your flight leaves Heathrow in two hours."

He had never unpacked. "Yes, sir."

"Stick with Adams. You'll lead our efforts. We're spread pretty thin in that area, as you well know, but I'm sure you're up to the job."

He would have to be.

4

ODESSA, UKRAINE

When the ambulance finally picked up Yuri Tvchenko's body, Jake still wasn't completely certain what had happened. The Odessa police had assumed the most obvious affliction. A stroke or a massive heart attack. But Jake knew better. Tvchenko had been murdered right in front of a hundred witnesses. He even suspected the cause of death, for Jake had seen nerve agents tested on animals before, and while with the CIA, watched confiscated Soviet films where they had conducted research on prisoners. Even worse had been when Jake had entered the small Iraqi village after it had been bombed with chemical weapons by its own air force. He could never erase that from his conscience. Somehow, someone had injected an agent into Tvchenko's system right before his eyes.

Jake rubbed his right hand. Where there had been a spot of blood earlier, just after Tvchenko collapsed, there was now a red puffy area a few millimeters wide, like he had been pricked by a rose thorn and it was now infected.

Jake scanned the room for Chavva. She was the last to have direct contact with the scientist before he crashed to the floor, but she was nowhere to be seen. He couldn't imagine her killing the scientist, yet she might have seen him talking with someone else. Although he was officially in Odessa to protect MacCarty and Swanson, he could never stand by when something like this dropped in his lap.

Standing at Jake's side were MacCarty and Swanson. They seemed to be in shock. Neither had ever seen a man die in front of them, and the violence of a nerve agent death had been a most brutal initiation for them.

"That was disgusting," Swanson said. He looked at his drink, uncertain if he should finish it.

"Death is rarely pretty," Jake said. "Listen, I'm going to head back to my room."

MacCarty nodded and started to drink his champagne. He was closer to drunk than sober.

"I wouldn't drink that if I were you," Jake said. "We don't know for sure how Tvchenko died. Whatever entered his body could have come from an airborne agent. Something could have sunk down into your drink." He knew this wasn't the case or more people would have been afflicted. Yet, just to be safe, it was a good idea to keep the two of them on their toes.

MacCarty slowly set the drink on a table. "Well, we've got a shitload of meetings tomorrow anyway. We can always grab a drink at our hotel. Bill and I will be along shortly."

"I should probably accompany you. That's what I'm here for," Jake said.

Swanson smirked as if to say he could handle himself.

MacCarty slapped Jake on the shoulder. "We'll be all right, Jake. We'll take a cab."

The three of them were staying six blocks away in the Chornoye Hotel off Primorski Boulevard. Jake figured they couldn't get into too much trouble with a short ride like that. As he drifted off across the room, he continued searching for Chavva, but she was definitely not there. In fact, neither were any of the Israeli businessmen.

· Out in the lobby, Jake made a quick phone call. When a man answered the phone, he excused himself in Ukrainian and hung up. It was his signal for the Odessa station chief to meet him immediately at a predetermined spot.

Jake stepped out onto Primorski Boulevard and started walking east. Tall trees lined the wide promenade, yet he could still see the lights from the harbor below. With such a warm evening, many others were out walking. Young couples, groups of girls and boys, and the frequent drunken old men staggering here and there. After three blocks, he turned south on Pushkinskaya down along a narrow park. Two blocks later the Volga sedan pulled up to the curb and a door opened. Jake slipped in.

Soon, Tully O'Neill turned left and headed toward Shevchenko Park. Neither said a word.

Jake had never worked for Tully O'Neill, since Tully had only recently taken over in Odessa. He had heard that Tully had worked for years in Bucharest, Sofia and Kiev as an operations officer. Odessa was his first assignment as station chief, which made him a late bloomer to the old agency, having first worked as a bureaucrat in Defense and the State Department. He believed he got a break with the new Agency because he wasn't one of the good old boys. In fact, at fifty, he would have normally been in charge of a much larger operation. The years showed in his receding hairline, long gray hair, and reddened eyes that seemed to droop from lack of sleep and too much alcohol each night.

Yet, Jake had heard through the grapevine that Tully was a man to be trusted. He would put everything, including his life, on the line for a friend. Jake hoped that wouldn't be necessary.

Tully finally pulled over on a secluded street on the north side of the vast park with a view of the large ocean cargo vessels, and he cut the engine.

"Well, what's up?" Tully asked.

"You didn't hear?"

Tully gave Jake a blank stare.

"Someone just killed Tvchenko."

Tully smashed his hands against the steering wheel. "God dammit. How?"

"At the dinner tonight," Jake said. "A nerve agent pellet or something. I'm not positive." He shook his head.

Pulling a cigarette from inside his coat, Tully offered one to Jake, who refused. He lit a Marlboro and inhaled deeply. "You know this town as well as I do, Jake. What do you think?"

Jake shrugged, and then rubbed his hand again. The puncture was stinging now.

"What's that?" Tully asked.

"I'm not sure. I got it when I shook hands with Tvchenko just before he died."

"Let me look closer." Tully pulled Jake's hand toward him and turned on the dome light. In a moment he said, "Son of a bitch! It's a message."

"What the hell are you talking about?"

"Here, look." Tully pulled a small Swiss army knife from his pocket and opened a tiny, pointed blade that looked extremely sharp. He started toward Jake's hand with it.

"Wait a minute," Jake protested. "What do you plan on doing with that?"

"Trust me. It won't hurt much."

Right. Famous words spoken by dentists to patients and young boys to virgins. Jake slid his hand back toward Tully, reluctantly. But Tully was right; it didn't hurt. It was much like removing a sliver from a puss-filled wound; the pressure was removed as Tully extracted something minuscule from his palm.

"What the hell is that?" Jake asked.

"Wait. I'll show you." Tully set the object in his cupped palm and spit on it. Then he removed a tiny, clear item that resembled a piece of rice from his pocket, along with a jeweler's eyepiece. He lined the three items up and peered into them closely. He slowly raised his head with a puzzled look. "Tell me what you see," he said to Jake.

Jake shifted his head over. "Halabja," he muttered. That's all it said. Just one word scribbled hastily, as though the writer were jotting down milk or eggs on a shopping list.

"Does that make sense to you?" Tully asked.

Jake settled back into his seat. "Just the obvious reference to the Iraqi village." Obvious indeed. Tvchenko had to be referring to Halabja, Iraq, the city bordering Iran that was bombed with nerve gas and mustard gas by Saddam Hussein's own forces in March of 1988. As many as five thousand Kurds—men, women and children—were killed within hours. Jake not only knew about the devastating events of that day, he had actually seen the bombing while working on special assignment in Kurdistan during the height of the Iran-Iraq War. He was there to confirm or deny the use of chemical and biological weapons. He would never forget the faces. Especially the children.

Tully tucked the tiny message into a plastic Ziploc.

"What does Iraq or the Kurds have to do with this?" Jake asked.

"Maybe Tvchenko planned on selling his new weapon to Iraq."

"We're not even sure he had a new weapon," Jake reminded him.

"He was still into nerve agents." Tully took a long drag on his cigarette and let the smoke out in one quick stream. "We need to get to his apartment before the police." Tully cranked over the car and sped off.

"Where does he live?" Jake asked.

"The Russian Quarter."

It was nearly midnight. The residential streets that Tully took were almost deserted. Jake realized that for Tully being in Odessa for less than a month, he already knew his way around the city quite well. In ten minutes, they were parked along a tree-lined boulevard, with old brick apartment buildings on both sides.

"Which one is his?" Jake asked.

Tully snubbed out his cigarette and pointed toward the second floor across the street. "You still have the Makarov?"

Jake patted under his left arm.

"Let's go."

They got out quietly. The street was lit only by a few short lamp posts. Many of the lamps were burned out.

They slipped inside and made their way upstairs.

At the top of the stairs, Tully drew his gun and pointed toward apartment 2A. Jake followed his lead. The door was unlocked.

Inside, the two men scanned the darkness for any movement. Nothing. Then Tully, who had been in the apartment one other time, closed the curtains and clicked on a small table lamp. The room was completely destroyed. There was sofa stuffing scattered about the floor, desks overturned, lamps stripped of bulbs, and papers blanketing an area near a far wall.

"Who the hell did this?" Tully whispered.

Jake sniffed the air. "Something's not right here." He moved toward a small kitchen off to one side, clicked on the light, and peered inside.

"What's the matter?" Tully was right at his side.

"I'm not sure." Jake moved back into the living room and then saw a door at the far end of the apartment. There was a black cord, a telephone line perhaps, leading under the door. "Where does that lead?"

"A small lab," Tully said. "Tvchenko did some research here."

Tully was about to open the lab door when Jake grabbed his arm. "Do you smell that?" Jake asked.

Tully shook his head. "Smells like old books or something."

"Not that. There's something else. I've smelled it before, but I can't place it."

Frowning, Tully started to shift the door lever downward.

"No!" Jake screamed. "Let's get the hell out of here, now."

"We're not done yet."

"That's my point," Jake said, pulling Tully out of the room by his arm.

They had just gotten to the outside hallway and closed the door, when they heard the phone ring. A second later, the door blasted outward into Jake and Tully, as the entire room exploded in flames.

On the ground, Jake shook his head and looked at Tully at his side. He was unconscious. Jake grabbed him by the coat collar and dragged him to the stairs. Then he hoisted him over his shoulder and carried him downstairs.

Outside, Jake stuffed Tully into the passenger side, pulled the keys from his pocket, and hurried to start the car. By now, other residents of the apartment building were making their way out of the front door and through windows.

As Jake drove off, he heard the sound of fire engines and police cars making their way to the fire. Jake drove only a few blocks, turned up a side street, and parked between two cars.

Tully was finally coming out of a groggy rest. "What the hell happened?" He reached inside his jacket for his cigarettes and retrieved a crumpled package. "Shit." He found one that was bent but not broken, and lit it.

"The place blew up," Jake said. "I realize what I smelled now. It was isopropyl alcohol, combined with ammonium fluoride. The cord under the door was the trigger. Someone had to be watching the place, saw us go in, and waited a few minutes to make the phone call. We were pretty damn lucky, because the air would have surely been toxic—probably with Sarin, a nerve gas. Or something like that."

Tully puffed on his cigarette, his hand shaking uncontrollably. "You saved our ass." Then he thought for a moment. "We've got to go back."

"Are you nuts?"

"We've had the place bugged for two weeks with a remote, sound activated tape. Our tape machine is across the street in another apartment. Armstrong changes the tape twice a day, in the morning and in the evening. We might have caught who did this on tape. Drive."

Jake started the car and headed off.

Tully directed Jake to round the block and end up across the street and behind the building where Tvchenko's apartment was burning. They could both see the smoke, white and puffy now, streaming over the building roofs. The Odessa station kept a room on the second floor with a direct view of Tvchenko's apartment. The officers never entered the building from the same street that the scientist would, but instead from a side door, parking on an entirely different street. That way they could come and go without anyone noticing.

"Stay here," Tully said, as he got out and slid a watch cap over his head. With his dark wool coat, his hands stuffed into his pockets, and now the cap, he looked like a merchant marine just off a ship.

Jake kept his eyes open, scanning the rearview mirrors, and continually peering toward the door Tully had entered. He wondered if someone had hung around after calling Tvchenko's apartment, and then followed them there.

In a few minutes, Tully exited the building carrying an old leather suitcase. He shoved it into the back seat and got into the front. "We're off."

Jake started driving, checking the mirror every few seconds. So far, they were alone. "Did you close down the place?" Jake asked.

"Yeah." Tully searched for another good cigarette, but not finding one, he threw the pack to the back seat.

"Those things will kill you anyway," Jake said, smiling.

Tully laughed. "Yeah, like this job won't do a number on our ass first." He pulled a cassette tape from his pocket, shoved it into the player, and hit rewind. When it stopped, he pushed play.

The first thing they heard was a door opening and closing and the sound of footsteps on a wooden floor. Then the sound of things flying, ripping, tearing. And finally whispered words.

"What was that?" Jake asked.

Tully stopped the tape and rewound it slightly. He played it again, only louder. "What language is that?"

Listening carefully, Jake cocked his ear toward the speaker. Then there was a louder sentence, and it became clearer to him what was being said. He smiled.

"What is it?"

"It's Kurdish," Jake said. "I only understand a little. It's sort of a cross between Farsi and Arabic, with a little Turkish thrown in. I learned some working in Kurdistan during the Iran-Iraq War."

"Halabja?"

"Exactly," Jake said. "The Kurds must have something to do with the message Tvchenko passed me."

"What do you suppose they were looking for?"

"I don't know. Maybe Tvchenko was about to sell them something. A new nerve gas. Or even a biological strain. But he was killed before the deal went through. So they go to his place, look for the formula, and set a bomb."

"Why bomb the place?"

Jake shrugged. "Maybe they figured if they couldn't have it, nobody would."

It made some sense. But Jake was still confused as to why Tvchenko had passed him the message, and what the Kurds wanted with Tvchenko's information.

One thing was certain. He'd make it his business to find out what was going on.

5

Tully had dropped Jake off at the Chornoye Hotel, saying he'd meet with him for lunch. Jake planned to sleep in. It had been a long night, with Tvchenko's death and Jake and Tully almost getting blown to pieces. The problem was, he had been so tired and pumped up from the night's events, that he had not slept well at all. He had tossed and turned, checking his watch every half hour.

By seven in the morning, he had decided the hell with it, get up and face the day.

He went to the bathroom, thought about shaving, and then decided against it. He was drawing the bath water and relieving himself when he thought he heard a noise in the room. Looking around he realized he had left the Makarov under his pillow. He was standing in his black jockey underwear. Nothing else. There was nothing in the bathroom he could use for a weapon. Damn. Not even a plunger.

Opening the door a crack, Jake peered out into the semi-dark room. He could only see the door to the hall, the window, which gave the room its light, and a chair next to the wall mirror.

Jake closed the door and thought. Had he really heard anything? He turned off the faucet and splashed around with his hands, as if he had stepped in and taken a seat. Then he moved behind the door and waited, his right fist clenched and ready to strike at head level.

He didn't have to wait long. In a moment, the door handle slowly lowered, and then the door swept into the room. Jake expected to see a gun, but did not. Instead, a brown leather pump stepped in, followed by dark hair.

Jake grabbed the door handle, quickly opened the door, and started to swing at the person's head, but pulled up short.

"Jesus Christ!" Jake yelled. "What in the hell are you doing here?"

It was Chavva with a shocked look on her face, having just jumped back against the sink. She was dressed in a black leather waist coat and brown slacks. She relaxed and crossed her legs at the ankles, looking Jake up and down.

"I'm sorry if I scared you," she said. "I tried knocking, but there was no answer. So I let myself in. I could hear the water running."

Let herself in? It had been late when he got in. Had he forgotten to lock the door? He didn't think so, but it was possible. "I'm sorry I almost hit you. It's just—"

She raised a hand. "It's my fault. A bath is a sacred place. I shouldn't have come." She started for the door.

"Wait." Jake closed the door. "Why are you here?"

She hesitated. "I thought we'd have breakfast. Talk. Get to know each other better."

Standing in his underwear, Jake felt a chill across his

body. He studied her large, round eyes, those moist lips, her perfect body. "Let's talk in the other room," he said.

She agreed and they both went into the main room, her taking the chair by the mirror, and Jake sitting at the head of the bed nearest the pillow with the Makarov. He wasn't sure why. He had no reason not to trust Chavva, other than the fact that she was so mysterious and had been the last person to actually touch Yuri Tvchenko before his death. Besides him, of course.

Jake slipped a T-shirt over his head, cutting the chill. He waited for her to say something, staring right at her, taking in every square inch of her.

Finally she said, "That was terrible last night... Tvchenko's death."

She looked visibly disturbed, as if she would cry, or had cried over the man's death.

"Were you two friends?"

She shook her head. "No. But it was a horrible way to die. The twitching." She shuddered.

Jake had seen so many people die, perhaps he was a bit too familiar. Too insensitive. Maybe that's why Chavva had disappeared after the man collapsed.

"It must have been worse for you," she said. "Him falling into your arms like that. Did he say anything before he died? Did he know he was dying?"

He thought about that. He hadn't even considered how Tvchenko had felt. How would it feel knowing you were dying? Jake had been shot before. Once, when he was grazed in the head, he had felt as though he were floating from the ground, and imagined himself rising to heaven. If such a place even existed, he wasn't entirely sure he'd be heading in that direction. He wondered about others he

had seen die, or having died recently. The worst of all had
been in Halabja. With those people, mostly innocent civilians, whose only crime was having been born a Kurd, he
could read their contorted faces. There was the mother
who had searched for her fifteen-year-old daughter, and
collapsed in the street gazing upward to Allah. What had
she done? Jake found himself staring at Chavva.

"I'm sorry," he said, thinking of her questions again.
"I'm not sure what he was thinking. I guess he must have
known he was dying, but assumed it was a heart attack or
something."

"He didn't say anything to you?"

"Like what?"

"I don't know. Maybe ask you for help."

"Why would he ask me for help? A stranger."

"I thought you said you knew him."

That was strange. They hadn't even discussed
Tvchenko. "We had met years ago," Jake said. "But I'm
sure Tvchenko didn't even remember me." Jake was rubbing the cut on his right hand where the scientist had
passed that single word, Halabja, scribbled on a tiny note.

"How'd you hurt your hand?"

"What?" He looked at his hand and thought quickly. "I
cut myself yesterday on a metal railing heading down to
the Catacombs," he lied. He had been to the vast expanse
of tunnels on the outskirts of the city, nearly a thousand
kilometers in all, while working out of Odessa with the
Air Force. They were dark and dreary places quarried in
the 19th Century, the stones used to build the city. He also
knew that anyone who needed a place to hide, or had been
in trouble for some reason or other, had used the
Catacombs. His briefing upon first arriving in Odessa

included a warning to stay away from them. There were no bodies buried there officially, but many had lost their way in the mazes, never to be heard from again.

"The Catacombs," she said, skeptically, like she had questioned his working for the fertilizer company. "I've heard they can be a dangerous place."

Jake shrugged. "You can get killed walking across the street. Sometimes you have to take chances." He realized he had summed up his philosophy on life in two sentences.

They looked at each other for a moment. Then she slowly rose.

"I'm sorry to come here and bother you," she said.

Her face seemed to reveal so much, yet nothing at all. Her lips would quiver, as if she were about to say something, and then she would hold back. Jake was entranced with her. He felt like he knew her, had some tie with her, but he couldn't figure out how. They had met twice, three times now, and each time had been strange. He met her at the door, feeling a bit funny letting her out in his underwear, considering they hadn't done anything.

She stood in the hallway outside, about to say something.

"What about coffee?" Jake asked.

She looked toward the elevator and then at her watch. "I should get to the conference, really. My boss is expecting me by eight."

"You have twenty minutes. I could throw on some pants." Jake smiled.

She looked down at his underwear. "Then I wouldn't be able to see your nice butt."

Now she had embarrassed him, which was hard to do.

And her use of the word "butt" came out awkward with her accent.

"How about lunch?"

Jake was about to confirm, when he realized he had set up a time to meet with Tully. "I'm sorry. I can't. Dinner?"

She shook her head. "My boss wants us to discuss the conferences we attend over dinner. There's supposed to be an interesting talk on a new grass hybrid that grows quickly in arid climates."

"Sounds fascinating."

She gave him a smirk he hadn't seen before; something between disturbed and annoyed. "Like fertilizer."

"Exactly. Maybe we could see each other after dinner for a drink."

"Perhaps." She started to leave, and then turned again. "Which conference will you be attending?"

He thought fast now. He hadn't planned on going to any of them. "I'm not sure. I might slip in and out of a few."

She nodded and swept off down the hall, and he watched every swaying step.

Lunch would actually be the first meal of the day for Jake. It was a fairly nice day. A bit overcast, but no real chance of raining. Jake had walked ten blocks to the Pecheskato Cafe off of Deribasovskaya Street. It was eleven a.m.

Tully was already inside the crowded restaurant, sitting at the bar with a vodka sour in front of him and a cigarette hanging from the side of his mouth.

"You look like shit," Tully said, shaking Jake's hand. "What can I get you?"

"A beer."

Tully waved to the bartender and ordered a Czech Pilsner.

They ate a quick lunch at the bar, Tully washing his down with two more drinks. When they were done, Tully seemed a little uneasy.

"What's wrong?" Jake asked.

Tully lit another Marlboro. "I've got to get back to the consulate."

"Did you send the tape off to Langley?"

Letting out a puff of smoke, Tully nodded. "Yeah, I've got to do that also. Could you do something for me. You know, if you've got time."

"I have to meet MacCarty and Swanson at four," Jake said. "I think they're both a little nervous after Tvchenko's death. They want me around until they head in for the night. After all, that's what I'm here for."

"Right. This won't take long." He scribbled something on a beer coaster and handed it to Jake.

Jake looked it over. It was an address. Not a great neighborhood, if he remembered correctly. Residences mostly. Cheap communist housing. "What about it?"

"Pick up a woman there. Petra Kovarik. Tvchenko's research assistant."

"What about your own guys?"

Tully inhaled deeply and then slowly let out the smoke. "They're all inexperienced. Except for Quinn Armstrong, and he wasn't in yet this morning."

Jake checked his watch. "I see you run a tight ship, Tully."

"Fuck you. I had him out looking for her all night. After we almost got our asses fried, I figured we better bring her in."

"She was working for you?"

"Yeah. Our main source on Tvchenko. She'll know what he was working on."

"Why didn't she tell you before?"

Tully thought about that, finishing his cigarette and snubbing it in the ashtray. "I don't know."

Jake smiled. "She was working both sides?"

"That's what I want to find out. Bring her in and we'll have a little talk."

Jake agreed. He had some time to kill, and besides, he didn't like the idea of someone trying to blow him up. Maybe she had set off the bomb. Jake left Tully at the bar and wondered if he'd order another drink or go back to the office to work like he had said.

6

Petra Kovarik lived in a crowded, congested section of Odessa where immigrants from former Soviet republics like Bulgaria and Romania were cramped into tiny apartments. Many of the brick row houses and concrete slab buildings were occupied by wives of Black Sea sailors, who were gone most of the year and didn't seem to mind the squalor when they were there, for they had seen far worse in ports with names that most Ukrainians had never heard of.

Jake had taken a cab, paid the man, who was glad to leave, and stood on the sidewalk gazing two blocks to Petra Kovarik's apartment building. He figured it was better to get out early and walk a short distance to her building. Who knew if someone else might be looking for the woman?

He slowly walked off toward her place. It was closing in on noon and the streets were fairly vacant. Two young boys were having a stick war along an iron fence, and they didn't seem to notice him pass. Cars that were parked on both sides of the street were mostly old Volgas or Trabants, the communist answer to the Volkswagen.

Kovarik's building was a four-story concrete monstrosity with balconies enclosed by metal railing that were currently being used as clothes lines. The steps leading to the front door had chipped away already, even though Jake suspected the apartment building was no more than thirty years old.

Inside, Jake checked the mailboxes in a foyer area. Above each box was a button, where, supposedly, guests would call up to an apartment and the occupant could decide whether to buzz the person in. The problem was, someone had bashed in the speaker and ripped the electronic lock from the glass door that was now opened wide.

There was a P.K. on the box for room 222. Jake headed up the scuffed wooden stairs. At the top, he noticed the hallway was dark. The far wall was a bank of glass blocks that had somehow been darkened and now let in very little light. The ceiling paint was peeling and chips scattered about on the wooden floor. The overhead lights were either off or burned out. He checked a switch. Nothing.

Jake started down the passageway, wondering if he should draw his Makarov. He thought of the kids playing down the street and imagined more were probably lurking about. He left the 9mm in its holster, but unzipped his leather jacket.

Since the even numbered rooms were on the right, Jake realized that Petra's room would be the last one on the right. As he got closer, he thought about Tully. He had seemed extremely strange, or nervous. Jake didn't really know him well enough to understand which.

As he reached the door, he could hear movement inside. It wasn't just a woman's feet crossing wooden floors, though. Things were flying and ripping, and now he thought about Tvchenko's apartment. Had the Kurds beat him to the place?

He slid his hand to the Makarov and started to draw it, when the door burst open and a startled figure smashed into him, knocking him back across the hallway to the door on the opposite side.

Jake scrambled to recover. Pulled the gun.

Two men had passed him and were sprinting down the hall.

Jake took aim in the darkness and hesitated. He didn't know who they were. They hadn't tried to shoot him.

By now the men were around the corner and taking the steps downstairs by twos or threes.

He peered toward the opened door, but couldn't see much. He stepped inside and closed the door behind him, his gun still drawn. The light switch didn't work.

Thinking about Tvchenko's place again, he sniffed the air. Nothing.

He bumped into something. A sofa? Now he suspected he was in the middle of the living room. The windows were covered with shades that let in tiny strips of light between them.

Suddenly, there was movement and the gun flew from his hand. Then a kick to his stomach.

Jake swung around in the darkness with a high round-house kick, connecting on some body part. A face? There was a thud to the floor, and Jake was immediately on top of a body. He grabbed for the neck with his left hand and punched twice at the face rapidly with the right.

The man below him settled.

Jake crawled across the floor to a small table, groped around, found a small lamp, and clicked it on. Then he found the Makarov on the floor by the sofa leg.

Lying on the floor behind him was a man in his early thirties, perhaps younger. He had dark hair just off his shoulders and he needed a shave, much like Jake. He wore faded blue jeans and a black sweatshirt. The man seemed around five-ten, medium build, but it was hard to tell with him sprawled across the carpet. Then Jake noticed the Nike basketball shoes.

He searched the man for I.D. Nothing. He rolled him over, checked him for weapons, and found an empty leather holster under his left arm, but no gun. The jeans were Levis, hard to come by in Odessa. Shit. He had to be an American or a Brit. Jake rolled him back. He had blood coming from both nostrils and a reddened left ear, probably from his kick.

Jake slapped the man a few times and he started to come around.

In a moment, the man raised himself to his elbows. He was having a hard time breathing. He blew out through his nose and dislodged a blood clot into his hand.

"Who the fuck are you?" the man asked in Russian.

Jake realized he had the Makarov pointed at the man. He aimed it away. "I thought I'd ask you that question," he said in English. "Since you hit me first."

The man rose to a sitting position and wiped his nose on his sleeve. "You're American. You don't look it."

"You do," Jake said. "Who are you?"

The man hesitated.

Jake pointed the gun at him again.

"Quinn Armstrong."

"Shit." Jake reached down for the man's hand. "I'm Jake Adams. Tully sent me."

The man looked at him reluctantly, and finally took Jake's hand and pulled himself up. He was still a bit shaky, so he took a seat on the sofa. "I thought you were a lot older."

"Who told you that?"

"I don't know. The way Tully talked, you were some legend. He spoke highly of you. Now I know why." He rubbed the side of his head.

Jake didn't know what to say. Finally he asked, "Where's Petra?"

Quinn shook his head. "I have no idea. I checked her normal hang-outs last night. She's not into the night club scene, but she goes to a few Jazz joints for the music. What the hell did you hit me with?"

Jake looked down at his brown hiking tennis shoes. They weren't much to look at, but they were comfortable to walk in and held up nicely against a man's head, or any other body part. "Sorry about that."

Quinn shrugged and continued. "I've been hanging around here since late last night. I must have fallen asleep on the couch. When I heard the door open, I got up to meet Petra. But it wasn't her. Two guys burst in and the biggest one cold-cocked me. I came around and saw a figure at the door. I took a swipe at the gun, and here we are. What do you mean Tully sent you?"

"Which word don't you understand?"

"It's just that he told me about you a few days ago," Quinn said. "Said you were old Agency, had worked covert ops, former Air Force Intel, the whole spiel. Said you went private a few years back, and were babysitting a couple of Bozos from Portland. Hardly the kind of thing you'd expect, considering your background."

"Did he also say I liked to kick the shit out of smart asses?"

"Afraid not. If you're referring to me, I'm not feeling really smart right now."

"Hang on a minute." Jake went to the kitchen and found some ice cubes, which he wrapped in a small towel and brought to Quinn. "You've got a helluva bruise forming under your ear. Put this on it."

Quinn took the ice reluctantly and set it against his upper jaw. "Did you get a good look at them?"

"No such luck. They plowed into me on their way out, but the hallway was too dark. The first one out was big, but he moved like a much smaller guy. Like a linebacker. He wasn't Ukrainian or Russian. I'm guessing he was one of the Kurds that ransacked Tvchenko's apartment." Jake looked around the room, which was destroyed much like the scientist's place had been. "He does a good job."

Quinn glanced about. "What were they looking for?"

"Other than Petra? I'd guess whatever she and Yuri Tvchenko were working on. You were her runner. Did she talk to you about their work?"

Armstrong had his eyes closed, in obvious pain. "She had her suspicions. She was a decent lab technician. Did what Tvchenko told her to. That's it. She said he was extremely secretive. Would only tell her what she needed to know to complete her experiments."

"You believe her?"

Quinn opened his eyes and glared at Jake. "Of course. I trust her."

"Where is she then?"

"I don't know!" he yelled. Quinn mulled over the question for a moment and then settled down. "Maybe she heard about Tvchenko's murder last night and got scared. She said he had changed a lot lately. So the guy gets himself killed, she starts thinking it had something to do with the research, and she goes into hiding. So, Tully sent you. Why are you involved?"

Jake wasn't sure about that himself. He had taken on the job watching over MacCarty and Swanson because that's what he did now, take care of people who didn't think they could do it themselves. It was true that the complexity of those assignments were usually less than exciting, but what the hell, it was a living. Every now and then over the past three years he would get a case that seemed easy at first but quickly turned into something else. Maybe this was one of them.

Looking the room over again, Jake finally said, "Who knows why we do the things we do? Did Tully tell you about last night? At Tvchenko's apartment."

"Yeah."

"Well, I guess I don't like people trying to dismember my body," Jake said. "I'm not ready for that yet."

"Makes sense." Quinn looked at the gun in Jake's hand. "Is that the Makarov Tully gave you?"

"Yep."

"It's a piece of shit," Quinn said. "I'll try to get you something better." He felt for his own gun, and not finding it, he said, "I guess we both need a new one. Those bastards took my brand new Glock 19."

"I'd prefer a CZ-75, but a Glock will do, if you can swing it."

"I'll ask for it in our next pouch due in from Rome." Quinn rose and brought what was left of the ice pack to the kitchen and threw it in the sink. When he returned, he said, "Let's head out and get a beer. I've got a few ideas left on where to find Petra."

Jake holstered the Makarov. "Sounds good."

7

It was Jake's idea to go to the Odessa Hotel for a beer. Quinn didn't care, he just wanted a beer to take his mind off the bruise that had formed on the side of his head. He had to be in some pain.

The Odessa Hotel was a few blocks down Primorski Boulevard from his hotel and perhaps a kilometer down that same street from the Maranavka, where Tvchenko had been killed the night before. The Odessa was nearly the same age as the Maranavka with less than half the charm or opulence. The red carpet in the lobby was worn and frayed and the oak counter in need of varnish.

Moving into the bar area, it seemed like night had already settled on the town, since half of the overhead lights were either turned off or missing.

They nudged up against the hotel bar, and considering the time of day, late afternoon, the place was fairly crowded. Picking up a couple of local pils at the bar, the two of them found seats at a table back in a corner.

"How's your head?" Jake asked.

"They didn't teach that move at the academy."

Jake shrugged. "I knew that before I joined the old

Agency."

Quinn rubbed the bruise gently. "Nice."

They stared at each other for a moment. Quinn scratched his finely cropped goatee that made his chin look like a sharp chisel. The pointed angles stretched his head out, making it appear longer than it was.

Finally, Jake asked, "What do you know about the Kurds?"

"You separate it from the whey to make cheese."

"Funny guy."

"Hey, I used to work on a dairy farm in the summers in high school."

Jake took a sip of beer and kept an eye on the door. He had had more than one reason choosing this place. He hoped to run into Chavva between conferences. But neither she nor any of her Israeli friends were there.

"The Kurds?" Jake repeated.

"I know nothing about Kurds."

"What about Petra?"

Quinn took a long sip of beer. "I don't know where she is. I'll hit as many places as I can tonight to see if I can find her. I'll bring her in and ask her about Tvchenko."

Great. Jake leaned back and thought for a moment about his questioning. What did it matter to him? He was damn near interrogating the man, someone who should have been asking him questions about his association with the dead scientist.

"Why did Tully ask me to go pick up Petra?"

"How the hell should I know!" Quinn's voice raised above the normal din of voices, bringing stares from a few men at the nearest table.

"Don't get pissed at me," Jake said. "I was just doing

the guy a favor. He thought you were—"

"What? Incompetent?"

"Sleeping...after staying up most of the night looking for Petra. Listen, I don't work for the agency anymore. I was just trying to help out."

Quinn rose to his feet and finished his beer. "Maybe you should go back to babysitting."

Leaving Jake there by himself, Quinn stormed out of the bar. That went well, Jake thought.

He finished his beer and then wandered toward the lobby. At the front desk, he asked for Chavva's room. There was nobody there by that name. Then Jake described her in great detail. The man at the counter assured him that if someone like that was staying there, he'd know about it. Outstanding. She had said the Odessa Hotel. Why would she lie to him?

Jake left the Odessa and walked to the Chornoye Hotel, where he and MacCarty and Swanson were staying. It was nearly four, the time he was supposed to meet his boss and sidekick.

Checking the front desk for messages, there was only one from MacCarty saying the meeting at four was cancelled. He and Swanson had another conference they wanted to attend, hoping to wine and dine someone from Kiev afterwards. That was fine with Jake. He pocketed the note and went up to his room. It had been a long night and a long day and he figured he could use a quick nap before dinner.

8

Bill Swanson was a nervous man, fidgeting in the high-back wooden chair at the end of the bar. He had gotten a call from a man an hour ago, a contact he had talked to only twice by phone, and Swanson had agreed to meet him, as long as it was a public spot.

The Chornoye Morye Bar was only a block from his hotel, and he had told his boss, Maxwell MacCarty, he was hitting the sack early and would see him in the morning. MacCarty had no problem with that, since he was tired from all the lectures that day, and trying to negotiate a deal for a plant in Kiev. Swanson thought he should have done the same, considering his lack of sleep the night before following Tvchenko's death.

Having gone through two vodka collins in the fifteen minutes he had waited for the man who had said he'd be there at eight o'clock, Swanson was getting nervous and impatient. He checked his watch again. It was ten after eight now.

The problem was he didn't even know what the man looked like. There was a man down the bar a few chairs, an older man who seemed like a daily fixture there, gruff and in dire need of a shave. Was it him? Doubtful. The man he had talked with sounded dignified, as if he were a businessman like him.

As he scanned the room again, he noticed there were only four other people in the place. Two younger men at one table holding hands across the table. Fucking queers, Swanson thought. The other two were about mid-forties and rather boisterous, speaking English. British accents. It couldn't be one of them. No. His contact was late.

That was fine. It gave him time to think. How would he deal with this man? He knew nothing about him, yet the proposition seemed too good to be true. The money had been waiting for him at the desk this morning, just as the man said it would after the first call. But what did he want now?

He ordered a third drink, and the bartender went to work on it in a slow, deliberate manner, something that would have gotten him fired in America.

"Don't turn around," came a deep, husky voice behind him.

Swanson had his back to the bathroom entrance, and the only other chair at that end of the bar was against the wall by that door. The man must have been in there watching and waiting. Waiting for him to go to the bathroom, he thought. He shifted slightly and tried to see the man through the corner of his eye, but it was useless.

"What do you want?" Swanson asked.

"The money wasn't for your good looks," the man said.

Swanson's drink came and he paid for it. The bartender asked the other man what he wanted. Nothing, was all he said, and the bartender went away with a disturbed look, as if he had seen a gun. Did the man have a gun?

"Well, what can I do for you?" Swanson asked, and then took a drink.

"Tvchenko. You were talking with him after his lecture yesterday, and at the party last night before his untimely death. I want to know what you found so fascinating."

How did this man know he had talked with Tvchenko? Had he attended the lecture? It was possible. There had been twenty or more men there, as well as four women. He racked his brain now trying to match the voice with those he had seen in the lecture, but he drew a blank.

"We talked about his work," Swanson said. "I was interested in his recent research with pesticides. I figured if it worked so well on Ukrainian bugs, why not Oregon bugs?"

"And?"

"And what?" Swanson started to turn but was stopped by a stiff object against the side of his face. It could have been a cane or an umbrella, or maybe even a gun. "What are you doing?"

"I told you not to turn."

Swanson swiveled his head back and took another sip of his drink. "Listen, I don't know what in the hell you want."

"You got the money?"

"Yes, of course. But I thought that was for what we had discussed earlier. Showing favoritism is one thing..."

"Shut up. Not so loud."

Swanson hadn't realized his voice had risen. "All right," he whispered. "What can I do for you."

"That's more like it." The man paused for a moment. "You have a man working for you. A Jake Adams. What does he know of all this?"

Swanson was wondering what "all this" was. "Adams knows Odessa. We had heard that the Ukraine was going through growing pains. Was a little wild. When we got our Visas the state department had warned us that businessmen had been murdered. He's here for security."

The man was silent, thinking about it. "What kind of background does he have?"

What was with this man's interest in Jake? What the hell difference did it make. He and Jake had been at each other's throats since they met. "Air Force intelligence, I guess. He used to work here."

"That's it?"

Swanson finished his drink. "Yes. As far as I know."

"Why isn't he here tonight with you? Protecting you."

Swanson laughed. "I thought it was stupid to hire him in the first place. A waste of money."

"Can I talk with him?" the man asked.

"Go right ahead."

"Where's he staying?"

"Same hotel as us. Across the hall. But—"

"I'll get back with you." The man stood up. "As I pass you, turn and head to the bathroom. Don't come out for two minutes. Don't try to look at me. Do you understand?"

"Yes, but..." Swanson felt something across his back, so he rose quickly and went into the bathroom. He waited there for a good five minutes. When he came out, he talked with the bartender. Asked him what the man had looked like sitting next to him. The bartender thought he was nuts, but he described him carefully, as if he would never forget the man. Swanson felt good about that. He had outsmarted the man at his own game.

9

Nearly twenty-four hours had passed since Yuri Tvchenko collapsed into Jake's arms, yet the Odessa police, who had ordered an immediate autopsy, had given no indication of the results of that examination. The problem was, there was no legitimate reason Jake should know the results and he knew it.

He had tried to rest, tossing and turning in his hotel bed, uncertain what to do next. On one hand, he couldn't help thinking about Tvchenko. What had he been up to? More importantly, perhaps, was his guilty feelings about MacCarty and Swanson. They were paying him to protect them, and he had been off all day looking into Tvchenko's death. It wasn't like he didn't try to help the two men. On the plane trip over, he had briefed them on ways to keep from becoming targets. But once the three of them had actually landed, and the two of them had seen that the city wasn't infested with ten-foot beasts, they figured they would be safe enough on their own. Jake had protested, relenting when he realized that the two men were adults; old enough to decide some things for themselves.

It was true that Jake would help negotiate any contract

if Bio-tech decided to build a business there or convert an existing facility. Maybe that was MacCarty's true concern. It was also true that Odessa had gotten more dangerous over the years. Tvchenko's death had proved that, as well as the intelligence briefings Jake had gotten from Tully his first day there. In the old days undesireables were simply whisked away, never to be seen again. Taken to some frozen Siberian resort, no doubt.

It was ten p.m. now. Jake waited in relative darkness at the base of the Potemkin Steps in the heart of the harbor region. He had always been told that there were one hundred ninety-two steps in all, but he had never found a good reason to count them.

Out on the street toward the harbor, cars frequently streamed by, their tires squealing on tight turns. Taxis mostly at this hour, carrying drunken sailors from one bar to the next.

Jake thought about the sleepless night before, where he and Tully O'Neill, the Odessa station chief, had quickly gone to Tvchenko's apartment, been nearly blown to pieces, and then discovered the tape with the Kurds. He thought about Tvchenko, trying to make sense of his death. Was it simply the GRU cleaning house? Jake didn't think so. Tvchenko must have been selling information to someone, until, much like a drug deal gone sour, that group decided they were getting a raw deal, or were being set up.

He regretted not finding Chavva at the Odessa Hotel that afternoon. There was something about her that was both disturbing and exciting. She had a certain naughty quality that transcended normal, rational behavior. He had never gotten her full name, just Chavva, like some movie star or rock singer.

Hopefully, Tully O'Neill had gone back to the office, made copies of the tape, and sent the original back to Langley by diplomatic pouch for a linguist to analyze.

Slipping his hand out of his pocket, Jake rubbed the scab in his palm where the cryptic note had been injected just before Tvchenko had crumpled into a convulsive ball. What did it mean? He knew nearly everything about the city of Halabja and its horrid past, but what was Tvchenko trying to tell him?

And what was he doing here in the dark? After his vain attempt to rest, he had gone down to the front desk in the lobby, where there was a message for him. It had only said, "Be at the bottom of the Potemkin Steps at ten p.m." Nothing more. Not who had sent it, or for what reason. Since going private, Jake realized he was alone most of the time. Back in his Agency days he would have been backed up with double layers protecting his back and moving in behind anyone approaching the area. But now he was on his own. Sure he could have disregarded the note, but what the hell, full living meant taking chances. And the note had been curious if nothing else.

He scanned the darkness for any movement, but there was only an occasional drunk sailor off in the distance at the pier. He felt for the Makarov under his arm. It reassured him, even though he had not fired the weapon. Would it work if he needed it? Hopefully Quinn Armstrong would get him a new piece soon.

In a moment, a large dark car approached slowly down the street and stopped, its lights blinding Jake from twenty feet away. The two back doors opened and two figures appeared—then there was the distinct clicking of automatic weapons chambering rounds.

Jake reached for the Makarov.

"That wouldn't be wise," came a harsh voice in broken English.

Jake slid his hand out from inside his coat and thought of dashing toward the harbor and diving into the water. "What do you want?"

"Answers."

"Who are you?" It was a stupid question and Jake knew it. But he thought he'd try.

"It does not matter. This will only take a short while. Assuming we get the right answers."

Taking a few steps forward, Jake tried desperately to identify the car. But in the bright headlights, it was impossible to tell the make for sure. It wasn't a normal pattern. More like someone had modified the light scheme. "Well? You ask the questions and I'll try to answer them."

"I'm afraid it's not that simple."

There was only a faint blowing sound, like a pellet rifle. Jake felt a pain in his neck, reached up and touched the dart, and that was the last he remembered.

10

His head swirled uncontrollably, as Jake tried desperately to lift his body from the cold cement. His knees ached. There was a sharp pain in his ribs, and he rubbed them now with his hand to ease the stabbing spasm that felt like a knife was still there imbedded in his chest. Then there was the swelling throb in his neck. All these problems were minor compared to his feelings of utter stupidity. How had he let himself get into this situation?

High overhead there was a single light, not bright enough to allow a good view of his surroundings. He could only see perhaps twenty feet in all directions. There were crates stacked high on two sides of the room, a crude wooden structure with windows, an odd attempt at an office on another side, and a high metal door on the fourth. Even through blurry eyes, Jake suspected he was in a warehouse of some sort. He could still smell the ocean, so he was probably in the harbor region.

Out beyond the light, he heard whispers. Then footsteps coming his way. He was on one knee and one foot, with a hand on his chest and the other trying to squeeze life back into his head. Feeling with his left arm, he realized the Makarov was gone.

Finally, he could make out three men heading toward him. They stopped ten feet away, but their faces were covered with white, cold weather masks, like those issued to Russian troops in the winter. The two outer men wore cheap wool suits, much like the old KGB or GRU would wear. The middle man wore a fine Armani, or a reasonable fake. The two on the outside carried submachine guns, but in the darkness and from that distance Jake couldn't see if they had rounds chambered. He supposed they did.

"Well, Mr. Adams," came a voice from the middle man. "I see you're with us again."

It was the same man who had spoken through the bright headlights. What type of accent was that?

"You've got me at a disadvantage," Jake said, struggling to rise. He winced in pain. Someone had done a number on his body while he was out.

The man laughed. "I'm afraid you're right." There was a long pause. "We need some information."

"Who's we?"

"I've heard you're a difficult man."

Heard, my ass. Read in a security briefing perhaps. "What do you want? Make it quick. I think one of your courageous buddies there broke my ribs." Jake squinted through the darkness to look for a reaction.

"You were the last man to speak with Yuri Tvchenko before he died," the man said.

"He didn't say shit to me!" Jake yelled, his voice echoing through the cavernous room. "Someone made sure of that," he added softly, with pain.

"Then why did you blow up his apartment last night."

Jake laughed and then started coughing. He could taste the iron of his own blood. So, they must have been at the apartment. They either followed Jake and Tully there, which was not likely, or they had been watching the place. Maybe they even set off the bomb. "Yeah, right. I got my ass fried there." He thought for a second. "Where were you when the whole thing went down?"

"I'm asking the questions here?"

"Who do you work for?" Jake asked, not expecting an answer.

"That's funny, that was my next question for you."

Jake glanced around the dark room for some escape route. "I work for Bio-tech Chemical from Portland, Oregon. We make insecticides and fertilizers."

"That's a nice little lie, Mr. Adams," the man said. His voice became more serious. "Whatever happened to Captain Adams, United States Air Force Intelligence? Expert in chemical and biological weapons?"

Damn! He knew more than Jake initially thought. But at least he hadn't mentioned the CIA. Time to shift gears. "Yeah, well the Cold War is over, remember. The military didn't need me any more. So, like all good capitalists, I went private."

The man considered this, then whispered to one of his men. The man walked up to Jake and swung his leg up quickly, catching him in the chest. Jake reeled to his back and landed with a crash to the cement. Then he buckled in pain. If the ribs hadn't been broken before, they were now.

After a minute, the man spoke again. "You could make things so much easier for yourself if you'd simply answer my questions truthfully."

"And then what?" Jake forced out. "Your boys take target practice." He had to stall. It was a gamble, but perhaps they wouldn't kill him.

"I assure you, my men need no practice," the man said. "Now, where were we? You were going to tell me everything you know about Yuri Tvchenko. What he was working on. Who he was selling out to. The whole story."

"You seem to know more about him than I do," Jake said, struggling to his feet. "After all, I've only been in Odessa a few days. I'm here to attend an agricultural conference. I just happened to be standing in the ballroom when Tvchenko was killed. I never even met the man," Jake lied.

"He was shaking your hand when he died!" the man screamed.

Jake stepped forward, directly under the light. "I had never met the man." He wanted the man to see his face when he lied. He had always been able to fool anyone with a straight face. First his mother, then his teachers, even his friends while telling a joke. He had also found it quite easy to fool a lie detector. The Air Force had never known this, but the Agency had its suspicions and did nothing. After all, that was a fine trait for a field officer.

The man in the middle was clearly frustrated. He reached into his jacket and pulled out an automatic pistol, pointing it directly at Jake's head. "I want the truth!"

Jake didn't flinch. If it had come down to this, dying in some squalid warehouse, then he was prepared. His parents had died. He had no wife. No children. Not even a girlfriend any more. He had dedicated his life to his work. First his education, then the military and the Agency, and now his private company. "Go ahead," Jake said. "I have nothing to live for. I work for a Goddamn pesticide company. So I'm basically a souped-up exterminator. I haven't had a date in over a year. And even then I didn't get lucky." He was really laying it on now. He peered directly at the masked leader and the pistol muzzle. "You wanta shoot me. Go ahead. I'm not worth that 9mm parabellum slug."

The man slowly returned his gun to its holster. "You seem to know a lot about guns, Mr. Adams. Why is that?"

"I grew up in Oregon. We're heavily armed out west."

"And why were you carrying the Makarov?"

Jake expected this question. "I've heard a number of businessmen have been shot in Eastern Europe and Russia lately. I was just trying to protect myself from...gangs."

The man whispered to his men. The two of them grabbed Jake by his arms and escorted him into the darkness. As they stepped outside, Jake could smell the saltwater and dead fish, and hear the light waves lapping against the wooden moorings. He felt a slight breeze across his face. Then there was a hollow thud as one of the men hit him in the back of the head.

Ten minutes later, Jake woke in darkness. His whole body was shaking. He was wet. He felt down with his hands, and realized he was lying on a course netting. Fishing nets. Suddenly he felt a hand squeezing his left arm, trying to pull him up.

"Get up, Jake," the man above him said. "Are you all right?"

He couldn't see the man yet, but he recognized the voice. It was British. "What the hell are you doing here, Sinclair?" Jake forced out.

The Brit pulled Jake up farther and stooped down to his

level. Sinclair Tucker was wearing a long wool coat, nice dress slacks, and brown oxford shoes. He had a strong jaw that he had not shaved in a few days, which was unusual for him. If there was anyone Jake knew who took personal hygiene seriously, Sinclair Tucker was the poster boy. They had spent a great deal of time together in remote Turkish villages, with no running water, except for a stream, and Tucker always managed to maintain a clean appearance.

"Well it's nice to see you too," Sinclair Tucker said.

Jake sat up and pain shot through his chest. "What brings MI-6 out on such a fine Odessa night? Wait a minute. I heard you went home for the holidays?"

"I bloody well did," Sinclair said, tipping his tweed driving cap to the back of his head. "I'm afraid my superiors had other ideas. The bastards forced me to leave in the first place, and then they ruin it once I've agreed. As if I had a choice."

"Can you help me here?" Jake reached his arm out to the Brit.

Tucker lifted Jake to his feet. The Brit was a wiry guy. Over six feet, but with no visible fat. He had surprised Jake with unusual strength on a number of occasions, as if his muscles were a secret.

"How'd you find me?" Jake asked.

"Superior British intelligence, I suppose."

"Now there's a triple oxymoron," Jake laughed, as he started walking down the pier. His balance was shaky and his head was still in a great deal of pain. He stroked the knot on the back of his skull, where dried blood was caked to his long hair.

Tucker was at his side. He swung Jake's arm over his

shoulder. "Actually, I had just gotten in from London and headed directly to your hotel. I assumed you'd know something about Tvchenko's death. You got into a cab just as I was pulling up. I followed you. I guessed you weren't going out on a late night tour of the city. So I thought you could use some backup."

Jake stopped quickly. "You saw the men take me?"

Tucker nodded.

"And you didn't do anything?"

"I took down the information on the car and followed it to the warehouse. I was in the warehouse when you gave them that bullshit story. You're a helluva liar, Jake. I had them in my sights. When they hit you and dragged you down the pier, I was afraid they'd kill you and dump you into the harbor. Luckily they didn't. They just left about ten minutes ago."

"Why didn't you follow them?"

Tucker laughed. "You dumb bastard. I came back to see if you were all right."

"Thanks."

"No problem."

By now they had reached the end of the pier. Jake could see a building a few hundred yards away, and he assumed it was the warehouse where the men had taken him. "Where's your car?"

Tucker pointed off into the darkness.

As the two men approached, Chavva sunk lower in the driver's seat. The car was in total darkness, so her reaction was from instinct. She had her window lowered, trying to hear what they were saying, without much luck.

She gasped when she saw one man helping the other. He

was having a difficult time walking. Someone had beaten him, she was sure.

A block away, the men piled into the little Zil sedan and then drove off. She thought of following them, but had a better idea.

11

The hotel room reeked of stale cigarette smoke from the two men chain smoking over the past hour. They had both been in the Israeli army, had fought little skirmishes too many to count, and had then found their way into the private service of the wealthy Tel Aviv businessman. The pay was better, they could still carry their pacifying Uzis, and so far they had not had to dodge any Arab or Palestinian bullets. They were playing a game of cards, both cheating badly, and catching each other with the dirty deed. If one or the other actually played it straight for a change, the other would surely lose respect.

Peering out the window from the twelfth floor to the vacant street below, Omri Sherut wondered how long she would be. He checked his watch again. It was nearly two a.m. He had called her an hour ago, and she had insisted on coming over. She didn't like handling anything over the phone, he knew. Unfortunately, she was far more persuasive in person. No one could say no to those eyes, and he had heard that even those were deceiving. She was a dangerous person. That was a fact. Her good looks did nothing to change that.

There was a faint knock on the door and the two men quickly dropped the cards and found their weapons.

Sherut waved them back to their game as he headed for the door, peeked through the view hole, and then opened it.

Chavva strutted in, obviously disturbed. She wore tight black jeans and a leather coat, and she swayed her hips with each determined step. She swung around toward Sherut. "Send the boys for a walk," she demanded.

Sherut hesitated. Orders were supposed to go in the other direction.

She glared at the two body guards, who were trying not to stare at her beautiful body, and failing miserably. "Get out," she yelled at them, swishing her head toward the door. "Keep an eye on the hallway and the elevator."

They didn't even look to their boss for help. They simply slipped on their overcoats and slid their Uzis into specially-made inside pockets. In a second they were gone.

Moving closer, Sherut wondered what was so important. Since his days with Mossad, so long ago now, he had taken orders from no one. He had built his successful business from the ground up, accumulating great wealth. He was only in Odessa now because of his friendship with the Mossad leadership. He was doing them a favor. How did this woman think she could make such great demands? Like a wife. He had been married once, until she started making demands much like this woman now. That one was gone as though she had never been born. It was an unfortunate accident. Who would have guessed the decks of a luxury cruise liner could be so wet and slippery at night?

"What's wrong, Chavva?"

She crossed her arms. "I told you Adams was not to be hurt. We need him."

"He's still alive. We didn't hurt him."

"That's not what I've heard," she said.

How could she know, he thought. He knew she was a resourceful operative. At least that's what his old friend at Mossad had told him. Warned him, as it was. He could not remember his exact words, but simply a feeling that she was not to be totally trusted. In fact, he had said, she herself had gone too far interrogating people. It was rumored that she could kill men twice her size with one kick, and had proven it many times. If she had heard that they had gone too far with the American, then she had more ears and eyes out there than he initially thought.

"We had to try to make him tell us what he knows," Sherut said, trying to calm her.

She turned away, wondering how to approach him. She needed their support. Didn't want it, but needed it. She was to give them a hand, yet work independently. She had her own ideas on how to make the whole thing work, regardless of Omri Sherut's plans. It was true that Sherut had worked as an officer in the past, but how many centuries ago was that? So what if he was a personal friend of the Mossad director. She suspected there was a greased palm here or there, but was in no position to prove it, and couldn't really care less one way or the other. It was all part of the game.

She turned around. "And? What does Jake know?"

"Nothing. I'm sure of it."

"He's not going to just give up the information," she said. "How can you be so sure?"

"The boys broke a few ribs."

She looked surprised. She had been right. Jake had been limping, being helped by that other man she had never seen before. She thought about the night they had met in Istanbul. He had not recognized her. How could he? It had been so long. He was a man she could let take her...do whatever he wanted. The thought of him being less than perfect disturbed her. "What did he say?"

"Said he works for a fertilizer company," Sherut said.

At least he's consistent. "What else?"

"He said he had never met Tvchenko. That he just happened to be standing next to him when he collapsed. I don't believe him."

"Why?"

"He was carrying this." Sherut handed her the Makarov.

She looked over the pistol, slid the chamber open. It was empty. "How did he explain this?" She popped the magazine out and extracted the first round. It was a brass jacketed hollow point. A standard round. If he was an operative, he would have untraceable hand loads with smokeless powder.

"He said businessmen were being killed every day in Eastern Europe."

She snapped the magazine into the butt of the gun. "That's possible. But I don't think so."

"That's what I figured," he said, feeling a little better about his talk with Adams. "He didn't carry himself like some businessman. Military intelligence maybe. Agency more likely."

She figured Jake Adams would be tough to crack. He had impressed her as someone with a great deal of conviction. No, perhaps a softer approach would work better on him. She smiled at the thought of seducing him. He would be both gentle and rough. A combination that was hard to find in a man. The truth is, she hoped it would come to this.

"What about his employers?" she asked.

Sherut pulled out a small piece of paper from inside his suit. "Maxwell MacCarty is the Bio-tech Chemical Company president. I met him at the conference. A capable man, but I don't think he would have anything to do with Tvchenko. His partner, Bill Swanson, is in charge of research for their company. He's another story. I don't think he's smart enough to be involved." He hesitated and thought about his meeting with the little fat and balding man from Portland at the bar earlier that night. He could be a problem.

"What's wrong with Swanson?" she asked.

"Nothing. I'm sure he knows nothing. Yet, he could be a problem for us."

She smiled. "Problems can be handled."

A chill came over him as he gazed at her eyes surrounded by dark, furled brows.

Jake Adams was standing before a full-length mirror in the hotel room with his shirt off. His ribs were definitely bruised, perhaps even cracked. It wasn't the first time and probably wouldn't be the last. When he had tasted his own blood earlier, he thought his lung had collapsed. But once he got back to his room, he realized he had been hit in the nose as well. So the blood could have come from that wound. Regardless, his ribs were in a great deal of pain. Pain he'd have to live with.

Tully O'Neill pulled a large roll of white medical tape from a first aid kit he had brought up from his car. Going on, the tape would be no problem. Coming off was another story.

Tully had hurried over after Jake's call. He looked like he had been drinking heavily. His face was red and his eyes had huge bags beneath them. He was dressed in blue jeans and an old brown leather flyer's jacket. Tully started toward Jake with the tape.

Jake saw him in the mirror. "No fucking way are you taping me." Jake gingerly pulled his shirt over his head, through one arm, then another, and let it fall to his waist.

Across the room, Sinclair Tucker sat backwards on a wooden chair, his hat propped back on his head. "They look broken to me," Sinclair said. "I think you should tape them."

"Stiff upper lip and all that rot, hey Tuck?" Jake said.

"Exactly."

The Odessa station chief seemed more serious than Jake had seen before, even after the bombing at Tvchenko's apartment. He gazed at Jake, the tape ready to go after Jake's chest. Looking at the dark bruises, he had to be wondering why Jake had taken a chance by going off alone. Although Jake had not worked with Tully other than the last few days, he had worked with others who had. Tully had told Jake when they first met that their mutual associates said Jake Adams took too many risks. But Jake also knew that he and Tully were alive today because Jake had sensed something wrong with Tvchenko's apartment where Tully had not.

Tully asked, "Who were they?" He paused and gave Jake a more critical glare. "And what in the hell did they want?"

Jake shrugged and the pain in his ribs made him wince.

"I didn't catch their names, and I didn't see their faces. The two with Uzis were pretty good size. As tall as Sinclair, but bulkier. Well trained I'd suspect. They knew some shit. Knew how to kick. Military or intelligence background, I'd guess. Style seemed familiar. I also heard one guy speak. I think he was trying to cover his accent, but I'd guess he was from the middle east. Perhaps Lebanese or Israeli."

"I got the make and license of the car," Sinclair chimed in. "An older Volga with local plates. Maybe your men could check it out, but I'm sure you'll find nothing."

Tully turned quickly. "Why's that?"

"Nothing personal, mate. I just suspect it was stolen. It had modified fog lights on the front much like the locals use in Crimea and the agricultural north. Rentals don't have those."

Tully had a disgusted look on his face. He had had a few run-ins with British MI-6. They had undone an operation he was running in Bulgaria during the height of the Cold War. He had lost nearly a year of hard work, and that was difficult for any officer to forget. Now here was a man he didn't know, an MI-6 officer, sitting there arrogantly thinking he was one of the boys in his inner circle, with complete access to everything he knew.

"Listen boys, we're not going to quibble over territory on this one," Jake said. "There's too much at stake. Tully, I've worked with Sinclair Tucker on a number of occasions in the past. He's damn good."

"Thank you, Jake," Sinclair said.

"Now, Sinclair. Tully here is the station chief. You don't get a position like that in our new Agency without attaining a certain level of skill." He thought for a minute and realized he was bullshitting himself. Many of those positions were filled because the person knew someone near the top. "I have complete confidence in Tully leading on this one."

Tully's eyes shot up. "Does that mean you'll continue to help out, Jake?"

Jake caressed his ribs. "I'd like a shot at the guys who did this to me, but I still work for MacCarty. And I haven't been doing a helluva lot for him lately. I know you're a little short, Tully. Let's just play it as it comes along. See what happens. When MacCarty and Swanson leave for Portland in a few days, then we'll talk."

"That's fair."

Sinclair Tucker went to a small brown refrigerator across the room. Inside were a few different types of beer, some bottled juice, and various airline-size bottles of liquor. "Anyone want something from here? Jake you look like you could use a beer." Sinclair opened two bottles and brought one to Jake. "How about you, Tully?"

"There's some vodka in there, Tully," Jake said.

"Why not."

Sinclair brought Tully one of the tiny bottles and handed it to him. Then he sucked down some of his beer.

Jake took a seat on the bed. "Have you heard from Quinn Armstrong, Tully?"

Tully downed the entire bottle of vodka. Then he said, "Not bad. Yeah, he said you two met at Petra's place. He's got one helluva bruise on his head. You caught him square."

"He told you it was an accident?" Jake said.

"Sure. But I think he's still pissed it happened."

"He'll get over it," Jake said. "Did you see him tonight?

Did he find Petra yet?"

Tully lit a cigarette and inhaled deeply. "I only talked to him for a minute on the phone. He was going to hit a few clubs tonight. We'll meet in my office in the morning. I'd like you to be there."

"It's the last day of the conference," Jake said. "That should keep MacCarty and Swanson occupied. What time?"

"Nine. Nine thirty."

"I'll be there. Now let's get some sleep."

They all finished their drinks and then Tully O'Neill left first. Five minutes later, Sinclair Tucker headed out as well.

12

NOVILLERO, MEXICO

With thick clouds overhead, the night was extreme-ly dark. Even the lights from the small village were barely visible, as the Cypriot fishing boat chugged slowly toward the pier.

For more than a week the boat had managed to avoid the American Navy and Coast Guard. The poor weather had helped.

Back in the shadows of an old wooden pilot house, Steve Nelsen, a huge man dressed in dark clothing with a zipper jacket with POLICIA stenciled in bright yellow on the back, peered around the corner, watching the boat make its way toward the dilapidated mooring. He was sure it was the right boat, yet it should have been here more than thirty minutes ago. Nelsen was pissed off even being in Mexico. When he had switched from the CIA's operations directorate to the intelligence section six months ago, he had sought a nice assignment in Europe, after hopping around the Middle East and Turkey for the last ten years. But he had made too many enemies in his

tenure there, and his boss, who was working on an ambas-
sadorship of his own, wanted him out of the way. He knew
too much.

Nelsen's partner, Ricardo Garcia, was no stranger to
night operations. He seemed to have the eyes for it, the
whites shimmering in the darkness like an animal's in a
car headlight. He too was dressed in black, camouflaged
in the darkness. He was a good foot shorter than his sen-
ior partner, but stocky, strong, and not afraid to mix it up
with bigger guys. He had been doing it all his life. Garcia
had only worked with Nelsen for a few days, having been
reassigned from drug interdiction in Columbia a few
weeks ago, and then two weeks of vacation in his home
town, San Antonio. Garcia wasn't sure what to think of
Nelsen yet, or how he'd react in a tight spot. But he
thought he was about to find out.

"Let's go, Dick," Nelsen whispered, as he headed
toward the pier. "Remember, on my command," he said
softly into his headset.

Garcia cringed but was right on the man's heels.

In a few minutes the boat was up against the pier, and
the captain watched his crew members tie the boat fore
and aft. The helmsman cut the engine. Cautiously, the
captain made his way from the pilot house to the port side.
Something wasn't right. There were two men in dark
clothes and heavy coats strolling slowly down the wood-
en planks. On another boat across the pier, two men were
straightening a fishing net at the stern. It was nearly midnight, and at that hour, he would have suspected the entire
pier to be empty.

Simultaneously, in chaotic seconds, the men walking

down the pier, those on the opposite boat, and others who
had been crouching out of sight, burst toward the Cypriot
boat, their weapons drawn. One man yelled orders for the
fishermen to hit the deck and keep their hands in plain
view. Others swept through the boat searching desperately for anything unusual. Within a minute, the entire boat
had been canvassed, with no weapon found. The four fishermen were taken into custody, and two officers remained
onboard to guard the vessel.

Nelsen watched as his men escorted the fishermen to the
van. He had been so certain. Something wasn't right here.
The captain of the boat had this knowing smirk, as a child
would when he had just gotten away with something. It
was definitely no fishing boat—with the hold converted to
extra fuel tanks. His men had also reported finding an
engine far more powerful than needed to fish. No, this was
the boat that left Johnston Island with the nerve gas. But
where was the bomb now?

Ricardo Garcia was next to him, wondering what had
gone wrong.

"What do you think, Dick?" Nelsen asked.

Garcia hated that name. Dick. This is the only man who
had called him that, since high school when he broke a
kid's nose for calling him it, and then softly adding "head"
at the end. He didn't want to make waves, having only
been together for a few days. Besides, the man was gigan-
tic. He wasn't only tall, but his muscles, which he exposed
as often as possible in tight T-shirts, were defined like
Arnold Schwarznegger's. Garcia shrugged. "It's got to be
the boat."

"Exactly! Let's see if we can't have a talk with these

boys," Nelsen said, squeezing Garcia's shoulder with his
strong hand, and hauling him off toward the car.

Five miles up the coast, a small launch had just come
ashore on a secluded beach. Four men, all dressed in
black, strained to pull the boat out of the rising tide. When
they finally had the boat completely on dry sand, they
gently tugged the heavy metal case from the boat and set
it on the beach.

Baskale ran to the tree line. Waiting there, as planned,
was an American-licensed Chevy Suburban with wide
tires and four wheel drive. The man drove the truck to the
beach without lights, and in a few seconds, the weapon
was loaded in the back and covered with blankets and
camping gear. The four men headed off in the Suburban
on an old dirt road.

CIA HEADQUARTERS

"What the hell do you mean there was nothing on it?"
the Director of Operations, Kurt Jenkins, screamed into
the secure phone. He was talking to the Mexico City station chief who had just gotten word from his officers in
the field that the Cypriot fishing boat appeared to be just
that. A fishing boat. Although it had been modified with
extra fuel tanks. His men, who were sure it was the right
boat, were heading out now to interrogate the fishermen.

Jenkins swiveled in his chair with the phone propped
against his ear and shoulder. He motioned for his assistant
Bradley Stevens to hand him the satellite photos that had
picked up the fishing boat coming ashore at Novillero. He
adjusted his tiny glasses on his nose, and then flipped

through the photos, listening to the station chief.

"You hold those men," Jenkins demanded. "Interrogate them thoroughly. You know what I mean." The director stopped on a photo to scrutinize it more carefully. Kurt Jenkins had worked his way up the old CIA chain. He had started his career as a satellite analyst, so he could read the obscure markings that to some appeared as specks of dust, but could be a hidden missile site, artillery, or really a speck of dust. "What is this?" The DO pointed to a spot on the dark photo.

The photo analyst, who had joined the assistant DO in briefing their boss, moved to the desk for a closer look. With a magnifying glass, the analyst crouched over the photo. "I don't know, sir. It could be another boat. A smaller vessel, perhaps."

"Just a minute, Walt," Jenkins said to the Mexico station chief, placing him on hold. The DO flipped to an earlier photo. "Why did the Cypriot boat vector down the shore like this?"

The assistant and the analyst shrugged. Then Bradley Stevens, the DO's most trusted assistant, a gangly man, reluctantly answered, "Maybe the captain was off course a little."

Jenkins glared at his assistant. "Bullshit. He's an experienced captain, yet he approaches shore nearly five miles from his intended course. I don't think so." The DO switched to the previous photo. "This is why." He poked his finger at the photo with the stray mark. The satellites had penetrated heavy clouds, so what was there was somewhat blurred.

His two men looked at each other.

The DO punched the secure hold button. "Yeah, Walt.

We just found out the Cypriot boat might have dropped someone ashore five miles up the coast. Get your officers there ASAP."

He listened carefully to the man on the other end.

The DO continued, "Yeah, we'll need some assistance from the locals on this one. Close down the roads in the region and check all flights from every dinky strip of dirt a plane can take off from. Need to know only. Call it drugs if you will."

He slammed the phone down and let out a heavy breath.

THE WHITE HOUSE

Sitting in plush, uncomfortable leather chairs in the Oval Office, members of the National Security Council had been convened for a special session by the president. Present were the president and vice president, secretaries of state and defense, the national security advisor, the Director of Central Intelligence, and the chairman of the joint chiefs.

The president, a large foreboding figure, swiveled around in his high back chair behind his large oak desk, his hands clasped together as if praying. In his short presidency, this was his first major crisis. It had been over a week since the incident on Johnston Atoll and the tension of not finding the bomb showed in each face.

"What do you have, John?" the president asked the CIA Director. As a former assistant in the operations directorate of the old CIA while on loan from the Navy, the president had come to respect and understand his intelligence briefings like no other president in recent history. Since he and John Malone had served in the Navy together, they had a special rapport.

The Director flipped open a folder. "We've been combing the Pacific for any boat that could have left Johnston Atoll, but we haven't found anything definitive yet. Just after the incident, it took hours for our satellites to reach proper positions. We assumed a maximum and minimum speed in any direction. The Navy has currently stopped and boarded twenty-one boats. Nothing. We also thought about a smaller craft hiding out on one of the islands or even picking up an airplane somewhere, but we're still looking into those possibilities. As you know there were a few major storms in the north Pacific just after the incident on Johnston, making it nearly impossible for our satellites and the Navy and Coast Guard radar. We positioned more satellites to track and photograph the entire region after the storms, and our analysts are continuing to study those as we speak." He hadn't been thoroughly briefed on the fishing boat seized in Mexico, and wasn't about to bring it up half-cocked.

"Have any terrorist groups claimed responsibility?" the president asked.

"No, sir," the director said. "Our Naval Intelligence people are still checking the backgrounds on the four vendor employees found executed in the walk-in freezer in Pearl Harbor. Nothing extraordinary, yet. They all appear to be victims."

"Dammit," the president said. "Who in the hell took the weapon? And, how much damage can they do with it?"

The Director shifted nervously in his chair. "We don't know who took it, sir. And the problem with the weapon they took is that it's a cluster bomb. They could crack it open and pull out individual bomblets. There are over a hundred bomblets, each over four pounds."

"How much damage could one bomblet do?" the president asked.

The director gazed at concerned faces around the office. "It's Sarin, a nerve gas. It could take out all of us in this room, the entire building, actually, assuming they had a method of dispersal."

"Don't they have an explosive charge built in?" asked the chairman of the joint chiefs, an army general.

"Yes, Bill. But they'd have to set it off with another charge. Unless they could drop it from a plane, which is possible, considering one of the terrorists had to fly the plane to Johnston."

"So, now you're telling me someone has a hundred little nerve gas bombs that they could conceal in their pocket?" The president shook his head.

"Yes, Mr. President. A big pocket. And this could be significant as well." The CIA director rose and placed a one-page message in front of the president.

The president quickly read the message. "How reliable is this officer?"

"Tully O'Neill is one of our best," the director said emphatically. "If he thinks there's something more to that Ukrainian scientist's death than meets the eye, we should listen. Yuri Tvchenko designed some of the Soviet Union's most horrid chemical and biological weapons."

"You think his death might be related to Johnston Atoll?" asked the secretary of state, skeptically.

"Anything's possible," the Director said. "Tully O'Neill, the Odessa station chief, checked Tvchenko's apartment in Odessa. He had a complete laboratory set up in a back room. But more importantly, the entire place had been ransacked. Furthermore, we've pinpointed the time his apartment was trashed to after the man's death. Just as our man was leaving, the place was bombed. He was nearly killed."

The president, uncertain what to think, looked at his other advisors in the room. "Does this mean anything, people?"

They all answered with blank stares.

The Director continued. "Sir, it could mean that the man was killed prematurely. Tvchenko was under investigation by our officers, and an agent we had recruited at the university there. The agent said Tvchenko was about to make a breakthrough with a new chemical insecticide. Very deadly. Sarin, the older nerve gas taken from Johnston, is basically a strong insecticide. Which is why we think Tvchenko was still working for the Russians. Or someone else. It seems that Tvchenko was also hurting for money and could have been looking for a buyer."

"Dammit," the president said. "Anything else?"

The Director shifted his eyes. "No, sir."

"What are you going to do about this?" the president asked openly.

The Director waited, and when nobody said a word, he took the question. "Sir, we're in a bit of luck. One of our former officers, Jake Adams, is in Odessa. In fact, he was with O'Neill when the bomb went off at Tvchenko's apartment. He saved my man's life."

"What's his background?" the president asked.

"Adams was in Air Force Intelligence before he joined the old Agency. He was an expert in chemical and biological weapons. He helped verify the withdrawal and destruction of them from the Ukraine after the break up of the Soviet Union. He holds a bachelor's in geopolitics and a master's in international relations."

"He's private now? What does he do?"

"He runs a security business out of the Portland, Oregon area. Computers mostly. But companies hire him to accompany them overseas, where they are trying to establish new companies or overseas subsidiaries. You may have heard about the computer chips he safeguarded from German and Hungarian companies over a year ago."

"He did that?"

"Yes, sir."

"He's not a damn intellectual idealist is he?" the president asked.

Malone smiled. "Not really, sir. Adams was a trapper in Oregon in his youth. He spent his summers guiding canoe trips deep into Canada. He's more of an outdoorsman than an intellectual. During the Iran-Iraq War he was on the ground behind enemy lines checking for chemical weapons use. He's tough and can handle anything that comes his way."

The president appeared reassured. "Very well. You've sold me, but will he help us out?"

"You're the president. If you want, you can reinstate his commission." The director smiled.

The president laughed. "Let's not start by pissing him off. Just ask your man, O'Neill, if he'll help us out. Give him whatever he needs. Let him lead if it'll make him happy. And find that chemical weapon from Johnston Island."

"Yes, sir. I'll make it happen. And we'll find the bomb." The director left, and the other council members followed him out the door.

13

ODESSA, UKRAINE

It was just a few hours away from the start of the third and last day of the Odessa Agricultural Conference. MacCarty and Swanson had ordered a western-style breakfast at the hotel restaurant. Both had tried the continental version for three days, with hard bread, salami, and numerous cheeses, and had found it difficult to stomach those things so early in the morning. So on the last day, they decided to deviate from the normal menu and force the hotel to their needs. They would eat bacon and eggs with fresh orange juice. At least that's what they hoped the waitress had understood.

MacCarty sipped a cup of Turkish coffee. "Have you seen Jake Adams lately?" he asked Swanson.

His assistant shook his head. "Nope. I don't know why you're paying him. He hasn't done a thing for us." Swanson drained the last of his coffee and waived for a waitress to bring more, but the woman seemed to ignore him.

"I think he'll pay off eventually," MacCarty said.

"When we start negotiating a deal for our new plant, he'll become indispensable."

"Maybe." Swanson said. He had always been the one MacCarty depended on. Now this outsider was the one who would move the company forward to new markets. Become indispensable. He thought about the night before at the bar, where he met with the man he never saw, yet had managed to get a description from the bartender. It had been such a rush. Dangerous, but exciting. Why would anyone pay for so little information? It made no sense. Nor did Yuri Tvchenko's death. The same could be said for their company wanting to deal with such an unstable, backwards country. He looked around him and saw America in the 50s. Low tech. Shit! No tech.

Back in the kitchen, a dark young man in a white chef's outfit swept through and checked the order sheets. Most of the slips had been sitting there, unattended, for ten minutes. It was the young man's first day on the job. First hours actually. Each slip had a number on it corresponding with a table in the dining area. He verified the table number, double checked it to be sure, and then told the head chef he would like to try this one.

Reluctantly, the head chef agreed. He had baking to attend to. And besides, he had had it with special requests from ungrateful foreigners. The Japanese had wanted one thing, the Norwegians something else. Now the Americans. Let the new kid handle it.

The new young cook pulled a slab of back bacon from a refrigerator, dropped it to the cutting board, whacked quickly with the cleaver, and then slapped six pieces onto the grill. It might not be what the Americans were used to, but it would have to do. Then he cracked four eggs, and they sizzled instantly on the hot, flat surface. He slid a small salt shaker from the front pocket on his smock, glanced over his shoulder briefly, and then shook out a great deal onto the eggs and let the contents dissolve. He flipped the eggs once. In a moment, he carefully set the eggs and bacon onto each plate and handed them to a waitress.

Disturbed, the older woman, whose job normally consisted of running coffee and refilling juice containers, snatched the plates from the young man and swept out through the swinging doors.

The young man excused himself to go to the bathroom. Once in the back bathroom, he poured the remaining contents of the salt shaker into the toilet. He wrapped the shaker in a handkerchief, smashed the glass container into a thousand pieces and dumped it too into the toilet, and then he flushed everything. Next, he stripped off the white smock, rolled it into a ball, and stuffed it under his right arm. Then he casually walked out and left the building from a back exit, throwing the chef's clothes into a dumpster.

After nearly fifteen minutes of waiting, the older woman plopped the plates in front of the Americans and refilled their coffee cups. The eggs looked slimy and the bacon was more like a chunk of fat with tiny strips of brown thrown in for color. Neither looked cooked very well, but by now the two of them were extremely hungry. Besides, the continental fare had already been removed from the buffet tables. There was no turning back now.

"Ummm... This looks good," MacCarty said.

Swanson didn't seem to mind. He was already working on the eggs.

MacCarty reluctantly took a bite of eggs. He noticed a strange flavor, but figured it was simply a difference in the spices used in the Ukraine. Swanson was scooping the eggs in as fast as his fork would work.

"You don't think these taste a little funny?" MacCarty asked.

"Probably free range chickens," Swanson said, his mouth full of eggs.

MacCarty ate one egg and switched to bacon. It wasn't bad. It reminded him of the bacon he used to make on hunting trips in eastern Oregon.

In just a few minutes Swanson had eaten every bite on his plate and was eyeing the leftovers MacCarty couldn't stomach. Then they sat back and washed the food down with a final cup of coffee.

It didn't take long for Swanson to start feeling funny. In less than five minutes he felt pressure in his stomach. Then his chest felt like it would explode.

MacCarty, who had eaten half as much as Swanson, felt fine for now. But he could see that something wasn't right with Swanson. His eyes seemed to enlarge. He was sweating profusely. Much more than normal. When Swanson's arms reached for his chest, MacCarty thought his assistant was having a heart attack. Then Swanson grasped his own throat and crashed to the floor, and MacCarty started yelling for help. In seconds the half-full dining area erupted into panic.

Sitting across the dining room at a table by himself, Omri Sherut watched the Americans. He had been able to pick up much of their conversation. But when the fat little bald man, who had thought he was so smart the night before, started gasping for air, Sherut knew it was time to leave.

He threw down his cloth napkin to the table, disgusted.

14

It was a clear, cold spring morning in Odessa. Jake stopped by a small coffee shop to meet with Sinclair Tucker prior to his morning meeting at Tully O'Neill's office.

Sinclair rushed in and took a seat across from Jake, nearly fifteen minutes late.

"Still on London time?" Jake asked, looking at his watch.

"Sorry, Jake," he said. "I had to stop by our front office to read a message. I see you've started without me." He nodded toward two empty cups of espresso in front of Jake.

"Yeah, I didn't get much sleep last night, as you know." The problem was he didn't feel like eating a thing, since his ribs were killing him, and he figured the thick coffee might at least fill the void in his stomach.

Sinclair Tucker ordered tea. "How are the ribs?"

Jake tried not to think about the pain, but it was difficult. "I've felt worse. I'm pretty sure they were only cracked or bruised."

A young woman delivered the tea to Sinclair and smiled

at both men as she swayed back toward the counter.

"I think she likes you, Tuck."

"Let's not go down that path again," Sinclair said. "Remember that good looking waitress in Adana? The one with the eyes so big we thought they had to be glass?"

"So."

"So, I'm not going through that again."

Jake laughed. "How could we have known she was a man?"

"You bastard. You knew! That's why you let me have her...it...whatever."

"I suspected," Jake said. "That's all."

Sinclair shook his head. "Listen, Jake. I've got a problem."

"That's obvious. I'm sorry. Go on."

Hesitating long enough for a sip of tea, Sinclair said, "Quite the jocular fellow even with bruised ribs." He paused to choose his words. "I haven't been given much support here," he said. "I was hoping you'd help me out. After all, we're on the same team here."

"True. But I'm not sure what I can do for you. I don't know anything yet."

"But you will," Sinclair said. "And I'd appreciate any help you could give me. Back me up, if I need it."

It wasn't a question Jake found difficult to answer. They had history, and that meant more in this business than nationality. They had gone through so much in the past. The aftermath at Halabja. The refugees at the enclaves in Turkey following the Gulf War. It seemed somewhat strange that many of the times their paths had crossed the Kurds had been involved. And now even here, in Odessa, the Kurds had brought the two of them together.

"You know you can count on me, Tuck," Jake said, patting his old friend on the shoulder.

Jake made it to Tully O'Neill's office at the consulate by nine-thirty. Jake had been to the office before when the old station chief had occupied the place. Things had changed a great deal since the height of the Cold War, he could see. There used to be large plants everywhere. Beautiful leather furniture. Nice paintings. But now, as if some bad joke had been played on the office, all that was fine was gone. Tully's desk was an old chunk of wood, worn down by time like a rock in a raging river. The walls were a drab earthtone and needed paint. Tully had tried to cover bad spots with certificates and photographs of him in various cities. The carpeting had been ripped up, exposing an oak floor that needed a good sanding and coat of lacquer. Only the Persian rug looked somewhat new.

Tully was standing before the window overlooking a back courtyard that consulate employees used for breaks and to eat lunch on nice days. He was wearing a tweed suit, the best that Jake could remember him looking since they met a few days ago. In Tully's right hand was a copy of a message he had just finished reading.

Jake took a seat out from Tully's desk in the center of the room.

For a moment, neither of them said a word.

Finally, Tully moved away from the window and took a seat behind his desk in a high-back chair that squeaked with his weight. He lit a cigarette and let out a deep breath of smoke.

"What the hell's going on?" Jake asked. "It's like a damn morgue in here."

Tully shuffled the papers he had set on his desk. "This classified message came in thirty minutes ago," he said, taking another puff on his cigarette. "From our CIA director. It seems he wants you to lead this investigation."

Jake shifted up in his chair. "What? I'm not one of you any more."

"He's aware of that."

"Besides," Jake said. "How in the hell does he even know I'm here?"

Tully smiled. "I'm afraid that's my fault. I had to mention you in my report on Tvchenko's death. The Director mentioned you to the president, and he insisted on asking you to work this for us."

"The president?" Jake said. "He doesn't know me."

"Afraid so," Tully said. "He heard about something you did a few years back. Something dealing with computer chips and Germany and Hungary."

Jake thought that case had gone unnoticed. "So, what do they want from me?"

"Like I said. Lead."

Jake looked shocked. He thought he'd help out a little if he could. But lead? "Why?"

"Let's face it, Jake. You're an expert in chemical and biological weapons. You know Odessa better than any of us. And you even have first-hand knowledge of the Kurds. You should lead. Besides, as you know, the station chief can't afford too much exposure. It looks bad if we're ejected from the country for spying."

This was true, Jake knew, but it was still shocking. What about Quinn Armstrong? It should have been his case.

"You can handle it, Jake," Tully said.

"Thanks for your confidence, Tully, but I didn't seem to

do things right last night. I've got the bruises to prove it."

"You're still alive. That's something."

Jake thought about being in charge. In charge of what? He had no idea what Tvchenko had been up to. He barely knew the man, yet Tvchenko had walked directly to him, planted the note with Halabja scribbled on it into his hand, and then collapsed with his version of a break dance. Someone had either jumped the gun or was now trying to cover their tracks. Jake suspected the former. Maybe Tvchenko's buyers had slipped and told him what they planned on doing with his newest nerve agent. Tvchenko suddenly realizes he cannot follow through with the deal. He panics. The other side panics. And now there's some terrorist group out there looking for what they had been promised. That was a helluva lot to place on any one man, and Jake was that man.

"What kind of assets do you have here?" Jake asked.

Tully lit a cigarette from his first, and savored the first inhale. He blew out the smoke. "Pretty green, I'm afraid. Other than Quinn. And you've met him." He smiled.

"Great!" Jake knew he could at least count on Sinclair Tucker. Then he remembered that he had come to Odessa to protect and help MacCarty and Swanson. He had no idea where his investigation may lead. Would he still be able to help those two? "What in the hell was Tvchenko up to?"

Tully propped his cigarette to the side of his mouth. "We need to pull in the source that worked with Tvchenko."

"Petra Kovarik? Has Quinn found her yet?"

"No. He's making a few phone calls right now in the communications room," Tully said. "He's a good man,

Jake. Use him. He knows more about Yuri Tvchenko than anyone else in our office."

"Why didn't they give him the lead on this one?"

"He was working Petra Kovarik," Tully said. "She was getting nervous. We had to back him off for a while."

"You think Quinn's agent was feeding him garbage?"

Tully swished his head and cigarette smoke rose up into his eyes. "We don't know. Quinn was playing with her, ready to set the hook, when Tvchenko gets killed."

"So, you think she might have told Tvchenko she was leading on some American?"

"Right," Tully said. "In fact, we speculated that she was romantically involved with Tvchenko, but we weren't certain. Quinn told me she wasn't much to look at, but she had a body that would stiffen a blind monk."

Jake thought for a moment. He needed to talk with this source. If she was as close as Tully said, she would have known what Tvchenko was up to. Someone had to know where she was. He checked his watch. It was close to ten o'clock. "We've got to find Petra Kovarik."

Tully leaned back in his chair. "What do you make of this woman disappearing?"

Jake rose from the chair and paced across the Persian rug. "Truthfully," he said, swinging around toward Tully. "I'm not certain. But I'd guess she might work for the GRU. She could have been doubling you. When you got a little too close, she, or some of her buddies, decide it's time to kill the scientist."

Tully exhaled a cloud of smoke. "I was thinking the same thing."

"Orrrr..." Jake took a seat. "She could have been legitimate. She and Tvchenko were lovers, let's say. The GRU figures she knows everything Tvchenko knows. So they nab her for insurance. Maybe she breaks, tells the GRU Tvchenko is selling his newest chemical agent to another source. The GRU gets pissed and has the scientist killed."

"It's possible," Tully admitted. "But wouldn't the GRU still need Tvchenko?"

He had a valid point, Jake thought. You don't want to kill your main source without some assurance that you no longer need him. "That would mean that the GRU has everything they need from Tvchenko. But I don't think they did. Why trash Tvchenko's apartment? And Petra's? We probably won't know for sure until we talk to her. Does she have any relatives?"

"Quinn's checking that as we speak," Tully said. He had just finished his cigarette and was staring at the pack on his desk, wondering if he should light another.

There was a knock on the door. "Come on in, Quinn," Tully yelled.

Quinn Armstrong strolled in carrying a small bag and took a seat in a wooden chair against one wall. He gave Jake a sullen glare. The bruise on his left jaw was black and blue and still raised somewhat. He was wearing khaki pants and a dull brown shirt under a black, unzipped mariner coat. If he were walking down Deribasovskaya Street in Odessa, one would surely take him for a local. He crossed his legs, exposing black work boots. He groomed his little goatee between his fingers.

"What'd you find out?" Tully asked Quinn.

Hesitating for a moment, Quinn shifted in his chair. "She has no relatives. It's one of the reasons I recruited her. Our Kiev office checked with a few of her friends there, but none of them have seen her in nearly a month.

Not since she came here to work with Tvchenko. We know she had been spending more and more time at his apartment."

The way Quinn said it, Jake thought there might have been more to their relationship. He knew that often happened when officers ran agents of the opposite sex.

"Do you have any idea where she might have gone?"

Quinn wouldn't look at him. "Possibly. I just remembered this morning about a friend Petra spoke about here in Odessa."

"Great!" Tully said. "Let's check the place out."

Just then the phone rang and Tully picked up. "Yeah." His faced became serious and he shook his head. "Thanks," he said, and slowly hung up. He sat for a moment with his hands folded across his lap.

"What is it?" Jake asked.

"Bad news." He was looking for the right words. "The two you came here with. Maxwell MacCarty and Bill Swanson. They've been poisoned."

"What!" Jake rose quickly. "Are they all right?"

"Uncertain. They're at the Polyklinik."

"That's a butcher shop," Jake protested. "They've got a better chance with a veterinarian."

Quinn rose and faced Jake. "It's not that bad."

"I wouldn't trust them to cut my nails," Jake said. "Remember, Quinn, I used to work here."

Tully came around his desk. "Come on guys. I won't have any fucking turf battles. Quinn, you either work with Jake on this one, or I'll have you transferred. I hear Grozny is looking for someone. Jake. I can't tell you anything. The director has put you in charge. But if you want total cooperation, and I think you know what I mean, then

I suggest you get along with Quinn."

Jake was thinking it over. He had nothing against the guy. Quinn was the one who had come in with an attitude. But Jake never took shit from anyone. Respect was gained through personal experience, not hearsay.

Jake loosened up a bit and let out a deep breath. "Fine. Quinn what do you say we take a quick run to the wonderful Polyklinik to see the great job they're doing on our poisoned Americans. Then perhaps we could check out the friend of your agent."

Tully shook his head. "Get the hell out of here."

When Jake and Quinn were gone, Tully lit another cigarette. "Fucking testosterone."

15

Neither Jake nor Quinn said much on the ride to the Odessa Polyklinik on Sudostroitelnaya Street. Quinn Armstrong was driving Tully's gray Volga sedan, a car that had seen one too many potholes, and looked like it had been parked by a blind man, with dents on the bumpers and quarter panels. They had set aside their differences, whatever they might be. At least verbally.

In fact, Quinn had given Jake a brand new Glock 19, fully loaded, with two extra magazines with hollow points, and a new leather holster. On the drive Jake had put on the holster, and he was now checking over the gun. It felt good in his hand. He loved the Glock.

Jake guessed the silent treatment had something to do with the CIA director putting him in charge of the investigation. The problem was, Jake hadn't really agreed to head up the investigation. While he had been contemplating it, he had heard about MacCarty and Swanson. Now Jake had this tight feeling deep in his gut that said he had screwed up royally not sticking closer to his employers. He knew that he couldn't have avoided what happened to them, but he still felt responsible. He had been hired to protect. Another part of him realized that he too could have been poisoned if he had been with them.

Quinn pulled up to the curb and parked across the street from the Polyklinik. Jake shoved the new Glock into its holster and zipped up his jacket.

The outside of the hospital hadn't changed much since the last time Jake had seen it. While in the Air Force there, he was forced to go to the Polyklinik for stitches to his scalp following a bruising game of 'touch' football. The consular general had sent over a syringe, needle and thread, and even bandages, because he knew those at the clinic would not be sterile. The hospital was one of those communist-built structures of steel and glass, slapped up in the fifties, that could have been designed by a four-year-old. The workmanship was so shoddy that the cement abutments and window ledges were already crumbling. Probably not enough rock in the mixture, Jake thought.

"It's not that bad," Quinn said. "In fact, maybe they should look at your ribs." He smiled with his hairy chin protruding out comically.

"Yeah," Jake said, "that's gonna happen today. Let's go."

They locked up the car and skirted across the street between traffic.

Inside, there was a waiting area with dirty cloth chairs, worn and tattered at the edges, and high ceilings that lead nowhere. A skylight would have been nice.

When they reached the information desk on the first floor, they glared at each other to determine who would ask the questions. Quinn deferred.

"I would like to see two Americans who are being treated here," Jake said in his best Ukrainian. He smiled at the older woman behind the counter.

She returned his smile. "Names please," she said, her English strained.

My god, how many Americans did they have there, Jake wondered. "Maxwell MacCarty and Bill Swanson."

She checked a paper chart on a clipboard. "Room 306. Down the hall. Take the elevator to the third floor. You can talk to the nurse there."

"Thank you," Jake said, and started to leave.

"You might want to take the stairs," she said. "The elevator is slow and breaks down periodically."

Jake nodded and smiled at Quinn as they strolled down the corridor, as if to say, 'see I told you the place sucked.' They took the stairs.

The third floor was even less impressive than the first. The linoleum floors were an off white, and scared and scuffed with black marks. Probably from gurney wheels that didn't work.

They immediately went to the nurses' station. Jake asked a young nurse in a bright white uniform, cap and all, the status of the Americans. She was reluctant to give any medical details. Only that there was no change. They would have to wait and see. The doctor would be by in thirty minutes, if they wanted to talk with him, they could wait down the hall in the waiting room. They couldn't see the Americans without the doctor's approval.

After waiting fifteen minutes in a small room down the hall, finally an older man in a white doctor's smock came around the corner. He was a slight man, completely gray, with a sunken face, as if he hadn't eaten in months.

"How may I help you?" he asked in Ukrainian.

Jake rose to greet him. "I'm Jake Adams. I work with Mr. MacCarty and Mr. Swanson. This is Quinn Armstrong with the U.S. consulate here in Odessa. How are they doing?"

The doctor looked at the two of them skeptically. "Mr. MacCarty is able to talk," he started in broken English. "However, Mr. Swanson is worse off."

"What exactly did they ingest?" Quinn demanded.

The doctor backed away somewhat. "The results are not back from toxicology. It was something they both ate. Perhaps the pork. We're really not sure yet. The police have taken samples from the restaurant and talked with the staff." He hesitated for a second. "You'll have to talk with them for those results."

"May we see them?" Jake asked.

"For a moment." The doctor stepped off down the hall, and Jake and Quinn were right at his heels.

The hospital room was something that might have been around in America at the turn of the century. There were six beds, four on one side of the room and two cramped in a small corner as an afterthought. The lighting was poor. A few of the long florescent bulbs were dark on both ends, burned out and forgotten. The tile floor might have been white at one time, but was now a harsh gray. On the wall next to MacCarty's bed was an ancient black phone with a frayed cord. There was one window with wire mesh across it in a diamond pattern. Jake wondered why the mesh was needed on the third floor. Perhaps the gloom had prompted patients to jump.

All the beds were occupied.

Bill Swanson was in the far corner. Tubes ran from nearly every opening in his body. But there was little elec-

tronic monitoring equipment like that found in American
Intensive Care Units. Only one machine, an older contraption with red dialogue numbers, checked his heart
rate.

Maxwell MacCarty lay in the other corner bed next to
Swanson. He did appear in better shape than his col-
league. He had more color in his face. Less tubes.

Jake stepped alongside MacCarty's bed. "How you feeling, Max?"

"Just fucking great," he whispered. He was barely audible.

In the basement, in a small room adjacent to the boiler
room, two men sat in wooden chairs with headsets on. The
wall was a large mass of telephone wires. They had tapped
into the phone on the wall of room 306. The recorder was
sound activated. They could hear and record anything that
went on in the room.

"Sound familiar?" one of the men asked the other.

The other smiled and nodded. "Yes. That's Jake
Adams." He picked up a phone and dialed quickly. In a
moment he said, "Adams is here with another man. Yes,
we're recording it. I understand." He hung up.

"What did she say?" the first man asked.

"Keep recording. Call her when they leave. She'll follow them from here. She wants us to meet later with the
tape."

The tape recorder whirred.

Jake introduced Quinn Armstrong to MacCarty. "What
happened?" Quinn asked.

MacCarty slowly related his story. How they were both

sick of continental breakfasts and wanted something they were both used to. When he was done, he admitted it would be nice to get back to Portland, with or without a firm contract. He said that he had eaten only one egg, but Swanson had cleared his plate.

Jake considered that. Why would someone deliberately poison these two? Someone obviously knew who he was, and perhaps even what he was doing. Did they think MacCarty and Swanson were actually working with him? It's possible. Or maybe it was unrelated. Maybe someone didn't want those two opening a plant in the Ukraine.

"Who have you been dealing with on opening your plant here?" Jake asked.

MacCarty's eyes wandered toward Swanson in the other bed. "A man named Victor Petrov. He works with the Agricultural Ministry here in Odessa. We were to talk today with him one last time before signing the deal. I guess he'll have to come here now." His eyes drifted up.

"I can arrange it if you like," Jake said, glancing back at Quinn. "But right now you need rest."

He nodded his head.

As the two of them were walking down the third floor corridor, buzzers went off and nurses started running toward the room with MacCarty and Swanson. Jake tried to get back in the room, but they closed the door.

Outside, back in the car, Quinn sat behind the wheel staring straight ahead. "Swanson did eat much more than MacCarty," Quinn said. "Perhaps MacCarty will pull through."

Jake shook his head. "I don't think so. The only difference between the two of them was when they'd die, not if.

MacCarty's system is trying desperately to fight the inevitable, but he's only delaying death. I've seen how they look before. The moment I saw Swanson I knew he was dead, just waiting for the monitor to confirm it. MacCarty will look like that within three or four hours. I'll bet on it. It was ricin. Twenty-five thousand times as toxic as strychnine. It takes less than two micrograms to kill an adult."

"What about an anecdote?" Quinn asked.

"No good. It consists of glycoprotein bands that divide into two peptide chains that attack the cells. One chain binds the ricin to the cell's surface and allows the other chain to enter. The white blood cells go crazy trying to get rid of the poison. Death follows due to toxemia. Plus, it's almost impossible to trace in a postmortem, even if you know what you're looking for."

"Jesus Christ. How do you know all this?"

Jake was drifting off, thinking about his two employers suffering in the hospital. Swanson was already gone. Sure he had been a pain in the ass, but he didn't deserve to die like that. And MacCarty. What would Jake say to his family when the bodies were returned to Portland. They'd want answers, and he wasn't currently in a position to explain their deaths. When he realized Quinn was staring at him, he said, "What was that?"

"How do you know so much about poisons?" Quinn asked.

"College. University of Oregon. My first two years I was a bio-chemistry major. Then I switched to geopolitics."

"Why?"

He had only revealed that to his closest friends. But it

wasn't a secret, really. "I don't know. I had enough for a minor and almost enough for a major in bio-chemistry, but then I had second thoughts about hiding myself in some lab after graduation, only coming out to go to and from work. I think it would have driven me nuts after a few years. So I said the hell with it. Decided to look at various peoples of the world. I continued that by joining the Air Force after graduation."

"Intel right?"

"Yeah. Human Intelligence. But I also had a decent computer background, so they used me for that also. I was in Germany when my boss found out I had a substantial background in bio-chemistry. They were looking for people to work on a verification team in the former Soviet republics during their drawdown of chemical and biological weapons. He asked me if I'd like to be on the team, and I said yes. I didn't know at the time they'd ask us to go all over the place. Turkey. Iraq. You name it, I went there."

Quinn looked at Jake. "Where to?"

"Let's go see if we can track down Petra Kovarik," Jake said. "You said she had an old friend in Odessa."

"That's what I heard." Quinn started the car and pulled out into light traffic.

16

DURANGO, MEXICO

The tin roof on the ramshackle house was getting pelted by a pre-dawn rainstorm. Back when the former DEA had a more formidable presence in Latin America, they had seized the tiny house off Mexican Highway 40 from a group of marijuana growers. The drug dealers wouldn't need the place while serving ten to twenty years in a Mexican prison.

The two CIA officers had taken the Cypriot captain and his three mates to this place on the orders of the Mexico City station chief, who had simply relayed the message from Langley. The orders were immaterial, really, because Steve Nelsen was leading the investigation and had already planned on his special form of "suspect awareness," as he called it.

Ricardo Garcia was in a back room with the Cypriot, asking questions and trying to soften him for what he knew would be an interesting interrogation. At least from what he had heard about Nelsen in a few days. It didn't take long for rumors to spread.

Two former DEA agents, who now worked in the criminal intervention department of the CIA, and also two former FBI special agents, working in that same department, stood around the periphery of the main room, their guns hanging prominently from leather holsters under their arms. In the old days, it would have been cooperation by three agencies that none of them had seen before. Now all six of the men were part of the CIA. Nelsen didn't like it one bit, even though he was in charge.

The three young seamen had been separated and interrogated. They spoke very little English, and only one of the CIA officers, Nelsen, could understand the Turkish. Nelsen spoke Turkish, Arabic, Spanish and Italian. None of the seamen knew a thing, Nelsen was sure. Answers from them had come easy, with only a few initial smacks across the head. They had been hired in Famagusta, Cyprus late one night after getting drunk with the captain, who had continued to buy them drinks. The next morning they had found themselves below decks on the fishing boat, pitching heavily, as they steamed through the Mediterranean. They had all come to fear the captain, and knew they were stuck. He would have knocked them over the head and thrown them to the sharks if they had rebelled. They were unanimous on that point.

Garcia pulled the Cypriot captain into the room, and strapped him to a wooden chair with leather belts. The remaining agents surrounded him to intimidate him. Nelsen was sure the captain knew something. Nelsen's men had found an abandoned skiff five miles up the coast from Novillero. There were four sets of footprints in the sand leading to truck tracks. Someone had carried something heavy, since their footprints were so deep, and their steps shifted sideways at short intervals.

Nelsen had asked Langley to run the captain's name through the Agency database. Just a few minutes ago he received a fax with the information. He sat across the small room now reading the curled pages.

The captain was really Atik Aziz. The name he had given was one of many aliases. He was fifty-two. Had been a captain in the Turkish marines when he took part in the invasion of Northern Cyprus in 1974. He had continued to fight there, helping set up an independent state through brutal suppression of anyone who apposed him. When the independent Turkish Cypriot government became more moderate over ten years ago, Aziz set out on his own to make his fortune. But by then he had left behind more bodies than any of his peers. Old habits were hard to break, Nelsen noticed in the report. Aziz was used by the highest bidder to ferry terrorists from Lebanon to strike the Israeli coast. He ran arms for the Palestinians from Syria. Aziz was a new-age pirate, and he looked the part with long, disheveled black hair, streaked with gray, and his scruffy face. His jeans and cotton jacket were frazzled, and his deck boots scuffed beyond repair. But more than the external was wrong with this man. He seemed to have this knowing radiance that emerged from a turned up smirk that exposed crooked yellow teeth. Nelsen would soon wipe that from him.

Nelsen rose from the wooden chair across the room and ripped off his jacket. His thick muscles rippled through his T-shirt as he adjusted his pants on his hips and checked for his 9mm under his left arm. He slowly approached the Cypriot, his eyes centered directly on the pirate's ugly scowl. He knew how to play the game. Intimidation.

Make the guy feel like his next breath depended on him.

Stopping a few feet from the Cypriot, Nelsen stretched his six-four frame, and then cracked his knuckles. He was a tall, imposing figure.

Rain smashed against the roof overhead.

"Where's the weapon, Aziz?" Nelsen asked with a deep snarl. He wasn't only big, but he could act with the best of them. Not even agents who knew him could tell if he was really pissed off, or simply playing the game.

The Cypriot gave him a bewildered look, as if he didn't understand English.

Nelsen looked at his partner, Garcia, who shrugged. Nelsen grabbed the man's hair, raising him and the chair from the ground, the leather straps cinched tightly across his chest. The man screamed. Nelsen dropped him and then pinched and twisted his left ear.

"Listen you fucking little terrorist," Nelsen said in Turkish. "I'll start ripping pieces from your body if you don't start talking. I want to know who hired you? Who has the weapon? Where's the weapon now? And what these men plan on doing with the weapon."

There was pain on the Cypriot's face as sweat appeared on his forehead. "I don't know what you're talking about," the man answered in broken English.

Nelsen tightened his jaw. "So, the briefing was right. You do speak English."

"Who are you?" the man asked.

Nelsen let the man's ear go, and then slapped him across the head. "I ask the questions, fuckhead." He paused to let Aziz feel the pain. "Now. Which question do you want to take first? How about, where's the weapon?"

The man shook his head. "I don't know."

Nelsen smacked him again. "Wrong answer. Try again."

The man looked at Nelsen sideways with his eyes, as if to say that he'd kill him if he got the chance. "I was never told that. That was not my job."

"And what was your job, exactly?"

"Delivery," the Cypriot said softly.

"I believe that," Nelsen said. "You've done such a good job for the Syrians in the past. Did the Syrians hire you?"

The man shook his head swiftly. "I don't know."

"Bullshit! You don't know who wired a hundred thousand dollars into two separate Swiss accounts?"

This riled Aziz. He shifted his eyes away quickly. Then, realizing he'd opened himself up, he slowly turned his gaze back to the American. "I never ask names. Deals are worked through middle men."

"So you simply take the money and do as you're told." Nelsen went to hit the man, and pulled up short. The man flinched backward. Nelsen smiled inside. He had been trained to intimidate through psychology, and his size had given him a great advantage.

The other officers in the room had been silent, their faces grave with concern. It was a carefully planned game, and they all knew the rules.

Nelsen pulled a pair of pliers from his back pocket. They were shiny and new with sharp teeth. He clamped them open and closed a few times to make sure they worked fine, then he slowly lowered them toward the man's crotch. He stopped for a moment six inches away from his penis, and imagined how it must have been shrinking to hide between the man's legs.

"I suppose you'd like to keep that one piece of equipment," Nelsen said smiling.

The Cypriot shifted his eyes downward, the sweat on his forehead bubbling out. "Please, I don't know anything else," he pleaded desperately.

Nelsen moved the pliers closer. "Give me the names of the men you picked up at Johnston Atoll."

"I don't know them."

"Bullshit! You spent seven days on the Pacific with those men, and you never caught their names?"

The man thought hard, keeping an eye on the pliers. "They only used single names," he forced out.

"First or last names would be nice."

Although there was a tape covering the entire interrogation, one of the former FBI agents pulled out a notebook and prepared to write.

"Go ahead," Nelsen said.

The man shifted in his chair and looked around the room. "They'll kill me, you know."

Nelsen knew that was a possibility, and didn't really give a shit. The man helped terrorists escape with over a hundred nerve gas bomblets. Maybe he deserved to die. "Let's hear the names."

"Mahabad," the man said slowly, deliberately, as if the words themselves would kill him. "Ragga. Baskale. Ruwanduz."

Nelsen looked at the officer taking down the names, and he indicated he had them written down. Something wasn't right with the names. "What nationality? Are they Turks?"

The man didn't answer.

Nelsen clamped down on Aziz's trousers and started pulling upward. "Answer!"

"Various," the man screeched in a higher pitch. "I didn't understand their language."

He didn't understand, but he knew. Nelsen was sure. "Who were they?"

The man refused to answer.

Nelsen reached down deeper into the man's crotch, grabbed something soft, and clamped down lightly.

Aziz screamed. "They were Kurds. They were Kurds."

Nelsen let up. "Kurds?" He thought for a moment. What in the hell were Kurds doing in the North Pacific? And now in Mexico? What did they want with the nerve gas? He had a feeling Aziz, the Cypriot, would remember a little more than he was telling, but it would take time to get the answers. Nelsen knew he had one advantage. He had softened him. Opened him up. Answers always came easier after that.

17

ODESSA, UKRAINE

Jake and Quinn had no problem finding the apartment where they suspected Petra Kovarik was staying. It was a tiny place off of Sverdlova Street, not far from the train station.

Quinn parked Tully's Volga against the curb, shut down the sputtering engine, and hesitated for a moment, looking up at the five-story brick building.

It was a hundred-year-old building that hadn't seen many improvements since it first opened. Jake guessed it might have been a decent address at one time, but time had decayed it like acid slowly dripping on metal.

Jake thought of similarities this building had to Petra's own apartment building. This time he hoped he had gotten there first. He had been beaten to Tvchenko's place, almost paying with his life, and someone had gotten to Petra's place first also. Both times he had been directed to the apartments by Tully O'Neill, and the timing couldn't have been worse. Well, that wasn't true. Someone could have set off the bomb at Tvchenko's a minute earlier.

Jake got out and headed up the stairs, with Quinn right behind him.

On the ride from the Odessa Polyklinik, Quinn had explained that Petra might be staying with Helena Yurichenko, a violinist with the Odessa Symphony Orchestra. She and Petra had been best friends while growing up in a small town outside of Kiev. Petra had gone on to the university to study bio-chemistry, and Helena had studied at the conservatory as a musician. Helena Yurichenko had lived in Odessa for nearly nine years. At first she had lived like a queen with the support of the great Soviet Union, but then came the split, and the money became more scarce. She was barely making it now, Jake could tell.

The inside of the building was in worse disrepair than the outside. Plaster was chipped from the walls in the corridor and the stairwell. The wooden railing needed varnish. It wouldn't take too much, but the place definitely needed a sprucing up.

Jake grabbed Quinn's arm, stopping him. "Hang on, Quinn. Let's take it easy. It seems like every apartment I've entered in Odessa, someone's tried to cut my stay short."

"I don't think anyone knows about Helena," Quinn said.

"If we do, someone else might."

Quinn was thinking it over.

"By the way, how did you find out about Helena?"

Quinn started up the stairs, but Jake pulled him to a halt. "I want an answer," Jake said.

"That's right. You're in charge."

"You got a problem with that?"

"I read the message."

"And?"

"It's bullshit! You're not even with the Agency."

"Keep your voice down."

"Is that an order?" He whispered loudly.

"I think maybe I kicked you too hard yesterday," Jake said. Or maybe not hard enough, he thought.

They stared each other down for a moment in the subdued light of the stairway.

"I finally remembered," Quinn said. He let out a deep breath and shook his head. "I was such an idiot. A month ago, just after Petra came down from Kiev, I went to the symphony. Rimsky-Korsakov. The Russian Easter Overture. Anyway, I met Petra there. Just happened to sit next to her. She pointed out Helena to me. Said she knew her and had been friends with her since they were kids. She only told me her first name, and I didn't even remember that until this morning. I had to track down her address through the locals. I've got a few contacts."

Jake considered this. "Great. Let's see what she knows."

Jake stepped past Quinn up the stairs.

As they rounded the stairs from the second to the third floors, the sound of a violin echoed down to them. Getting closer, Jake felt the hairs on the back of his neck prickle from the beauty of a soft Vivaldi concerto. The sound became louder as they reached room 302.

Quinn looked at Jake, as if wondering whether he should knock on the door and disturb such a luscious, dynamic tone. Jake couldn't imagine any neighbor complaining about the noise, for it was such a mesmerizing and overpowering sound.

When she stopped playing, Jake quickly knocked. He couldn't hear if someone had moved to answer the door, so he started to knock again, when the door opened a few inches, bared by a metal security stop.

Peering through the opening was a set of wide blue eyes against a pale face. Long straight hair swept down as far as Jake could see. She was staring at Jake, uncertain what to think of him. She held her violin bow in her right hand like a sword.

"What can I do for you?" she asked in Ukrainian. Her voice seemed to resonate and flow much like her violin.

"I'm Jake Adams, and this is Quinn Armstrong," Jake said in Ukrainian. "We'd like to speak with Petra."

She started to close the door.

"Wait," Quinn jumped in. "Tell her Quinn is here. We are friends."

She looked at Quinn now, as if she recognized the name finally. Her eyes switched back and forth nervously. "She is not well," she said in English.

"Please," Quinn pleaded. "It's urgent that we talk with her."

She muttered something and closed and locked the door.

"What the hell was that?" Jake asked. He wasn't fluent in Ukrainian, but he usually understood more than he could speak.

Quinn smiled. "She told us to go fuck ourselves."

"Really? And she looked so sweet and innocent."

"Musicians can be brutal. She'll be back."

He was right. A minute later the door opened again. This time all the way. The blonde stood back and motioned with a nod of her head to enter.

Inside was totally different from the entryway. The walls were freshly painted ivory white. There were plants everywhere soaking up the sun streaming through tall windows. There wasn't much furniture. A small sofa. A chair with a stand and music in front of it. Her violin lay in its open case, cradled in soft red velvet. The lack of clutter made the room look much larger than it was.

There was a small kitchenette off the living room, and a little wooden table with two chairs. Jake and Quinn stood in the middle of the room, as Helena closed the door.

She was wearing a sweater that extended just over her buttocks. Her legs were covered in black tights with stir-rups over tiny feet in pink stockings. Jake realized that she was a very small woman, perhaps five feet two, yet she stood tall as if she were much larger. Overall, she was an extremely attractive woman.

"Would you like something to drink?" she asked in her version of English, moving into the kitchen area.

"No, thank you," Quinn said. "I need to speak with Petra."

Her eyes shifted toward a closed door. "She'll be out in a minute."

Jake moved over and looked at her violin. "Your music was beautiful."

She came closer, as if defending her violin like a moth-er would her child. "It's all I have. I would die without it." She stroked the velvet near the violin's neck.

"Passion is something lacking in this world," Jake said, gazing into her eyes. "We need more people who love what they do, instead of those who simply do what is expected of them."

She thought for a moment. "You do understand. That's a rare quality."

"For an American?"

"For anyone," she corrected, smiling through teeth that

could have used braces. It was her only imperfection.

Finally, the door opened and Petra Kovarik came out. Her hair was dark and wet and had just been combed. But her face was blotched with red. She had been crying. She wore tight clothes displaying a perfect body. Jake understood Quinn's attraction, if his hunch was correct. And the way Quinn was looking at her, Jake was probably right. Officer had fallen for agent.

Quinn met her in the center of the room and they kissed on both cheeks, then quickly on the lips. He whispered into her ear. She took a seat at the kitchen table and Quinn took the other. Jake moved closer to listen, and Helena sat on the sofa and crossed her legs.

"Have you heard about Yuri Tvchenko?" Quinn asked.

She nodded her head, but kept her eyes in a constant stare at the table. It was as if she were peering down through the floor, through the ground, and on to hell. She was scared.

"Who would want Tvchenko dead?" Jake asked.

She looked up at this man she had never met. "Who is he?" she asked Quinn.

"I'm sorry. This is Jake Adams. He's a friend of mine who knew Yuri. They had worked together a few years back. He was with Yuri when he died. He's trying to help me find his killer."

She seemed to relax with that last revelation.

Quinn started again. "What was Yuri working on? You must have been part of that."

She hunched her shoulders. "We were working on new pesticides," she said. Her English wasn't perfect. It flowed with a childlike quality. "It was for agriculture. You spray the fields with this strain and you wipe out the entire bug population. And the larvae and eggs are also affected. They become sterile."

That was the story Jake had already heard, but there had to be more to it. "Who was he dealing with? Who wanted to buy the strain?" Jake asked.

"I was never involved with that," she said, looking not at Jake but Quinn. "Yuri was a very secretive man. He trusted no one. We worked together. That is all."

"You weren't lovers?" Jake asked.

She laughed.

Quinn gave Jake a quick glare, as if he had just asked a nun how many men she had screwed.

"What's so funny?" Jake asked.

She tried to hold back her laughter. "Yuri would rather fuck his test tubes. He had no time for women. Besides, he liked men. Young men."

Quinn looked somewhat surprised. "You never told me that before."

"You never asked."

Jake turned and smiled at Helena, who looked bored on the sofa. He swung back to Petra. "What are you hiding for?"

Anger swept across Petra's face. "I don't trust the men." After she said it, she covered her eyes with her hands.

"What men?" Quinn asked.

She started sobbing. "The men who started showing up at the lab," she forced out.

"Here in Odessa?"

"Yes."

"When?"

"It started a few months back," she muttered. "One man. Then two came a few weeks later. They were not like those who had come in Kiev all the time. These were different."

"How?"

"They were more desperate looking. They were Arabs I think. From the Middle East, anyway."

"So you were still working for Tvchenko?" Jake asked, already knowing the answer.

She nodded. "At his apartment."

"What about at the private institute?" Quinn asked. He looked more concerned now.

"The original strain was worked there. But he was moving in other directions, and he wanted that closer to him. Where he had all the control. He came to Kiev and got me just over a month ago."

Jake thought for a moment. "But you said the men started coming a few months back."

She shifted her eyes up at Jake. "That's what Yuri told me."

"What did they say when they came?"

"I don't know. They talked in the other room. I stayed in the lab."

Quinn was sitting back now, as if he were looking at an unfaithful wife.

"You're a bio-chemist and you have no idea what in the hell Tvchenko was up to?" Jake yelled. "I find that pretty hard to believe."

She threw him an indignant glance. "It's true."

"What about chemicals," Jake said. "Was he working on any new chemical agents?"

She shrugged. "I don't know."

Jake knew she was lying. Tvchenko's apartment was full of chemicals. He may have been working on biological strains at the private institute, but unofficially he was working on chemical agents. Jake thought for a moment. Tully O'Neill had had Tvchenko's place wired. Why hadn't he mentioned there was a woman there? That other meetings had taken place in the apartment? If she did know what he was up to, then she was one hell of a liar. Regardless, she had a good reason to be scared. Whoever killed Tvchenko, must have seen Petra at the apartment. They would have to assume she knew what Tvchenko knew. She was in danger.

Jake pulled Quinn aside, explaining how he thought Petra was in danger.

"But she doesn't know anything," Quinn pleaded.

"It doesn't matter. They don't know that. Whoever they are just wants to plug holes." Things were becoming clearer now for Jake.

Quinn looked at Petra, who was slouched back in her chair brushing her fingers through her wet hair.

"How can we protect her?" Quinn finally asked.

He wasn't thinking straight, Jake could tell. His eyes flicked back and forth from Petra to Helena and then off to nowhere.

"We'll have to get her out of here," Jake said. "What about the consulate?"

Quinn swished his head quickly. "I can't hide a Ukrainian citizen in our consulate."

"What about a safe house? You still have to have a few of those hanging around. If not, set one up."

It was the only way.

"You'll have to bring Helena with you," Jake continued. "If we found her, so will they. Better yet, I'll come up with a place for them."

It wouldn't be easy to sell that to Petra, and Jake knew it. But until they had all the answers, there was no other way. Besides, Petra knew more than she was saying. Once they had her on neutral ground, she might open up.

18

BERLIN, GERMANY

It was noon and the sun was trying desperately to poke through the heavy clouds.

Sitting at an outdoor table at a restaurant on the edge of Alexander Platz, Gerhard Kreuzberg took a long chug on his liter of bock beer. He gazed around the square at the sharp-edged buildings that were supposed to be the highlight of socialism, but thought only about how ugly the place was. It was no wonder communism had failed. It was far too gloomy. Only the flowers that separated the walkways were appealing to him. Primrose stretched along one strip like a sea of red. Grape Hyacinth across another side in a dazzling purple. Then tulips and daffodils in every color lined the edges. Bees and hornets buzzed around from flower to flower in a choreographed dance. Kreuzberg took in a deep breath and could distinguish a blend of the flowers, but not any particular individual flower. He had always liked gardens.

Kreuzberg had been the foreign relations minister under Helmut Kohl for over six years before retiring from public service when Germany's new president took over. He had served the public ever since graduating from Berlin University in the late fifties. He had been most fortunate to live in the Western corridor when the Russians, Americans, British and French divided his great city. And now he had returned to his native home, to a city that was still not whole and equal. That's why he came to Alexander Platz to eat lunch once a week since moving back to Berlin. He needed to see what had been so bad, what he had fought so hard against.

Two men sat at a corner table sipping coffee and keeping an eye on the man sitting alone. One man was young, his eyes passionately intense. The older man, in his early thirties going on fifty, leaned back and sipped his coffee. He knew for sure his target from the photograph was the man drinking the beer and eating by himself. Their contact had been right. He ate here every Wednesday after his driver had dropped him off and drove the silver Mercedes away.

If everything else went as planned, the man would eat his meal and walk toward the Weltzeituhr, check his watch against that large international clock, and then continue on toward the television tower, where he would gaze up at it in amazement. His driver would pick him up at exactly one thirty off of Unter den Linden. He was like clockwork.

The older man tried to ignore him, but it was too difficult. He was too excited. He had worked for years in Germany, trying to bring their cause to the world stage through peaceful protest, and then not so peaceful bombing of travel agencies and airline offices. Now, to be

called on for this.... The older man smiled and took a sip
of coffee.

   Kreuzberg ate a simple meal of currywurst and French
fries soaked with mustard. He loved the smell of curry
even more than the taste. His old colleagues in Bonn had
always wondered how he could eat that way, but he had
been doing it since his youth. Wealth and esteem had not
changed him so much that he could not enjoy plain food.
He remembered where he came from. His father had been
a simple shop owner, and had worked hard to send his
only son through gymnasium and on to the university.
   When he was done eating, he paid for his meal and
started walking across the wide square. There weren't as
many people out and about as normal, but still the area
was crowded. When he reached the Weltzeituhr, he
flipped his pocket watch from a vest pocket and gazed
down at it for a moment. His father had given him the
watch. It was not an expensive one, but it was the only
thing he had to remember his father by. He was nearly a
half hour earlier than normal. He had eaten his meal
quicker today. It was difficult to sit at a table alone. The
time simply stood still.
   Continuing on, Kreuzberg wandered closer to the nee-
dle-like television tower, Fernsehturm. It was the tallest
structure in a city where every building, except those few
that had been reconstructed from rubble, was no older
than fifty years.

   The two men kept their distance. When the German
stopped, they stopped, pretending to talk about something
important. In a moment they would be joined by the third

man circling out and approaching from the other side. It was a flawless plan. They could not fail.

When Kreuzberg paused to gaze up at the tower, he noticed the two men again. He recognized them from the restaurant, where they seemed to look at him with almost a sexual intent. Maybe not sexual, but surely passionate. Kreuzberg was dressed rather well in an expensive three piece suit. A British cut that he had had made in London on his last visit just a month ago. They were probably thieves. They were dressed in dark wool pants, black and brown shirts. All cheap and off the rack. They were Turks, he thought, looking to steal his wallet. He had dealt with thugs before. And now the city was full of them. The worst were the Russian Mafia and the Chechen thieves. They would slice the suit open to get the wallet instead of simply asking for it.

He turned and walked toward a more crowded area, where he would meet his driver. They would never try anything in front of all these people.

In a moment, he reached Unter den Linden. He checked his watch again. He had fifteen minutes and only three blocks to walk before he reached his meeting place. Now he wished he had asked his driver to eat with him today. He was a big man, and his mere physical presence would keep most thieves away.

The sidewalks were teeming with people walking off their lunches. Occasionally, a bicycle would ring its bell, warning a walker of its approach from the rear. Kreuzberg had nearly been run over a dozen times, so the bell always made him cringe.

He was a block from his meeting place now. There was

a large hedge to his right that skirted the sidewalk for an entire block. Birds chirped and fluttered within the thick bushes. One flew out quickly and nearly hit his head. He jumped back swiftly.

The flowers were gone. There was only a small strip of grass along the sidewalk, where dogs had urinated and defecated and the nasty odor rose up to tinge at Kreuzberg's sensitive olfactory nerves.

Just fifty meters now and ten minutes for his driver to show up. His driver was always on time or early. He expected nothing less of his people.

He had kept an eye out for the two men following him, but they had disappeared. Perhaps he had been too concerned. He relaxed a little.

When he was almost to his meeting place, he noticed a man approaching straight away. He had seemingly appeared from nowhere. He wasn't dressed as shabbily as the other two men, but he was dark like them.

Kreuzberg slowed his pace.

The man continued toward him, not even looking at him.

Kreuzberg tensed up again as the man was nearly upon him. But he was looking behind Kreuzberg.

A bell rang from behind, and Kreuzberg jumped to the side, turning quickly as the bicycle nearly hit him.

He didn't feel a thing when the man reached out to help him from getting hit by the bike. The man simply smiled, turned, and continued on down the sidewalk.

Kreuzberg felt silly. He brushed his suit and straightened it out over his hips. He even laughed slightly out loud. Why did they allow those bicycles on the sidewalks anyway?

In a moment he reached the spot where he would wait the last few minutes for his driver. But something was wrong. He felt a piercing pain under his left arm. Was it his heart? Had the man and the bicycle scared him that much?

The pain spread out and seemed to be invading his entire body. Now he started sweating. His breathing became labored. He was barely able to catch his breath. People walked by him, staring. He started to loosen his tie. His neck felt hot, like it would blow up.

He couldn't breathe. He grasped his neck with both hands, as if he were being strangled by invisible hands and he was struggling to remove the ghost's strong fingers.

Then his knees buckled. He hit the pavement with a thud. Now a young couple stopped and seemed to be saying something to him. He peered up at them with teary eyes, as if begging for help.

He twitched uncontrollably on the ground. But by now he could no longer feel anything. It was as if the world were spinning around at a hundred times its normal rotation, and he was at the center rising up a torrid, swirling tornado.

In a moment he lay still.

A silver Mercedes pulled up to the curb and the driver rushed quickly through the crowd. He peered down at his boss lying on the cold, hard cement, his eyes glazed over in horrid hope, looking up to the cloudy sky to God.

19

STATE OF CHIHUAHUA, MEXICO

Baskale had driven all night through some of the most treacherous terrain in northern Mexico, on dirt roads that never should have been built and were rarely maintained. The last fifteen miles had been without a road. The Chevy Suburban had held up well with its wide desert tires, laboring only occasionally when the sand became deeper and looser. Despite his best efforts, Baskale knew he was over an hour late. He had stayed too long at the drug dealer's house. He had driven with great determination, but he didn't want to crack even one bomblet open. One tiny fissure, one brief whiff, and they would all die. His mission was far too important to die that way, in some snake-infested desert.

The sun was inching up toward the horizon to the east, as the four men stood at the southern bank of the Rio Grande, staring across to the other side. They would have to cross in daylight now.

With binoculars, Baskale could finally see movement and then three quick flashes of light from a flashlight. He looked at one of his men and slapped him across the head when he didn't return the signal. The man finally flashed back twice.

In a moment they could hear a boat motor. Then, in the increasing light, a tan form headed in a straight line from the other side. As the boat got closer, it slowed and its wake settled down. At the last minute the boat turned upstream and the driver let it drift toward the shore, keeping the sputtering motor just above idle to keep up with the current.

The boat was a large, deep-hull fishing craft. Black lettering on the side read, 'Rio Grande Excursions.' The driver was a Mexican in his late fifties. His unshaven face was weathered with deep crevices; his long, scraggly hair speckled with gray. He had spent most of his adult life running drugs and people across the river. He didn't ask questions. He just took the jobs for cash. U.S. dollars.

Two of Baskale's men held the boat fore and aft, while a third waited back at the Suburban. Insurance.

Baskale stepped down the bank.

"I get my money up front," the Mexican said, his voice echoing across the river and back.

Baskale reached inside his jacket, felt the 9mm pistol, and then slid an envelope from his inside pocket and tossed it to the Mexican.

Holding the wheel with his knees, the Mexican flipped through the money quickly. It appeared to be all there. Besides, he would never consider quibbling with dangerous men. It was bad for business, and he knew it could get him killed. He smiled and slipped the money inside his shirt.

"Let's cross then," the Mexican said, grinning through

tobacco-stained teeth.

Baskale nodded his head to his man up the bank. The truck slowly backed down the hill toward the river, its brake lights flashing on and off every few feet. When the truck was six feet from the shore, Baskale halted the truck with a waving hand.

In just a few minutes, the four men opened the back of the Suburban, hauled the weapon out gently, and set it smoothly into the boat's flat bottom. The wooden planks creaked as the full weight settled in, and the pilot thought for a moment it would crash through to the metal hull. But it held. They would have to take two trips across the river, though. The boat was too small to handle the weight of the five hundred pound bomb, plus five adults.

They crossed the river. Baskale, his strongest man, and the Mexican.

Water sprayed over the bow when the boat hit swirling back currents, and Baskale wondered how deep the river was. He hoped they would not hit a rock and tip over.

On the other side Baskale had a dilemma. He had only himself and his strongest man to lift the bomb from the boat.

"You'll have to help us," Baskale told the Mexican.

The Mexican looked at him skeptically. "I don't know what that is," he said, barely above the sputtering boat motor. "I don't want to know. My money was for hauling people and equipment across the Rio Grande. Nothing about lifting. I have a bad back." The man tried on a grin.

Baskale quickly pulled out his 9mm and slapped the bolt back, chambering a round. "Your back could get worse. Hollow points do a terrible number on flesh and bone." He waved the gun for the Mexican to help lift.

With the boat slamming against the shore from the river's current, and with only three men lifting, it was difficult to hoist the heavy carton over the side of the boat. The large man on one end stumbled and nearly dropped it. Baskale gasped. He wasn't sure how stable the bomblets were. They had been extremely careful with it up to this point. On the long ocean trip, he had insisted they pack styrofoam around the edges to keep it from sliding in heavy seas. In the back of the Suburban, they had laid it on foam rubber and packed sleeping bags and clothes around it. That had done two things. Kept it safe from the bumpy ride, and made it look like American tourists camping their way across northern Mexico. Now, when they were this close, having reached America, he couldn't allow it to be damaged.

They set the carton on the soft sand and slid it away from the water.

The Mexican went back across for the other two men and the gear from the back of the Suburban. In a few minutes, they were back on the Texas side, the gear on the ground next to the bomb.

Baskale was gone. Then there was the sound of a vehicle approaching through the scrub brush. It was a Suburban, nearly identical to the one they had just abandoned. Only this one was a GMC and light tan, like the Texas sand itself. Backing down the embankment, Baskale stopped a few feet from the weapon. The men hurried to load the truck. They were getting good at this.

The Mexican, sitting at the boat console, reached for the throttle to crank the motor.

"Just a moment," Baskale said, pulling the bow into the sand. "You can have the other truck if you wish." He nodded across the river.

"Are you serious?" the Mexican asked, his eyes wide.

"Of course. It's worth a lot of money. Low miles. It would be good for your business. The keys are in it. Go take a look."

The Mexican was overwhelmed. He powered the boat in reverse, swung the bow around, and pushed the throttle forward to full speed.

By now the Suburban was full, the men inside ready to leave. Baskale stepped to the driver's side and one of his men handed him a small transmitter.

Across the river, the Mexican had driven the boat into the sand, beaching it, and was now climbing into the back end to check it out.

Baskale got behind the wheel and cranked over the engine. He looked into his rearview mirror and could just make out the man scurrying around inside the truck on the opposite bank. He pointed the transmitter over his shoulder and pressed the button.

The abandoned truck blew up in a ball of flames.

As the new GMC Suburban with the four men headed over the ridge, Baskale imagined the Mexican still flying through the air somewhere across the river, floating up toward his fool's heaven.

Leaning against the front of a dirty Ford Ranger 4x4, Steve Nelsen lowered the binoculars and looked across the hood at Ricardo Garcia, his assistant. Officially, they were supposed to be partners, but Nelsen had made it known that he worked with no one. He was in charge.

Nelsen had gotten the name of a possible contact from Aziz, the Cypriot, after a little persuasion. Aziz had overheard the name while crossing the Pacific. It meant nothing to him, he had said. But it was another story with Garcia, who had worked northern Mexico for three years as a DEA agent. As soon as Aziz said the name, Kukulcan, Garcia knew the man wasn't talking about the Mayan serpent god of the same name. Kukulcan, alias Miguel Blanca, thought of himself as a big-time drug dealer from northeast Chihuahua. He had a hacienda north of La Perla he had named the Presidio. But the place was nothing like a fortress. It was more like an oasis in a desert. An aberration of the contrasting terrain of cactus and dirt and scrub brush. The man himself, Garcia had said, was nothing more than a puppet for higher-level drug concerns. The old DEA and the Federalis had not been able to stick anything on him, yet they knew they could if they watched more carefully. They were afraid to take him out, knowing someone more powerful would rise in his place. Someone with more brains and more weapons.

The sun was rising quickly, and Nelsen wondered why there was no movement around the place. Had they been seen moving in? He didn't think so.

He stepped back to his driver's door, reached in, pulled out a small hand-held radio, and whispered into it. "Move in."

Garcia hopped into the pickup and checked his gun, a 9mm Beretta. He chambered a round, but left the safety on.

Nelsen started the truck and they headed down the dirt drive toward the house.

"Are you ready, Dick?" Nelsen asked Garcia.

That was all he could take. Garcia pointed his Beretta at Nelsen. "I think I'm gonna fucking kill you right now,"

Garcia said.

Nelsen didn't flinch. "Go ahead. Put me out of my misery. Get me out of this hell hole. What the hell's your problem?"

"Dick. Nobody calls me Dick. You understand?"

"Sensitive bastard, aren't you?"

Garcia turned the gun toward the dashboard. "Ricardo was my father's name. He died when I was nine. He... Just call me Garcia."

"No problem."

Nelsen stopped the truck nearly fifty yards from the front of the house and left the engine running.

By now the Federalis had worked their way into position surrounding the place, their M-16s with thirty-round magazines, cocked, poised and aimed at the house.

Nelsen had parked off to the side of two vehicles, blocking their passage up the driveway. There was an older Mercedes, dented slightly and dirty, and a 4x4 Ford Bronco with tremendous tires.

The Federalis moved forward, closer, crouched low behind yucca and sage.

Nelsen and Garcia in the Ford Ranger were to be the decoy, something for those inside to focus their attention on. The two of them waited and watched.

Four Federalis moved toward the front door. They screamed who they were, and then burst through the front door. When they went inside, others took up closer positions at the door, their weapons aimed and ready to fire, and even more were around back waiting for any movement out the rear doors.

In a few moments the team leader appeared at the front door and waved for the Americans to approach.

On their way to the hacienda, Nelsen felt his gun under his left arm, but left it in its holster.

At the door the team leader smiled, his camo paint cracking at the corners of his eyes. "Someone was here," he said.

Nelsen hurried inside. Immediately, he knew the Kurds had been there. One man sat at a table, a bullet hole in his forehead and a shocked look in his open eyes. Further inside, a man lay in his underwear in a bloody pool on a tile bathroom floor. The blood was still wet, but not frothy. In a back bedroom there was a naked woman curled against a window in a heap, a bullet to her temple, one to her left breast, and several holes in the wall behind her.

Garcia met Nelsen in the bedroom. "You don't think this was a drug deal gone bad?"

Nelsen shook his head. "No. Do you?"

Garcia looked around and then shook his head. "The man in the bathroom. That's Kukulcan...Miguel Blanca. The man at the table out front is his bodyguard."

"Looks like he fucked up in that regard," Nelsen said.

"You're right. I've never seen the girl before."

"Probably fuck of the week," Nelsen said. "Let's check the place over completely. There could be something here saying where the Kurds are going, and why."

Garcia agreed with a nod and headed back into the main room.

Nelsen moved in for a closer look at the woman. He stooped down next to her and moved a piece of hair back away from her eyes. She had been a pretty woman, he was sure. Young. Mid-twenties, perhaps. She exercised. Took care of herself. He liked that. She didn't deserve to die like this, to cover someone's tracks. He moved back from the woman and closed his eyes, trying to imagine the Kurds in this room. They wanted something here. But what? He traced their movements from the front room to the bathroom and then to the bedroom. The guy at the table had not known what hit him. Miguel Blanca must have seen it coming, but couldn't do a thing to stop it. And this woman. She had a scared look on her face. She had died last, scurrying to the farthest corner of the house. What did the Kurds want here? They were close, but where were they going with the weapon? Maybe Kukulcan was their transportation, and they were simply clearing their tracks from the trail behind them.

20

ODESSA, UKRAINE

"Well, Tuck. What do you say?" Jake sat on a park bench along Primorski Boulevard, his eyes focused on Sinclair Tucker sitting next to him. The Brit crossed his long legs and shoved his driving cap to the back of his head. Tucker was clearly thinking it over. Jake had asked him for a safe house to keep Petra Kovarik and her friend Helena until things settled down a bit. Tucker was unusually concerned, as if Jake were asking for more than he was. They both knew that MI-6 had places like this. Apartments or houses used to interrogate or hide agents or suspects for short periods of time. The problem was, the intelligence agencies all liked to keep the places to themselves.

Tucker smiled and shook his head. "You know, Jake, my boss would have my ass if he knew."

"He's in Kiev," Jake said. "You're in charge down here."

That was true, but Tucker still didn't like the idea of giving up his location. That was evident by his stiff jaw and the incertitude in his eyes.

Jake looked across the street at the front of Tucker's bogus company, Black Sea Communications. Jake had showed up unexpectedly and hauled him across the street. He knew that Tucker would have had the entire building covered with cameras and sound, so he'd have to talk across the wide street, with cars and trucks zipping by. The noise was more than any recorder could handle.

"Come on Tuck, I'm not asking you to kill someone," Jake said. "I just need a safe place."

Tucker didn't budge. He watched the people pass on the sidewalk in front of him. An older man. A woman with a young child in a rickety stroller. Two young men walking arm in arm.

"We're working together here," Jake pleaded. "I can do it without you, but I'd like to work with you. Remember, you asked me for cooperation."

That seemed to work. Tucker turned toward Jake. "Share what you find out from the women?"

Jake thought about that. He hadn't been told not to share information, and it was a common practice. A professional courtesy. "Sure. You'll know what I know."

"I'd appreciate that," Tucker said. "It appears like you had a jump on us with this one. With the scientist's assistant and all."

"What do you know?" Jake asked.

Tucker smiled. "That's a bit premature, Jake."

"Not really. You tell me what you know up to this point, and I'll give you what I know. Then we'll fill in the blanks as they happen."

"That's fair," Tucker said. He told Jake everything he knew. About Tvchenko's contacts with certain foreigners, that they still had not identified. How he had his men checking all known GRU agents in Odessa, to see if they had been pushing Tvchenko into developing new weapons. The jury was still out on that. He mentioned how they even had one of the agents working for them, but he couldn't give Jake the name.

When Tucker was done, Jake explained everything he knew, from the tiny note Tvchenko had planted in his hand, to his employers, MacCarty and Swanson getting poisoned, and finally to the point where he and Quinn had found Petra at the friend's apartment. He even speculated on the theft of the chemical nerve agent from Johnston Atoll being related to this case in some way. Only time would tell if he was correct.

"What are the Kurds up to?" Tucker asked.

"I don't know for sure," Jake said. "They've been pushed and shoved so many times they probably don't know for sure themselves. Their biggest problem traditionally has been their inability to agree on anything. Maybe the various factions and tribal leaders have finally united in a great effort for autonomy and a free Kurdistan homeland. If that's the case, watch out. That's twenty million pissed off mountain people. I've seen them fight. They don't understand the word surrender."

Sinclair Tucker rose from the bench and planted his hands deep into his pants pockets. "I'll tell you what, Jake. I'll contact our people in Turkey and see what they've heard."

"I'll do the same." Jake reached his hand out to shake, and received a key in his palm from Tucker. Jake folded it in his fist. "And?"

Tucker whispered the address and then immediately

skirted across the street between traffic and into his office building.

Jake slid his hands into his pockets, dropping the key among his own. He quickly memorized the address by repeating it over and over in his head, while strolling down the sidewalk toward Tully's Volga.

21

SOUTHWEST TEXAS

S teve Nelsen was flipping through the gears, barely keeping the Ford Ranger on the winding dirt road. Without the four-wheel drive, the truck would have careened off the road miles back.

Nelsen had heard over the radio about the Suburban blown to pieces on the bank of the Rio Grande, knew exactly what had happened, had quickly inspected the smoldering shell of a truck, and hurried to the nearest bridge to cross into Texas. He had had to drive five miles through scrub brush and then along a bumpy dirt cow path to reach a rickety old wooden bridge that had looked safe enough for a single walker, perhaps a young boy on a bicycle, but surely not a Ford 4x4 pickup cruising at high speed, followed closely by two Jeep Cherokees with four Agency officers. A lone Mexican customs agent had stopped them before they crossed the bridge, and Nelsen had nearly ripped his throat out while pointing his gun at the man's head, before Garcia had stopped him and explained calmly in Spanish that they were in hot pursuit of international terrorists and every second counted.

They were waved through on the U.S. side, after calling ahead on the radio first.

It was just after nine in the morning, and Nelsen suspected the terrorists had a few hours head start. His only advantage, he thought, was they would be driving the speed limit, maybe even slower, so they wouldn't attract the local cops. They couldn't afford to be stopped. Also, if they had crossed the river across from the bombed truck, then they would have had to drive across extremely rough Texas outback, so they would have been driving slow to keep the bomblets from breaking open.

Nelsen had called in his position for backup by CIA interior officers working out of the El Paso office. Four agents in two other vehicles were converging on their position, aided by Presidio County Sheriff's units and a pair of Texas Rangers. If everything went as planned, Nelsen would have the terrorists and the bomb boxed in. If he could keep the truck on the road.

He swerved dangerously close to the edge of the dirt track, nearly sliding down a steep embankment.

Nelsen's partner, Ricardo Garcia, sat in the passenger side of the truck cab grasping the armrest, his knuckles turning white.

"Catching the bad guys would require us living. Isn't that right?" Garcia asked.

Nelsen twisted the wheel furiously. "You can get out any time, Ricky."

"Yeah, right." Garcia glanced behind, but could only see dust. "Do you suppose the boys are keeping up?"

"They know where we're heading," Nelsen said. "Besides, they can't lose us. Just follow the dust cloud."

"How do you know where these guys are heading?"

Nelsen hated answering questions. If the Agency would let him work alone, he would. "Simple. These bozos aren't Americans, yet they've had help every step of the way." He paused for a moment, shaking his head, as if to say how in the hell did this guy get into the Agency. He continued, "They've been able to keep just out of reach. Somebody in America is supporting them. Sanctioning them. We checked out all possible subversive groups in Texas, and that wasn't easy. But we knew their nationality, or in their case their multiple nationalities. There were very few nationalized citizens. Those who were did not impose a threat."

"And you were going to tell me this when?" Garcia asked.

Nelsen disregarded his partner as he braked and braced for a sharp corner. The back of the truck fishtailed. He continued. "So what was next? Students. We checked the databases for every college in Texas, then we had agents, escorted by campus security, check out every one last night. We narrowed it down to five possibles. Then later to two. Both are Iranians. But they aren't Persians."

"Let me guess. Kurds."

"Exactly." Nelsen thought it over. He wasn't used to working with a partner. "Sorry, Garcia. I called this in after talking with the Cypriot. I just forgot to tell you."

The truck reeled around another corner, nearly crashing through a bushy clump of yucca. To the north, the landscape evened off slightly. To the south were jagged points of rock and dirt, topped by scrawny pines and cacti. Nelsen imagined it was a great place for rattlesnakes.

"Get on the horn and see if the locals have cut off the

other end yet," Nelsen ordered. "I don't want those bastards getting away."

Garcia switched frequencies and called in. The sheriff and his men were in place five miles away. They had two helicopters in the air, but had not seen any other vehicles yet.

"Fucking podunks! Give me that thing." Nelsen swiped the handset from Garcia. "Listen Goddammit. You tell those chopper pukes to get their asses in gear and open their eyes. Anything moves out on this wasteland makes one hell of a dust cloud. They should be able to see that for ten miles."

"Yes, sir," came the reply.

"Don't piss these locals off," Garcia warned. "They're libel to let the bastards slip through on purpose. Let them head off to a different county."

Nelsen knew he was right, but he hated to admit it. "If I catch them pulling that shit, I'll shoot them myself." He glared over at Garcia for an uncomfortably long few seconds, his eyes away from the dangerous road.

Garcia turned away.

The Suburban had been off the road behind high brush when four county sheriff's cars passed by in a hurry, lights flashing, just minutes before the cars had turned to set up the road block two miles down the open road. A lone helicopter swooped low across the foothills of the Del Norte Mountains a few miles away.

Baskale started the engine and then inched the truck up the embankment, the four-wheel drive digging the tires into the dirt, but not spinning. The map showed a crossroad ahead. Paved. The Suburban crept onto the dirt road, and Baskale checked the rearview mirror every few seconds. The truck headed northeast right at the speed limit. Baskale didn't want to bring any attention to his truck. He knew that the men were looking for him. Finally, a challenge. He smiled outwardly, but also felt he couldn't afford to get caught. Not before he was done.

In a few miles, Baskale turned north onto U.S. Highway 67. He had zig-zagged across nearly every dirt road in the county, and now it was time to make up for lost time on a few paved roads. He would head east after a few miles, then north again, repeating the pattern and staying away from any towns of size. He would change vehicles soon, and would have to kill again, covering his tracks. Nothing would be left to chance. There was too much at stake.

Baskale kept looking into his mirror, but there was no one there.

Nelsen slowed the Ranger down as he approached the road block. He skidded to a halt and slammed his hand against the wheel. "Fucking shit. Where the hell did they go?"

Garcia got out and started talking with the sheriff.

In a couple of minutes, the two Jeep Cherokees came up behind them, the entire vehicles covered in dust, with only spots on the windshields cleared by overworked wipers.

Nelsen slid out and unfolded a map onto the hot hood. He slashed his finger to the north across the map, figuring they had to have passed the sheriff cars somewhere along County Highway 169.

"It would help if we knew where in the hell those bastards are heading," Nelsen muttered to himself.

Garcia and the sheriff were at Nelsen's side now.

"What now?" Garcia asked.

"I want every road within a hundred miles blocked to the north at Interstate 10," Nelsen started, sliding his finger along the blue interstate line. "Every stinking little skunk trail. Cut off the county lines here and here," he said, swishing his finger like a knife across the paper. "Call in more air support from Goodfellow and Laughlin Air Force Bases in the east."

"We don't have authority for that," the sheriff said.

"No, but I do," Nelsen said, his teeth clenched. "You tell anyone who asks that this is by order of the Central Intelligence Agency. As you may or may not know, we have authority and jurisdiction over whomever we need."

The sheriff headed off.

"That'll piss off a whole shitload of Texans," Garcia said.

"It's my job to piss people off. If they don't like it, they can go work for McDonald's."

22

ODESSA, UKRAINE

Jake had hurried back to Helena Yurichenko's apartment, where Quinn was watching over Petra Kovarik. Quinn had been somewhat nervous, wondering what had taken him so long. Jake hadn't realized he'd been gone two hours, but he was running on cautious mode, watching his back as he drove through the city, doubling back, stopping at the curb quickly. After getting the key from Tuck, he had found a phone and called Tully O'Neill, finding out that MacCarty too had died at the Polyklinik an hour ago. With that knowledge, he wanted to be absolutely certain he didn't make any mistakes. He knew he had not been followed.

Then Jake drove Petra, Helena and Quinn to the MI-6 safe apartment, being equally cautious, handed the key over to Quinn, and told them all to stay put. He had something he needed to do.

Jake parked Tully's Volga at the curb on Primorski Boulevard a half a block from the Chornoye Hotel, the hotel where he was staying and seemed like a year since he had been.

He was tired and it must have shown in his eyes as he strolled to the elevator. As he waited for the elevator to arrive, he noticed the lobby was very active, with people from many different countries huddled in groups of threes and fours. Then he checked his watch and realized the last day of the agricultural conference must have just ended, and attendees had come back to the hotel to freshen up before hitting the town one last night.

The elevator dinged and opened. He got in and punched six. He was alone on the ride up. At the sixth floor, the doors opened and he got out. He slowly moved out into the dim hallway, where the carpet was worn through to the hardwood floor beneath it. Down a few rooms, yellow markers criss-crossed the entrance to two rooms across the hall from each other, MacCarty's and Swanson's. He hadn't been back there since seeing them near death at the Polyklinik earlier in the day. The local police had sealed the rooms until they were certain what had happened. As far as Jake knew, the locals hadn't determined if their deaths had been a simple accidental poisoning. But Jake knew better. Someone, for some unknown reason, had killed his employers, and he'd find out why. He had a feeling their deaths were related to Tvchenko's murder, but wasn't sure how or why.

He stood for a minute outside of MacCarty's room. MacCarty had been a nice guy. He didn't deserve to die like that. Swanson was a prick, but Jake still felt for the man. He had suffered tremendously. Why had someone wanted to kill them? Did they know something about Tvchenko?

Glancing up and down the hallway, Jake thought about breaking into MacCarty's room, going through his things, trying to find anything that wasn't right. Then he remembered that his room adjoined MacCarty's.

He went into his room and clicked on the light. He looked around quickly and realized something wasn't right. Clothing items were not where he had left them. He pulled his gun and moved slowly through the room. If someone was there, they could only be hiding in the bathroom. He stepped closer to the half-open bathroom door, and shifted his gun to his left hand.

With one sudden burst, he slammed his shoulder into the door and flung himself inside.

Nothing.

But something wasn't right. It wasn't just the maid service. Things were not in their normal place. He always made a point of placing items in a particular fashion, so if someone had been there looking for something, he'd know it.

Back in the main room, he opened the top dresser drawer. His folded underwear were rumpled and shifted to the side. Someone had flipped through looking for something. It could have been a maid seeking money, but Jake didn't think so. Yet, it might have been the local cops, since they probably knew by now that he had traveled to Odessa with the two dead Americans. He returned his gun to its holster.

Jake sat on the bed for a minute thinking about all that had happened in the last few days. How did he get himself into these situations? It had been a simple case. Fly with the two Portland men to Odessa to attend a conference. A cultural and technical exchange. Take in a few sights. See a few old hang outs. Babysitting. Then Tvchenko dies into his arms, Jake is almost blown to bits, he's kidnapped and beaten, his two employers are killed. What happened to simplicity?

As he was thinking back it reminded him that his ribs were still aching. There was pain with each breath he took, and any quick movement made it feel as though knives were stabbing and twisting through his chest.

He gazed across the room at the door adjoining MacCarty's room. He could get in there. It's the least he could do for the man. Look into his death. If he found why they had been poisoned, he might figure out what Tvchenko was up to. He was sure the three deaths were connected.

Moving over to the door, he checked the lock. It was one of those two-lock deals, where he needed the key from his room and from the one on the other side to enter. He unlocked his side, and just for the hell of it, tried his key in the other lock. No good. It fit in the hole, but didn't turn.

Jake didn't like to admit it, but he was pretty good at picking locks. He chocked it up to a less than stellar youth. He had never been caught at anything significant while growing up in his small Oregon town, but it didn't mean he wasn't into things. It just meant he never got caught. One of his favorite things was picking locks for fun. Once he got through a door, his friends would want to steal everything inside. But Jake wouldn't let them. For him the challenge was simply getting past the door. And he had gotten good at it.

In less than a minute, he was in MacCarty's room. It was dark inside. An identical mirrored image of his room. He had been in there twice on Sunday, the day before the conference began, so he knew where MacCarty had left certain items.

He moved around the room easily by the light from the window. The local police had flipped through MacCarty's suitcases, throwing his clothes across the bed. The liner was ripped from one suitcase. There was nothing there. He suspected there wouldn't be, even though he had no idea what he was looking for.

MacCarty had told Jake he was working a deal with Victor Petrov with the Ukrainian Agricultural Ministry. Yet MacCarty's briefcase was missing. He might have had papers in there saying what the contract included. He looked around the room one more time for the leather case MacCarty was rarely without. Perhaps he had brought it with him to breakfast and the authorities had taken it as evidence after the men collapsed into their meals. He made a mental note to search for the briefcase, and then went back into his room and locked the door behind him.

Jake wished he could get into Swanson's room, but he wasn't about to cross the police barrier. He had heard far too many stories about the local police, and he didn't have diplomatic immunity. If the locals took him in for questioning, he could be tied up in bureaucratic muck for years, while wallowing in some disgusting four-by-six cell with roaches and vermin his only friends.

Instead, Jake changed clothes. While doing so, he checked out the bruises on his ribs. They were at that purple and black stage, and still a bit swollen. The outer edges had started to turn a dull yellow, so he knew the healing process had started.

When Jake was done changing, he placed a few items in various locations, so he'd know if anyone had been there again. Then he headed out.

Back downstairs in the lobby, Jake wandered toward the front desk. There were still a number of people hanging around. He saw her and stopped in his tracks. Chavva was leaning against a tall marble stanchion. She smiled when Jake noticed her and moved toward her.

"What are you doing here?" Jake asked, as he moved closer to her. He wanted to kiss her on both cheeks as the Europeans always did among friends, but he wasn't sure how close they really were.

She raised her brows seductively. "My boss is staying here. There wasn't enough room at my hotel."

Jake thought about that. He had tried to find her at the place she said she was staying, but they had no record of her there. "You're at the Odessa Hotel?"

She swished her head quickly. "No, no."

"But you said the other day—"

"I said I was staying at The Odessa Hotel. What I meant was the best hotel in Odessa. I'm sorry for the confusion. Did you try calling me?" She looked genuinely disappointed.

"Semantics," Jake said. "So, you're at which hotel?"

"The Maranovka, of course."

It was the same hotel that the agricultural conference dinner had been held. The same place Tvchenko had been killed. That could have explained why Chavva had disappeared that night. She had simply gone up to her room. "Which room?" Jake asked.

She smiled. "I'm in 902. Please give me a call." Her disposition changed quickly from cheery to grave, as she looked past Jake. "I must go. I'll be in Odessa for only a day or so. I must see you." She brushed alongside Jake as she sauntered across the room toward the outside doors.

Jake watched her carefully, taking in her perfume that lingered in the air. She met up with the older man, Omar Sharif, or whatever his name was. At the businessman's side was a huge man wearing a long coat, opened in the front. Jake knew muscle when he saw it, and this man was with the Israeli for one reason. To intimidate.

Omar kissed Chavva on both cheeks and then stared across the room at Jake. In a moment, the three of them were gone.

Continuing to the front desk, Jake wondered about Chavva's relationship with the older man. He didn't think they were lovers. They would have kissed on the lips then.

There was a message at the desk for Jake from Tully. It simply said to meet him at the entrance to the catacombs just before closing. Jake checked his watch. It was four-thirty. The catacombs would close at six. Jake shoved the note into his pocket and left the hotel.

Great. That's just the place he wanted to go as darkness set in.

23

It was said that there were a hundred ways to get into the extensive catacombs on the outskirts of Odessa. When Tully had said the entrance to the catacombs, Jake had assumed the one that had become a tourist attraction to the east of town. Jake had been there a few times, and had even gone underground for a number of hours. They were dark and damp tunnels, a constant cold, regardless of the season. It could be ninety degrees outside and the catacombs would be forty-five and clammy.

The note hadn't said whether Tully would meet him outside or inside, so Jake stood around for a moment wondering what to do.

There was a small ticket shack that charged tourists to enter the tunnels, which had always bothered Jake. Why would someone want to pay to see man-made caves? He guessed they were interesting. When he had entered the catacombs years ago, he had gone at his own risk at a private entrance. That one had been used by resistance fighters hiding from Nazis, but had since been taken over by black marketeers and more recently, the Ukranian mafia.

Jake looked back at the small parking lot. Since Jake

had Tully's Volga, and there were five other cars there, which car would Tully be driving?

When Jake turned back toward the catacomb entrance nearly a hundred feet away, he noticed a man standing near the mouth. Tully? Jake drifted closer. The man went into the tunnel out of sight.

Jake paid for a ticket and walked toward the entrance. As he got closer, he could see lights slung down the side of the walls. The tunnel entrance narrowed and became dark. There must have been a turn at the bottom, he guessed.

The man had disappeared. Jake descended the slope and felt the gun under his left arm. Considering everything that had happened to him in the past few days, he was becoming more and more cautious. He wasn't taking any chances now.

Jake got to the end and sure enough, the tunnels turned toward the left and continued down. The lights were farther apart, making it impossible to see more than thirty feet or so in front of him. He thought about pulling the gun but decided against it.

The walls were jagged at the top and smoother at the bottom. The deeper he went, the more moisture on the walls. Why was Tully pulling him deeper into the catacombs?

For some reason Jake stopped. He wasn't even sure why. He just did. There was a passage that went off to his right. He could hear voices a short distance away. Two people talking in the darkness of that new tunnel. Jake looked back down the main tunnel with the lights, but saw or heard nothing.

He slowly stepped down the dark passageway. It was so

dark that it reminded him of the times in his youth when he used to pretend he was blind, covering his eyes and stepping through unfamiliar woods in the dark. He would feel with his feet as he stepped, stretch his arms out for tree limbs, and listen as night animals scurried in the crunchy undergrowth of darkness.

He slipped his feet forward, expecting to fall off a cliff into nothingness at any moment. He hugged the left side wall with his shoulder, his left hand stretched outward against cold rock.

He got closer to the voices.

He felt like he had started turning to the right. Then he saw the lights ahead, and he knew he had been rounding a bend. Two flashlights.

He stopped and peered at the lights shining at each other's face. He was too far away to tell if Tully was one of the men. The voices got louder. The men were arguing, Jake thought. What language? Russian? He couldn't be sure.

Jake started to step closer.

The men were scuffling. Something metal hit the rock floor. Flashlights swayed back and forth as blows were struck. One man hit the ground and the other was shining his light as if searching. Looking for a gun?

Jake drew his 9mm as he got closer. He was now twenty feet away.

A shot echoed loudly through the cave. Then another. One man had found the gun and was firing toward the other. The second man had turned off his light. There were two more quick shots. Then silence.

Jake had stopped after the shots. He didn't want the man with the gun thinking he was the target. His heart was pounding loudly. Could the man hear it?

He couldn't move, but Jake thought of something. He crouched down low against the wall and aimed his gun toward the light. When he was ready, he yelled, "Tully?"

The flashlight whipped around. "Jake?"

Jake held his position. "What in the hell is going on?"

"Did anyone pass you?" Tully asked, as the light moved toward Jake.

"No. He must have gone the other way."

Tully was now just a few feet away. He shone the light on Jake's face. "You can put down the gun."

Jake lowered his aim and rose to his feet. "What was that all about?"

Tully flashed the light on his own face. He had blood trickling from a cut lip. He motioned with his index finger to be quiet, and then he turned off the light and tugged on Jake to follow him.

They wandered back through the darkness toward the entrance. After they reached the lighted passageway, Tully let go of Jake and they hurried up toward the parking area.

When Jake reached the outside, he squinted from the brightness, and took in a whiff of fresh air. Then he looked at Tully. His clothes were soiled. His hair was messed up.

Jake returned his gun to its holster. Tully did the same. "What's going on?" Jake asked.

Tully wouldn't look at him. "It was a contact of mine. We were supposed to meet tonight at the train station, but he called to cancel. No reason. He wanted to meet me here instead. Something wasn't right, so I left a message for you to back me up."

They were through the gate now and almost to the parking lot.

"Why didn't you wait for me?"

Tully shrugged. "If it was a set-up, you wouldn't be in as much danger following me as you would standing next to me."

True. But he might have been more cautious. "What were you arguing about?" Jake asked.

They both stopped alongside Tully's car.

Tully was thinking the question over. "Money. He wanted more. I told him he needed to give me more before I could give him more."

"So, he tries to kill you?"

"I don't know why. He's a little touched, I think."

That didn't make sense, Jake thought. Why had Tully tried shooting the man? Jake looked at Tully more carefully now that his eyes had completely adjusted to the light. He was looking pretty bad. His eyes looked like a Mexican road map, the red lines streaking every which way. His hair was tousled and slimy-looking, as if he had used an entire tube of gel on it.

"I see my car is still in one piece," Tully said. "Did you find Petra?"

"Yeah, we did. Quinn is talking to her now. Seeing what she knows about Tvchenko's research. What about your contact? Is he going to get out of there?" Jake swished his head toward the catacombs.

"Shit, yeah. He knows those things inside and out."

"You got a ride?" Jake asked.

Tully shook his head no. "I took a cab."

"Let's go. I'm driving."

24

BRIGHTON, ENGLAND

The train ride from London to Brighton was much the same as it had been the last four years. Routine. Sir Geoffrey Baines, as chairman of Britain's foreign service, could have warranted a car and driver and a weekly apartment in London. But Baines would have none of that. He preferred to travel as he always had by train to London and then by taxi from Charing Cross Station to his office on Whitehall, across from the Houses of Parliament. He would only indulge his superiors and take a limousine on those rare occasions when he addressed parliament, even though it would have been only a short walk. Appearances.

He spent the hour each way by train from his home in the morning, and again at night, reading a good book. He would have gone over papers, had he not been required to leave them in a safe each night. And sometimes he even stretched his own rules, bringing less sensitive information home with him. Tonight was one of those rare times. He had been in meetings all afternoon, and only had time to scoop up the papers from his desk before hurrying to catch his train. Included in that mass of paperwork was a secure fax from Sinclair Tucker in Odessa. It was probably one of his routine reports on bogus letterhead from the communications firm. Anyone off the street picking it up would have to conclude it was the babbling of a child. Either that, or somehow the fax machine had gone haywire, replacing standard English for obscure, disjointed diction.

Baines was dressed somewhat down for a man with his power and prestige, wearing a modest wool suit, a putrid green overcoat, and scuffed brown oxfords protruding from his crossed legs. He was rarely without an umbrella and never without his felt derby hat, which hung over his umbrella handle at the corner of his seat.

He was reading a Thomas Hardy classic for the third or fourth time. Once never seemed to be enough. He was lost in the book as the countryside flew past the window to his left. His stop was just minutes away, and he was trying desperately to finish a chapter before he reached Brighton Station.

In a few minutes, the train slowed and then seemed to sneak along, until it finally came to a halt alongside the brick walkway of Brighton Station.

Baines had timed his reading just right. He slipped his book back inside his leather attache case, locked it securely, gathered up his umbrella, and popped his hat on his head. He swayed down the narrow aisle, his wide frame bashing against each seat he passed.

Once on the loading terminal, he turned instinctively to the left, and walked off toward the main station. He checked his watch. He was right on time. It was ten after six. Baines lived four blocks from the terminal in an old Victorian that dated back two hundred years. It had been in his family for a century, and would go to his son when he passed on. His son, who probably wanted nothing to do with the old house, since he had worked in Paris for eight years, was married to a young French wife. Deep down Baines knew the house would go up on the auction block, or be sold outright by his son. His wife would never leave France.

He found himself growing tired with each step he took toward home. He was seventy-two, but only death would make him retire.

His house was on Preston Lane. It was a three-story place with a second-floor balcony overlooking the street, and a third-floor balcony with a view of the back garden. As a young man, Geoffrey Baines had watched German planes fly over his house on their way to London. When he was old enough, he had joined the British Air Force as a pilot, and after crashing in Belgium while returning from a mission, he was offered a position in the intelligence service. He had been with MI-5 or MI-6 ever since.

Baines stood before his housea and gazed up at the balcony, where the door was open. That was odd. Perhaps Mrs. Jones, his housekeeper, had simply forgotten it. She wasn't normally prone to forget, but it was possible.

He went through the creaky metal gate and unlocked the front door. He placed his umbrella and hat on the wooden rack, instinctively, and then with some difficulty pulled his overcoat off and hung it over a peg by the door.

Looking into the library to his right, he noticed things shuffled around. Mrs. Jones could not have cleaned, he thought.

He started to turn toward the hall that led to the kitchen, when there was a flash of movement.

Something hit him in the face.

He reeled back against the wall and smashed his head against it. Then a punch in his stomach knocked the wind out of him. He slowly slid toward the wooden floor. Stars sparkled before his teary eyes. He could taste blood. The pain in his nose was overwhelming. He reached up and felt the blood pouring out over his lips, into his mouth, and down over his chin. He shook his head and tried to look up.

There were sounds above him. Men talking. Baines rolled to his side so his head was through the doorway to the study. Two feet away was Mrs. Jones's face, her eyes opened wide. She had an ice pick sticking out of her forehead and her throat was slit.

Baines reeled backward in horror. One of the men kicked him in the kidneys and Baines passed out.

When he came to, Baines was lying on the study floor. The two men were standing over his desk. They had opened his attache case and were shuffling through the papers. One of them noticed he was awake, and he slapped his partner and muttered something to him.

Who were these men? Baines studied them carefully. They appeared to be Arabs or Turks. He couldn't tell for sure. But the language wasn't right. He couldn't understand anything. Maybe it was because his brain was still not functioning after the blow to his nose. He tried to pull himself up to his elbows.

The largest of the two men started toward Baines, but the other one stopped him.

The smaller man smiled. "You didn't expect us?" He asked in a crude version of English, as he swept his arms out in a grand gesture.

"Who are you?" Baines asked. His throat was sore and caked with dried blood. His nostrils were nearly plugged as well.

"That doesn't matter," the man said. "Our relationship will end in a few minutes. You have to be asking yourself, why? Why me? Just remember that God has a reason for everything. If you were good in life, which I doubt, then God will send you to a better place. At least that's what you believe is true. Am I right?"

Baines didn't answer. He had always wondered what it would be like to die. He had a feeling he'd find out soon. When he was younger, falling from the plane after being shot down during the war, he had prayed to God to spare him. Bring him home to England safely. God had done just that. But now...in his own home. A place where everyone should feel safe. Yet he was not.

The man kicked him in the leg. "Are you still with us old man? You want to know who we are and why we're here. Well I'm not going to tell you. My people were killed for no reason, and your government did nothing to stop them. Nothing to punish them for their crimes. Now you will die wondering why. Why you? Why now?"

What was that accent? Baines tried desperately to think, but his mind wasn't working right. He was about to die. He knew that. If he had only carried a gun—

The smaller man nodded for his friend, and the larger man moved behind Baines, pulling his arms over his head. Next, the smaller man put his knee on Baines' chest. He withdrew a syringe from his coat pocket, and much like a cruel dentist would, he brought it in front of Baines' eyes. With one hand the man grabbed Baines' throat, and then he shoved the needle up his nose.

Baines tried to scream in pain. He shuddered.

Then the man injected a full shot of liquid into him.

The men let him go and backed off across the room to watch.

In a few minutes, Baines felt his head swirling even more. Then he started sweating. He felt so hot. His heart started racing. It felt like it would burst from his chest. He couldn't breathe. He grabbed his own throat and tried to squeeze air through it. All he could hear was a gurgling sound in his wind pipe. His head pounded now. Spinning. He was spinning. He tried to think of pleasant things. Good things that had happened in his life. His wife. The birth of his son. But there was only the pain.

He twitched on the floor, and the two men watched him, smiling, until he no longer flopped around. No longer moved at all.

Before the men left, the large man kicked Baines' flaccid body just for the hell of it.

They picked up the papers from the desk and were out the door.

25

ODESSA, UKRAINE

Jake was tired and confused. He was still somewhat chilled from the short time he had spent in the catacombs. He had dropped off a reticent Tully at the office and then drove to the small apartment to the east of Shevchenko Park. The place Tuck had loaned him. It was nothing special, and Jake hoped the two women wouldn't have to be there long. He had been extremely careful coming here, ensuring he wasn't followed.

He now had Petra alone. He was sure that she was important. She was perhaps the only person who might know what Yuri Tvchenko was up to. Her and the Kurds.

Quinn went back to the office to brief Tully O'Neill, and Helena was resting in the back bedroom. Quinn had told Jake before he left that Petra had told him nothing. But Jake wasn't sure that Quinn had asked the right questions. Perhaps he was too close to her.

Petra was on an old sofa cradling a cup of tea Jake had made for her. Jake leaned against the wall peering through a corner of the curtains to the street three stories down. It was starting to get dark and some of the street lights were beginning to turn on.

Jake went over and sat on the sofa across from Petra. He was finally alone with her. "Are you all right?"

She shrugged. "I was all right at Helena's apartment."

"No. They would have found you there." He thought she seemed less afraid than at Helena's place. More willing to talk.

"How long will Quinn be?"

"Not long. He had a few things to take care of." He wondered what she would be willing to talk about. Start with the things he already knew. That always worked best. "How long have you been a bio-chemist?"

"Ten years." She took a slow sip of tea, her eyes still trained on Jake.

"Did you work with Yuri the entire time?"

"No. I started at the university in Kiev as a research assistant for another man. He was nowhere near as brilliant as Yuri. He was uninspired. Yuri was a genius."

He thought about asking her again if she was in love with Yuri. He didn't believe what she had said earlier about him being a homosexual. But sex was irrelevant to what he was trying to find out. "What was the basis of your research at his apartment?"

She took another sip and stared off across the room over the top of the cup. "I thought I told you. We were seeking a better pesticide. Yuri was certain he could come up with a substance that would revolutionize the industry."

"Much like his chemical weapons program for the Soviet Union had?" It was a mistake to bring that up, and Jake regretted having said it.

"Yuri did what he was told," she sneered. "Those pigs

used him during the best years of his life. They worked him to death. And for what? To build more and more weapons that would kill more efficiently. He wasn't a murderer. He was a gentle man. He loved life. Especially since the break up of the Soviet Union. He always considered himself Ukrainian. He spoke Russian only when necessary."

Jake was certain now that Petra had more than a passing admiration for the man. She had loved him. "Tell me about the new pesticide."

"We were working with beans."

"Beans?"

"Yes. It was incredible. We would synthesize the beans in an alcohol-based solution, along with other chemicals. The result was a highly toxic, yet stable, solution much like sarin that would kill any bug that came in contact with it. Interestingly, some of the bugs would not die right away. They would carry the strain to others and infect the entire peripheral population."

Jake thought about the isopropyl alcohol he had smelled at Tvchenko's apartment prior to the explosion. "So what you were dealing with was sort of a cross between Sarin and Ricin?"

She gazed at him incredulously. "You know about these things?"

"A little," Jake said. "I have a background on some of the more common nerve gas agents and poisons." He quickly shifted gears back to the research. "So, then Yuri was sort of using his former research for commercial purposes? But how did he plan on keeping the strain safe for civilian populations."

She finished her tea and set the cup on a small table.

"Ahhhh...that was the difficult part. Because the bean base mutated and spread, it affected some bugs differently than others. Some bugs would live for days flying or walking around like normal. Then boom. They were dead. They would twitch and shiver and shake, become completely immobilized, and then die. We tested the bugs after, to see why some had been affected differently, but still had no answer. Yuri had his suspicions, though."

Jake thought about watching Tvchenko die right in front of him, twitching much like she had described. "What were his suspicions?"

She sat back farther into the sofa, as if she were a turtle hiding inside its shell.

Jake turned quickly toward the door. He thought he heard something.

A clicking noise.

He started to turn his head toward Petra, when the door burst open.

Jake dove to the ground, drawing his Glock.

Two men with silenced Uzis started spraying the room. Bullets hit the wall with thuds.

Jake returned fire, emptying half a magazine.

One man dropped, the other backed away.

Jake rolled across the floor behind a chair and listened, but all he could hear was ringing from the shots he had fired in the close quarters.

He rose quickly and made it to the side of the door, peeked around the corner, his gun pointing the way.

Nothing.

A door down below slammed and he could hear a car pulling away, its tires squealing. He turned to check the man lying on the floor on his back. He had a bullet in his forehead and another had taken out his mouth. A third bullet had penetrated his chest.

Then he remembered Petra, and he ran back inside.

Petra lay slumped back against the arm of the sofa, her hair covering her face. Jake checked for a pulse, but she was dead. She had been hit at least three or four times. It was hard to tell with all the blood.

Now Jake thought of Helena. She would be awake, hiding, frightened.

"Helena," he called out. "It's Jake. I'm coming in."

He went into the bedroom, and she ran and collapsed into his arms.

"What happened?" she asked.

Jake tried to find the words to say that Petra, her best friend, was dead in the other room. "Helena, I'm sorry. Petra is gone."

She peered up to him. "Someone has taken her?"

He shook his head. "No. She's been killed. I'm sorry."

She didn't believe him. She hurried to the living room and went immediately to Petra. She sat next to her friend, placed Petra's flaccid head on her shoulder. "You're all right," she said. "I'm here now. Everything will be fine."

Jake stared and became angrier with each moment. How could someone do this? She was a scientist's assistant. Whatever it took, he'd find the other man who did this, and especially the one who had hired them.

26

TEXAS

By now Baskale guessed every road in west Texas had been cut off. Which is why he had driven to the dirt airstrip, parked the Suburban alongside the twin engine Beechcraft, and was preparing for take off.

The airstrip wasn't on any map, since it belonged to the Chihuahua drug dealer. The dealer had used the private airport to run product across the border, and to fly in American goods that he couldn't find in Mexico. The dealer had told Baskale about the place and given him the keys to the plane just prior to being shot. Baskale couldn't have someone staying behind and giving up his position. Especially someone as weak and pathetic as Kukulcan.

His three men had helped load the bomb onto the plane, and then they had split up into two teams. Baskale and the biggest of his men would fly off in the plane, and the other two would leave in the Suburban, quickly ditch it for a tiny car, something that could never carry a five hundred pound cluster bomb, and then meet again at the predetermined location. The authorities were looking for four terrorists in a large truck with a deadly bomb. Now the two in the small car would be a couple of Israeli tourists touring the American west. At least that's how their passports would read. Baskale and his most trusted man had become Americans. They had drivers' licenses with a Dallas address, social security cards, Visa and Mastercards, and even pictures of wives and children, which they surely didn't have. They were entrepreneurs who had opened a business five years ago, where they converted old homes into stately estates, at a considerable profit. They had just bought the plane off an old man who had lost his pilot's license due to his eyes. Their cover wasn't perfect, but then Baskale didn't think he'd have to explain it to anyone.

In a few moments they were airborne, and Baskale watched the other two men driving away in the Suburban. He would beat those two to the next location by a good four hours, maybe more. He only hoped they wouldn't run into any trouble.

Nelsen was dumfounded. He had cruised up to Interstate 10, was driving east at sixty-five miles per hour and listening to reports across his radio that they had still not found the men. He was beginning to question his own insight. Perhaps they had stopped somewhere to wait it out. Sit tight until dark, hide the bomb, split up into four directions, and return later for their precious nerve gas bomb. Or, worse yet, they could break open the bomb and split the bomblets four ways. It was possible, but not likely. So far they had kept on moving, staying one step ahead of him. He didn't think they would change their pattern.

They were in a hurry to go somewhere. But where? And why? That would take some thinking.

Garcia had hitched up the laptop computer to the cellular phone and was accessing everything the Agency knew about the Kurds. Perhaps they would get lucky and figure out why they were in Texas with a nerve agent. His fingers clicked along across the keyboard.

"You're pretty good at that," Nelsen said.

"My mother is a journalist," Garcia said. "She taught all of us to type before we could even scribble our own names. I must admit, it's come in handy over the years writing up reports and searching databases."

"What you coming up with on the Kurds?"

He clicked a few more times, and then punched the enter button. A history of the Kurds blinked onto the screen. Garcia scrolled up to more recent history, from 1980 to the present. On the right of the screen was a side bar with general statistics. "I had no idea there were so many Kurds. Shit, twenty million?"

"That's right," Nelsen said. "I don't think most people realize that. I spent some time in Turkish Kurdistan while working out of the Ankara office. The Kurds are a hardy lot. Goat and sheep ranchers mostly. Mountain people. The Turks simply called them Mountain Turks. They denied them their own language. They aren't allowed to officially speak or write the language. But they do, and there's not a damn thing the government can do about it. I scouted the area once after Turkish troops were sent in to stamp out a minor uprising. The Turks got their asses whipped trying to fight in the mountains. The Kurds are a tough people. But we've got the advantage here. They don't know Texas and America like we know it. They're on our turf." He hoped he could believe his own words.

Nelsen slowed the truck slightly as they ran into light traffic at the Fort Stockton exits. He noticed that there were city police blocking the on ramps, just as Nelsen had ordered.

Garcia clicked away on the computer. "I guess they've got this area blocked off."

"Yeah, but they could be anywhere. Think. Think. What would you do?"

Garcia shrugged. "I don't know. Sit low. Assuming I don't have to be someplace at a certain time."

Nelsen thought about that. He had been puzzled for the last few days on where the Kurds were going, what they were trying to accomplish, and he had been stumped over the entire case. There was no logical reason the Kurds should want to bring terror to American soil. Yet here they were. But just maybe... "Ricardo, punch up the Gulf War time frame."

In a few seconds the screen blinked the information. "What do you want to know?"

"What does it say about after the ground war? March 1991. I seem to recall that the U.S. pulled up short, to the displeasure of many, and tried to let some of the internal forces finish off Saddam Hussein. It didn't work of course, because Iraq had secretly held back and withdrawn some of its best trained Republican Guards. Hussein knew he was beat and didn't want to have the coalition completely destroy his best army. I visited some of the safe havens set up within Iraq after the Kurds had been forced to retreat. It was a total zoo."

"That's almost exactly what it says on the Agency database," Garcia said.

Nelsen smiled. "That's because I helped write that portion. But in light of that knowledge, what could you conclude about the Kurds?"

Garcia studied the screen as if he'd missed something. "I don't know."

Nelsen slammed his hand against the steering wheel. "Dammit. I've been such an idiot." He shook his head. "Me of all people. I should have figured it out."

"You want to let me in on your little secret?"

"Bush. They're after former President George Bush. He lives in Texas. Houston."

"Why would they want to kill Bush?"

"Because they're pissed off at him. Bush let the Kurds down. Everybody knows it. He should have intervened when the Kurds were being pushed back into the mountains of Turkey and Iraq, but he just let the situation take its course. He thought the Kurds were stronger than they were. Didn't fully realize that Hussein had kept his best troops standing by. He didn't respond to their plight until thousands had frozen and starved to death."

Garcia still looked confused.

Nelsen jammed the accelerator to the floor. Then he grabbed the cellular phone, switched it back to voice, and punched in a number. He called CIA headquarters and was holding for the assistant manager of external operations. It was true that they were now operating on the turf of internal operations, but it had started outside the U.S. so they had first authority. In the old days, the FBI and CIA would be butting heads now. But now they were all on the same playing field. Internal and external would work as one. At first the assistant DO had thought that Nelsen's story was incredulous, to say the least. But slowly, as Nelsen articulated his position, he shifted toward his field officer's reasoning. It was incredible to think of terrorists trying to assassinate a former American president on U.S. soil with one of its own nerve gas bombs. Incredible, but highly likely.

When Nelsen was off the phone with CIA headquarters and concentrating on the road, thinking about how they should proceed, a smile came to his face.

"What's so funny?" Garcia said.

"The Kurds. They have an ironic sense of humor."

"How's that?"

"Face it. They could have easily just flown a few terrorists to Houston, armed them, and sent them loose after the former president. But they don't. They go through this elaborate scheme stealing a nerve gas bomb, killing a whole bunch of people in the process. Then they spend almost a week on the high seas, probably puking their guts out, and land in Mexico. Then they drive north with the bomb leaving bodies in their wake. Why? It seems like an awfully complex assassination." Nelsen smiled and raised his brows at his partner.

Garcia considered it. "So, they want to kill Bush with his own weapon?"

"Exactly."

As they cruised along the nearly deserted highway, Garcia gazed off to the scrub brush and sage to his right. Then he turned to Nelsen. "What if we're wrong?"

Nelsen gripped the steering wheel until his knuckles turned white. "I'm not wrong."

27

ODESSA, UKRAINE

Jake had hurried off with Tully O'Neill's Volga and Helena in tow. After driving just a few blocks, he abandoned the car and slid onto a city bus, watching to see if they had been tailed. He got off near the train station and stole a cab waiting outside, while the driver was drinking coffee at a small kiosk. He had no idea where he was heading, only that to stay in one place wasn't an option. He still wasn't certain how the gunmen had known they were at that apartment. He was sure he wasn't followed. Yet, somehow the men had found them, and he didn't want to take any chances with Helena. The gunmen had to assume Petra had told Helena something, and they couldn't chance leaving her alive. The same went for him.

There was also no time after Petra's murder to call Tully and Quinn to tell them what had happened. Part of him didn't want to call. It would have been like an admission of failure, and he had experienced far too much of that in the past few days. He began questioning his own competence. Yet, deep down, he knew that it would have been nearly impossible to totally protect MacCarty and Swanson. He knew also that if an assassin or group of assassins wanted someone dead, they'd find a way to make it happen. All he needed to know was, why? Why were these people being killed?

He was feeling pretty rotten about Petra, especially. After all, she had died right in front of him. He had reacted too slowly. From now on he would trust only himself, regardless of personal sensibilities and Agency priorities. If the Agency wanted his help, it would have to put up with his rules.

Helena was resting against his shoulder in the front passenger seat of the cab. She had been incomprehensible the entire trip, mumbling in Ukrainian and Russian. Even in her great distress, Jake noticed she was beautiful. She was a lost little girl without her pacifying violin, which had been left behind at the last apartment as they left rather abruptly.

The cab wound through the country road to the northeast, and the lights of Odessa were only a glow behind them now in the rearview mirror.

In a few hours they reached the outskirts of Nikolaev. Jake found the train station and parked the cab a few blocks away, wiped his prints from anything he had touched, and got Helena out from the curb side.

She was leaning against him as they walked toward the station. At the window, he bought her a ticket to Yalta. She had no idea why, but also had no strength to protest.

The train would leave in fifteen minutes. Jake escorted her to a private compartment, sat her against a window seat, drew the curtains closed, and took a seat next to her.

"Listen, Helena," Jake whispered. "You're going to Yalta. Here's your ticket." He stuffed the yellow stub into her coat pocket.

"I don't know anyone in Yalta," she cried. She looked like a little girl who had lost her parents at a shopping mall.

"Good. That's perfect. No one would guess you'd go there. I want you to go to the Summit Hotel. It's just four blocks from the train station. Pay cash for four days." Jake slipped her a wad of cash. "I want you to stay there, eat there, sleep there, and don't leave. If anyone questions why you are traveling alone, simply tell them you are waiting for your husband to return from sea. He's a merchant marine. I'll come there to pick you up."

She gazed up to him. "You won't leave me there?"

"Of course not. I'll be there in four days. That should give me enough time to find out who did this to Petra and what they want."

She tried to smile, but her lower lip trembled.

Jake thought about Petra and Helena being alone for all those hours before he and Quinn had found them. Had Petra confided in her? "I have to ask you something. Did Petra ever talk about her work?"

She swished her head no.

"What about Tvchenko. Did she talk about him?"

She thought for a moment. "Only about how he made love to her. You knew they were lovers."

"I suspected it. So, Petra probably did know what Tvchenko was up to?"

"Maybe, maybe not. Yuri was very secretive. He was a good man. I'm sure of that. I don't see how he could have been involved with making bad weapons."

Jake stared at her. If circumstances were different, perhaps they could get to know each other better. He found himself extremely attracted to her, both mentally and physically. She was a delicate flower without any thorns.

"Are you sure there's nothing you can tell me to help me find out what in the hell's going on. Think. It's important."

Helena shrugged. "I don't know anything. I'm a musician."

There was a last call for the train to Yalta over the speakers. Jake kissed Helena on both cheeks and started off. She pulled him by the collar and kissed him passionately on the lips.

"Jake, please don't leave me."

"I have to go." He didn't want to, though. It would have been so much easier to simply take the train to Yalta with her, spend a few days making love to Helena in the hotel, and then.... "I'll meet you in Yalta. I promise."

He pulled away from her, and she slumped back to her chair.

Out on the loading gate, Jake was walking away but felt as though something was penetrating the back of his head. He turned to watch the train pull away. Helena's face peered around the curtains, a desperate glare, as if her soul was reaching out for him. In a moment the train was out of sight picking up speed.

Jake went back to a different window and bought himself a ticket to Odessa. He had an hour to waste, and he felt like a stiff drink of whiskey, even though he couldn't stomach hard liquor. Besides, he needed a clear head. He was confused. In the last few days a prominent scientist had died in his arms, he had nearly been killed by an explosion in that man's apartment, he had been kid-napped, shot at, and been forced to steal a cab. He had killed a man only hours ago, yet he felt nothing for the dead man. He was nothing. Nothing more than flesh and blood without a soul. Jake was protecting a woman he barely knew, and he was still no closer to finding out what in the hell was going on. His boss had been poisoned, and he had no real reason to stay behind and continue investi-gating. No reason but pride. He would never run away from a fight, like some whimpering dog that had been bit on the butt.

Somehow his position at the apartment had been com-promised. Someone had given him up for dead, and only Quinn Armstrong, Helena, or Petra knew where they were. And, of course, Sinclair Tucker. Jake hadn't been careless enough to let someone follow him there, but it was possible. Especially if Tully's Volga had been tracked somehow. It was more likely that someone had sold him out. His jaw clamped his teeth tight with that thought.

28

WASHINGTON, D.C.

Kurt Jenkins, the CIA Director of Operations, ush-
ered his assistant into the study of his Georgetown
home and quietly shut the French doors behind them.
Jenkins' wife had answered the door, and when she saw
that it was work, had stormed off to the dining room to
feed her two young children, while she screamed for her
husband up the banister. It was another meal her husband
would have to re-heat in the microwave.

Jenkins tried to keep his home life and Agency duties
separate, but sometimes that was impossible. When he
had shuffled down the stairs, he understood why his wife
was so disturbed. With just the sight of his assistant,
Bradley Stevens, in the foyer, he knew something was up.
And it was probably not good news.

"What do you have, Brad?" Jenkins asked, pouring two
glasses of whiskey straight up.

Stevens was a tall, slim man who walked like a stork.
His thin face and crooked, long nose, were accented by
tiny circular spectacles, identical to the ones his boss,

Jenkins, wore. Stevens was a Princeton honors graduate in political science who had decided on law school at age ten, but had put it off to serve his country for a few years. A few years had turned into ten, with Stevens hopping from Defense to the State Department, and now the Agency. He was in his early thirties now with no intention of going back to school. He liked what he did. It was important work. And besides, he too had a wife and two children to support. He was Jenkins' right hand man. His eyes and ears in an organization where paranoia was endemic.

Bradley Stevens took off his glasses, breathed on them, and then started wiping them clean with a special cloth he always carried in his pocket. "Not good, boss," Stevens said, settling into a hard leather chair. He put his glasses back on, accepted the glass of whiskey, and held it in his unsteady hand.

"Don't spill that, Brad. It's older than your children." Jenkins took a sip of whiskey. "Well?"

"Odessa. Tully O'Neill, the station chief, called secure about an hour ago. The woman who worked with Tvchenko, Petra Kovarik, has been murdered."

"How? Did we get anything from her?"

Stevens shook his head. "We're not a hundred percent certain. She was being watched by Jake Adams when at least two gunmen smashed through the safe house door and started firing."

"Jake Adams?"

"Yes. He used to work for the old agency, and was a captain in Air Force intelligence before going private a few years back. He's the one who saved Tully's ass a few days ago. The director put him to work for us."

"Yeah, yeah, go on."

"Adams and Quinn Armstrong were watching the two women. Armstrong stepped out for a minute when the shooting took place. It appears that Adams escaped with the other woman, a friend of the scientist's assistant."

Jenkins took another drink of whiskey. "Where are they now?"

"Uncertain. The only blood in the room was from Petra Kovarik. Adams shot one of the shooters, but that guy's not talking."

"Who is it?"

"No name, no I.D., but Tully seems to think he's either a Turk or a Kurd, maybe both."

"Shit! Have we come up with a tie with the nerve gas theft from Johnston Atoll? What in the hell is going on in Texas?"

Stevens shifted in his chair and took his first drink of whiskey, nearly choking.

"Well?"

"I'm not sure. But Steve Nelsen has his theory."

"President Bush. I know, I already heard that one. If he's right, he's a hero. If he's wrong, then he's pissed off a whole bunch of people."

"It makes some sense."

"That's a hell of a memory on the part of the Kurds," Jenkins said. "Why wait so long? It's been years since the Gulf War."

"The Kurds are a patient bunch, sir," Stevens said. "They've been pushed and shoved for a long time. Maybe they're sick of being bullied. But that's not all. There was a businessman killed in Berlin a few days ago. Gerhard Kreuzberg."

Jenkins' eyes shot up. "Kreuzberg? The German foreign minister a few years back?"

"Yes, sir. Under Kohl. In fact, he was the foreign minister during the Gulf War."

"And you think—"

"It's too much of a coincidence not to think it."

"What would they gain by killing Kreuzberg?"

"Legitimacy. Revenge. Kreuzberg wouldn't allow Germany to get involved any more than they did."

"But he had German law on his side," Jenkins assured his assistant.

"True. But that's never stopped the Germans before. It wasn't only that. He stood by when Germans started killing Turks in Bonn, and Cologne, and Frankfurt. Many of those were Kurds. They set themselves on fire on the autobahns in protest, and Kreuzberg did nothing. He couldn't. The average German was backing him, because Germans had lost their jobs to Turks, jobs they didn't want to do until there were no others to be found. The country was combining with East Germany, with more labor problems. Kreuzberg had to make a strong stand. The Kurds felt betrayed."

"So they kill him years later?" Jenkins asked.

"Maybe they're finally unifying like the Palestinians did under Arafat."

"That's three operations in two weeks. That's some great unity." Jenkins paused to finish his whiskey and think. "This is all just a theory."

"A pretty good one."

"What do you recommend?"

Stevens straightened the tiny glasses on his nose. "Our German contacts say Kreuzberg was killed by a poisoned pellet. Probably Ricin."

"Ricin? Who still uses that?"

Stevens shrugged. "I don't know. But it's interesting. All those people on Johnston were poisoned. Tvchenko was probably killed by a Sarin-based formula, and now the German. Tvchenko developed some of the most deadly Sarin weapons, and then went far beyond that stage. Tully O'Neill said that Tvchenko was working on a new pesticide. Sarin is similar to commercial insecticides and pesticides. Maybe Tvchenko was trying to double dip. Make one version of the formula for commercial use, and the other for military use as a nerve gas."

"Is that another theory?"

"Perhaps more than a theory," Stevens said. "Tully said Tvchenko's apartment smelled of isopropyl alcohol, a precursor for Sarin."

"Isopropyl alcohol is used all the time by chemists."

"True. But not in great quantities."

Jenkins was thinking it over. There was still no logical reason the Kurds had started on this road of terrorism, but it was becoming clearer that they had. Stranger still is that the Kurds had not claimed responsibility for any of the acts. It was more or less an unwritten law that the guilty bastards with blood on their hands would be proud to extol praise on themselves to anyone who would listen, that it was they who had brought terror to the super countries. Yet, they had remained silent. "So, what will the Kurds do next?"

"We'll have to research who's pissed them off."

Jenkins rubbed his temples. What was going on? He would have to trust his field officers, Nelsen and O'Neill. If Nelsen thought Bush was in danger, they'd better do everything within their power to safeguard him. And this Adams in Odessa. What was he up to? The Kurds were a problem that would not go away easily this time. Who had pissed them off? That was the problem. The list would be long.

"Fire off a call to Nelsen pronto," Jenkins finally said. "Tell him I want a plan to keep Bush safe on my desk in the morning. He can use whatever means possible. Extreme prejudice." Jenkins pointed his finger directly toward his assistant's skinny nose. "Also...I want O'Neill to brief me on Adams. I want to know if Tvchenko's assistant told him anything before she was killed. Brief O'Neill on the German and Nelsen's theory in Texas."

Stevens rose from his chair and started toward the door.

"Just a minute," Jenkins muttered. "Talk with our people in Berlin. Brief them on what's going on in Odessa and Texas. Explain what we think is a tie to Johnston Atoll."

"Yes, sir." Stevens let himself out.

Jenkins poured himself another whiskey and stared into it. This was perhaps the most important case he'd ever worked on. Certainly the most important since the new Agency was formed six months ago. When he was sworn in as Director, he had had this great feeling of pride. Yet, he had also felt apprehension, since he knew that so many people would depend on his judgment. He only hoped he was up to the task. He slowly put the glass to his lips and let the whiskey slide down, warming him all the way to his gut.

29

ODESSA, UKRAINE

Omri Sherut was backed against the warehouse wall, anger giving way to a reassuring gaze, as he kept his eyes peering into Chavva's.

"I had nothing to do with it," Sherut said. "My men weren't involved."

She had met with him on short notice after finding out Tvchenko's assistant had been gunned down while being watched by Jake Adams. She had a 9mm automatic pistol trained on Sherut's balls, and she imagined his dick was looking for a place to hide.

Sherut's huge bodyguard was about to pounce on her, until the Israeli businessman waved him off.

"Who in the hell killed her? And why?"

"I don't know," Sherut said calmly. "Probably the same people who killed Tvchenko."

She thought about that. He could be telling the truth for a change. But why would the Kurds kill off their own puppet? "Tvchenko was developing something for the Kurds, right?"

Sherut shrugged. "That's what our intel says. He was working some deal."

"And the GRU?"

"Who knows? Maybe they killed them both. They could have found out Tvchenko was working both sides of the street and took him out."

She lowered the gun away from his crotch and backed up a step or two. "I don't think so. Tvchenko was too important to the GRU. They needed his expertise. They wouldn't kill him."

"So then it was the Kurds."

It made no sense. Why would the Kurds recruit Tvchenko only to kill him off? "Do you think the Kurds got everything they needed from Tvchenko?" she asked.

"It's possible." Sherut straightened his overcoat and smiled. "What about your friend, Mr. Adams?"

"What about him?"

"How does he fit into this equation?"

She looked over at Sherut's goon, whose face seemed to carry the same stupid appeal of wonder, as if his brain were too small to muster up more than one expression. "Can we get rid of him?" She shifted her head toward the bodyguard.

Sherut hesitated. Finally, he nodded for his man to leave. "Meet me at the car?" Sherut told him.

When the two of them were alone, Chavva moved closer to the man who was supposed to be her boss. Her face was inches from his, but her gun was poking him in the belly button. "You know more than you're saying," she whispered. "What has Mikhael failed to tell me this time?"

He wasn't one to back down from just anyone, but then

Chavva wasn't just anyone. Sherut's heart pounded and sweat beaded up on his forehead. "You know the director as well as I," he said. "He only tells us what we need to know."

"Bullshit! You two go back thirty years. You know something, you bastard." She slid her gun to the side and fired a round past his waist into a plywood wall.

He jumped. Then he realized he had not been hit. "What in the hell are you doing? We're on the same team."

"We work for the same man," she corrected. "I'm on no one's team. The next one goes right through you."

By now the bodyguard had heard the shot and was running toward them, his Uzi drawn and pointing his way.

She turned the gun toward Sherut's face and stuck the barrel into his mouth just as he was about to say something. She pointed at Sherut's bodyguard with her free hand. "I'd stop right there. Unless you want a quick lesson in cranial anatomy."

The large man skidded to a halt, uncertain what to do.

Sherut tried to say something, but all that came out was a gurgling sound.

She slid the gun out to his lips.

"You're fucking crazy," Sherut yelled. "Yosef was right."

She glared at him when he brought up the name of the assistant director of Mossad. The two of them had collided more than once over the direction of an operation. "So, Yosef has been talking about me? He's a pig."

"I'll let him know the next time we speak."

She looked over at the bodyguard, who had his Uzi pointing directly at her. She knew he couldn't fire without the possibility of hitting his boss with a stray round. Those guns were meant to put lead in the air, not for accuracy. She was getting nowhere fast, but she had not really expected him to fold over like a lamb.

"Where's your other man? His twin?" she said, flipping her head toward the huge bodyguard.

Sherut hesitated. "I had to send him back to Tel Aviv."

"Is that right?" she asked the bodyguard.

He didn't answer. He simply stood there with a stupid look on his face. She could tell he wanted to kill her.

She started laughing out loud. Her voice echoed through the empty building. She continued laughing louder and louder. She couldn't stop herself. It was as if she were back in her small little village again. She was trapped and couldn't escape. Only her laughter kept her from going crazy.

When she finally stopped, she realized she was curled up on the cold cement floor. The barrel of her gun was pointing directly up her nose. Once again she had failed to pull the trigger. She was still alive. Not a young girl. A grown woman. She leaned up and looked around. Sherut and his man were gone.

30

ODESSA, UKRAINE

On the train ride from Nikolaev to Odessa, Jake had tried to get some sleep. But it was impossible. He couldn't get his mind off of Helena and Petra and Tvchenko. And especially MacCarty and Swanson, whom he had vowed to protect. On one level he knew that the two of them had simply gotten in the way, were at the wrong place at the wrong time. To the contrary, he had failed. Failed miserably. And that was something he wasn't used to, nor would he ever learn to like. Petra had put her trust in him, even though she didn't realize the danger she was in. Realistically, who could have guessed that MacCarty and Swanson were in any kind of danger? That's what he'd have to keep telling himself.

Jake had also wondered again how those two men, three with the driver, had found where he had stashed Petra. He still had to check Tully's Volga to see if someone had placed a tracking device on it, but it was more likely that someone had given up his position. And only a few people knew where he had taken the women.

Jake got off the train and walked through the station corridor. It was nearly three in the morning, and there were only a few people up and about. Some had sprawled out across three or four chairs, covered by coats or news-papers. An older man sat against a stanchion staring off to nowhere and mumbling to himself.

After Jake was nearly through the large, cavernous ter-minal, he swung around quickly, as if he had forgotten something. When he realized no one was following him, he turned and continued out the building. His nerves were getting the best of him.

The outdoor kiosk, where the cab driver had been earli-er that evening as Jake stole his car, was closed and board-ed shut. He felt somewhat guilty about stealing a man's livelihood, but Jake would make an anonymous call say-ing where he could find the taxi.

The night air was cool and damp. Jake needed to walk and think.

He got a few blocks when he heard steps behind him. Was he being followed? He varied his pace and the person behind him did the same. The man was perhaps thirty yards back, Jake guessed. But Jake knew better than to look back. The moment he became too preoccupied by the one behind him, then an associate of his would step out in front. It was a common ploy used by thugs and intelli-gence agents alike.

There was a park ahead. A small park with trees close to the sidewalk. It was darker there, the lamp posts farther apart.

Jake stopped briefly, pulled out some papers from inside his jacket, as if he were looking at a map. He pulled the Glock from its holster and slid it under the papers.

Continuing on, Jake pushed the gun into his pocket, cocked the hammer, and gripped the handle tightly.

When he had stopped, the man behind him had paused briefly and then continued toward him with a slower pace.

The park was a half a block away.

Jake turned quickly and headed toward the follower.

The man was twenty yards away. Still in shadows. He stopped. Started to reach into his jacket.

Jake swung his pistol from his pocket. "Keep your hands clear," he said, his voice echoing through the darkness. "At your side." Jake was pointing the barrel at the man's head as he approached him quickly.

Shifting around to the backside of the man, Jake turned the older man with silver hair around a hundred and eighty degrees so he could see the park. See if there was another person approaching from the bushes. Jake looked the man over. He was wearing a fine suit with a wool overcoat. He had this knowing smirk, as if he was still in control even with the gun trained on him.

"You can put the gun down, Mr. Adams," the man said through a thick accent.

Jake kept the gun on him and reached inside the man's coat to see what he was reaching for. It was a beeper of some sort. Not a gun. A panic button maybe. He looked at the man again. It was the man from the party and his hotel who had been talking with Chavva. The Israeli businessman. Omar Sharif, or whatever.

Glaring at the man, Jake kept his gun trained on him. "Why were you following me?"

The man smiled. "I know who you work for. Perhaps I can help you."

"The men I work for are dead. Poisoned over their

breakfast eggs."

"I'm aware of that. I meant your real employer. The Agency."

Jake didn't flinch. "I don't know what in the hell you're talking about. Agency? I'm no journalist."

The man laughed. "I've heard you have a sense of humor, Mr. Adams. But I'm sure you know what I'm talking about."

Jake thought about the voice again—the inflection, the accent, and the way he said he had heard about him. It was the same man who had picked him up, brought him to the warehouse, and had his men beat him. He felt the pain in his ribs again just thinking about it.

"How do you know anything about me?"

"I have my sources."

"And you are?"

"A concerned businessman."

Jake looked around and noticed a dark Mercedes slowly making its way up the street from the direction of the train station. He pointed his Glock at the man's head. "I'd tell your driver to stop right there."

The man waved his hand toward the Mercedes and it came to a halt a half a block away, but the engine remained running.

"What exactly do you want from me?" Jake asked.

The man became more relaxed. He had that smirk on his face again. "I think we're on the same side here, Mr. Adams. You were the last person to talk with Tvchenko before he died. You were old friends I understand."

Jake lowered the gun to his side. "Hardly. We had met a few times. What do you have to do with his death?"

"I'm just curious."

Yeah, right. "So, how does Chavva fit into all this?"

The man smiled. "Yes, she has told me about you. But I have other sources. Chavva is a wonderful young woman. A bit ambitious, perhaps. But then aren't we all? She's not involved with this. She's simply another associate of mine."

Now there was a line of bullshit. Jake knew Mossad when he saw it, and Chavva and this man had it written all over them. They were at least agents of that organization, if not outright officers.

"I'm going to tell you once and only once...I know nothing about Tvchenko's death. We didn't even get a chance to speak. Even if we had, there wasn't a thing he would have told me. We had only met a few times. My only concern now is with the bastards who killed my employers. I'll find out who killed them. I owe them at least that much."

"And what about Tvchenko's recent project?"

Jake shrugged. "What's it to me? My job here is basically over."

"And you don't care what could happen to millions of innocent people?"

"Is anyone really innocent? Children perhaps."

"Children have died by gas before," Sherut said.

Jake studied the older man now, and wondered if that was a warning of past atrocities by zealots or fascists. He shuttered remembering the contorted faces of young children huddling with mothers in Halabja. The horror and certitude of death was imprinted in their tiny eyes. That was innocence. For their only crime was having been born a Kurd. "Yes, children."

"Stay out of it, Mr. Adams. You're a smart man. I'm

sure there must be someone in this world who cares about you."

It was interesting he should say that, because Jake was feeling quite the contrary right now. As if everyone was out to get him. It was a paranoid notion, but something he had no real control over. It was also interesting, because he had told this man at the warehouse he had nobody.

"I'll do what I have to do," Jake said. "You stay out of my way."

Slowly, Jake wandered off toward the park. He heard the faint sound of a car door slamming, and the Mercedes pulling away from the curb. He knew now that he would find the guilty bastards who killed MacCarty and Swanson, those who had gunned down Petra, and those who had killed Tvchenko. Someone had made the game more personal, and he would make sure he won.

31

ISTANBUL, TURKEY

By the time Sinclair Tucker knew what he was doing, he had followed the two men to the Odessa airport, taken the quick flight to Istanbul, and was now pretending to read a Turkish travel magazine while he watched the two men over the top.

The men looked like brothers, dressed in nice slacks, shirts buttoned down the front and leather jackets. Their hair was longer than most others in the terminal, and had not been combed, Tucker realized. Above all, they were calm.

Tucker had barely had enough time to call in his actions to his associates at the bogus communications company in Odessa, who had switched his call through to London. He was given a number for an Ankara contact, another MI-6 officer, who would arrange to help him once they were on the ground in Diyarbakir, which is where the men had bought tickets to.

The two men he was following were Turks. Kurds he suspected. Tucker had followed them to the safe house where Jake Adams was watching the two Ukrainian women. When the second car pulled up and two other men quickly exited toward the building, Sinclair had been nervous but unable to do a thing about it. He couldn't call Jake in the room to warn him. There was no phone, and he didn't have one either. That's what had streaked through his mind. After he heard the shots, and only one man had returned to the car, before it screeched off, horrible thoughts had gone through Sinclair's mind. He had wondered if Jake was all right, was still wondering. And he had realized that Jake had probably taken at least one man out.

Then Tucker had had only a split second to make up his mind what to do. He could follow the two remaining men who had done the shooting, or he could stick with the Kurds. He had chosen the later. Strangely enough, he had not even considered looking in on Jake. He had made that mistake the last time, when the men had kidnapped Jake and beaten him in the warehouse. Jake had been serious when he wondered why Sinclair had not followed the men. That was standard practice, after all. Yet, he couldn't help wondering if he had left Jake in that safe house bleeding to death.

There was also no way Sinclair Tucker could have known the men he was following would leave the country in such a hurry.

The Kurds picked up their small carry-on baggage and headed out the door to the ramp area. They would be getting on one of those interesting looking commuter planes, where the turboprop engines seemed to dwarf the rest of the plane, and where everyone got a window seat, whether he wanted one or not.

Dammit! He wanted to call Jake Adams. See if he was all right. He had promised to keep Jake informed. But there was no time now.

Sinclair flipped the magazine to the table and followed the men outside.

32

ODESSA, UKRAINE

The ninth floor hallway of the Maranovka Hotel was in near darkness, and Jake crept along one wall, sliding his left hand along a wooden border, while his right hand gripped his 9mm Glock tightly.

He didn't like being followed by the Israeli. How had he found him at the train station? Now he even wondered if Helena was safe.

The Israeli had made him think long and hard about the entire case. He wasn't sure if Tully O'Neill and Quinn Armstrong had told him everything about Tvchenko and Petra. The strange appearance of the Israeli businessman, if that's what he was, ripped his mind back to Chavva. She was a link to that man, and perhaps even knew more than him.

Which is why he was sneaking along the hotel hallway in the early morning with his gun drawn.

Jake reached room 902 and grasped the door handle. It was locked, of course. Should he knock? No. The hotel was old and the locks just as decrepit. Besides, he wanted her on his terms. He holstered his gun and slid out two small tools. Within a minute, he was inside the room with the door closed behind him, and he was standing against the wall waiting for his eyes to adjust to the darker room.

He had been in the hotel before, having stayed on the seventh floor while still with the Air Force inspection team. So he knew the layout of the rooms.

In a moment he could see everything in the room. There was a large bed in the center, a bureau on the far wall, and a small table with two chairs against a mirror on the wall he leaned against. The bathroom was in the far corner, where a dim light escaped from a half-cracked door.

There was a figure on the bed and it had just moved and settled again.

Jake moved closer. Was this the right way to approach her? What if she had nothing to do with the case? She could have him arrested, for one thing. But he couldn't let that stop him. After all, people had already kidnapped him and broken his ribs, tried to blow him up and shoot him, and the Israeli had followed him and warned him. No. This was the only way.

He stepped forward and the floor creaked.

He froze.

His heart raced and he waited a moment for it to settle down.

Moving forward again, he selected each foot placement as if he were climbing a rock cliff without a rope.

Now he was right over the bed and could just make out Chavva's beautifully sculpted face, with the lone sheet snuggled tightly to her neck.

He didn't want to do this, but he had to.

With one fluid motion, he jumped into the air and landed across her body, his hand over her mouth.

Her eyes opened in horror.

"It's Jake," he started.

But with one quick flip of her lower body and twist of her upper torso, she slipped to one side of the bed. Then her knee came up catching Jake in his leg next to his crotch. It was enough to throw him off balance and enough to free one of her hands.

She slapped him across his left ear, knocking him to the floor.

Then she was on top of him punching toward his face, which he had covered with his arms.

He bucked her to the carpet and they wrestled. Then Jake realized she was entirely naked. He had grabbed her butt to twist her over and found a handful of flesh. Then he had her from behind, one hand across her breasts and the other over her mouth, which was trying to bite his fingers.

"It's Jake Adams," he finally forced out. "It's Jake."

She seemed to settle down slightly, but her muscles were still tense, her chest heaving with each quick breath.

He couldn't see her face to read what she might be thinking. But he wasn't about to let go until he had a chance to explain himself.

"I'm sorry to come to you like this," he started. "But I was just warned by a friend of yours to stay out of the Tvchenko affair. I want to know why."

She didn't move beneath him.

"I'm assuming he's your boss. If so, nod your head."

She still didn't move.

"If I let you go, will you scream?"

She shook her head no.

He released his hand from her mouth.

"You fucking bastard," she yelled. "You scared me to death. The first time we meet you end up dragging a young girl from a party, and now this. Do you like scaring the shit out of women?"

He almost laughed at the way she said "shit," but he held back. "I'm sorry, Chavva. It's early. I couldn't wait until morning. I was nearly killed last night. And I'm getting pretty sick of being used for target practice or as a punching bag. My employers have been killed..." He trailed off into silence, and she twisted her head toward his.

He released her and she rolled to face him, not even attempting to cover her nakedness.

"Someone tried to kill you?" she asked softly.

"Afraid so."

"How?"

He thought for a moment. He didn't want to mention Petra, and especially Helena. "I was at an apartment with friends when two men burst in and sprayed the joint with automatic weapons. I..." He was going to say shot one of them, but didn't know how she would react to that.

"Why would someone do that?"

"I don't know," he said. "Maybe they think I know more about Tvchenko than I do."

He could see her eyes, large and bright. Tears had formed at the sides of both and she wiped them away.

"What's the matter?" Jake asked.

She nuzzled her head down to his chest. "I don't know," she sobbed. "I don't want anything to happen to you."

That was interesting, Jake thought. They didn't really know each other that well, yet he held her close to his body, his hand across the smooth thinness of her lower back.

"I don't understand," Jake said. "Why should you care what happens to me?"

She gazed up at him. "I don't know. There's something special about you. I knew it from the first time we met."

"In Istanbul?"

She hesitated. "Yes. There." She slipped up even with him and slowly pressed her lips to his. They were thick and moist and warm. She pulled back from him and lay on the floor, exposing her naked body to him. "Make love to me, Jake."

Her breasts were round and firm and rose from her perfect form, the nipples tight and hard. She reached over, took his hand in hers, and placed it onto her breast. And she moaned.

She slid her hand to his pants and unbuttoned his jeans and slowly lowered the zipper. Then she had a handful of his hardness.

They kissed as he quickly lowered his pants.

He entered her slowly and they meshed as one.

After a while, they lay on the bed, her face snuggled tightly into his chest. The sun was starting to rise over the Crimean Mountains, making it easier to see in the room.

Jake had not come to Chavva to make love, yet he was profoundly glad he had. What was her relationship with the Israeli businessman?

Stroking his hand through her hair, he watched her sleep. Her eyes were moving violently beneath the lids. She was shaking. Her lips tightened. Her breathing quickened. With one fast motion, her eyes sprang open and she screamed 'No...'

Jake wrapped his arms around her. "It's all right, Chavva. It was a dream. Only a dream."

She snuggled under his chin. "I'm sorry."

"For what? We all have bad dreams."

She smiled. "I guess you would know."

He looked at her in wonder. She was a beauty. A complex beauty. He had to ask her. "What are you doing in Odessa?"

Turning away from him, she said, "What do you mean?"

"Your boss. Omar Sharif?"

"Omri Sherut," she corrected.

"Whatever. He's definitely Mossad. He reeks of it."

She look puzzled. "What?"

"You know. In the encyclopedia you look up Mossad, and his picture is there."

She giggled. It was the first time Jake had heard her laugh. She had always seemed serious before, but this was an endearing side of her that he had not seen. He liked it.

"You are funny as well as handsome, Mr. Jake Adams," she said. "And, of course, you have other talents." She slid her hand to a new hard on.

"Whoa... But what about Sherut. What do you really do for him?"

"Not this. If that's what you mean."

"No." She was stroking him, and he was finding it difficult to concentrate on what he needed to ask her.

"Sometimes it's better not to talk at moments like this," she said. "Maybe later. But right now I think we better find a place to put this."

He couldn't argue with that logic.

33

After leaving Chavva's room that morning, Jake wandered down Primorski Boulevard, sat at a park bench watching the boats move about the harbor, and tried to put some perspective into his current situation. He was confused by the factions involved in the case, and by his own late-night encounter with the beautiful Israeli woman that he knew very little about. Maybe that was the attraction. Sometimes the heated passionate tryst was just what a person needed to feel alive again. Yet, Jake couldn't help wondering how this time had been different. Chavva seemed so familiar. So comfortable with him. It was as if they had made love a hundred times before.

She had told him very little about herself and the man she purportedly worked for, Omri Sherut. He was in reality an Israeli businessman, but his involvement with Mossad was uncertain as far as she knew. Jake had no idea if she was telling the truth. She had said that things were not always as they appeared. Perhaps that was her way of reversing or recanting her story. Jake knew that when he worked for the old agency, under the cover of a business-man, he had often denied any involvement with any

American government agency. It was a little lie that all intelligence officers had to give. Security over sanctity.

Jake ate a scant lunch from a street vendor and wandered around the city. It was a gorgeous day. Windy, with dark clouds swirling overhead, and only a slight possibility of rain showers from the west. He knew he better take advantage of the fresh air now, because he'd heard on the radio that thunderstorms were moving into the area that evening.

He thought about Tvchenko and Petra, and how MacCarty and Swanson tied into their deaths. But he was drawing a blank. He knew there was a connection. Only time would tell what that was. MacCarty had talked about a deal he was working with the Ukrainian Agricultural Minister, Victor Petrov.

Standing before an old granite government building, Jake gazed up at the thirty-foot columns across the front. There were wide steps, the width of the building, leading up to tall wooden doors. The place resembled a typical American county court house built around the turn of the century.

Inside, Jake found the room number for the Agricultural Ministry on a directory, and he headed upstairs toward the third floor.

The third floor was marble and wood, some of which needed a good shellacking. The ministry office was through a wooden door.

Considering it was a Thursday afternoon, there were very few people walking about. The office had a reception desk and four wooden chairs with a coffee table cluttered with old magazines. It seemed that waiting rooms were waiting rooms regardless of country.

Jake stepped up to a young woman at the desk and smiled. "Good afternoon," he said in his best Ukrainian. "I'm Jake Adams here to see Victor Petrov."

"You are American," she answered in English. "I am glad to know you." She held out her hand to shake.

Jake shook her strong hand. She was a fairly attractive woman in her late twenties, but her grip resembled that of someone who had worked a farm herself for years. Perhaps milking cows by hand.

"That's all the English I know," she said in her native language. "Is Victor expecting you?"

"No. But I'm sure he'd like to talk with me. I work for Bio-tech Chemical."

She raised her brows. Without saying a word, she picked up the phone and called her boss. She repeated the company name at the end, and then smiled and hung up. "He'll see you, Mr. Adams." She rose and let him through a door.

Victor Petrov was a large, thick man in his early sixties. He wore gray slacks and a white shirt with sleeves rolled up. His bright red tie hung loosely over his massive neck. He was grossly out of shape, but it was evident that he had been a magnificent specimen in his earlier years. He met Jake in the middle of the room and they shook hands. Then he offered Jake a chair and returned behind his desk, where he leaned back on an old creaky wooden behemoth of a swivel chair.

"What can I do for you, Mr. Adams," Petrov asked in perfect English.

Jake hadn't thought about where to begin. MacCarty had given him only limited information on the deal he had been working. "My employer, Maxwell MacCarty, told me you two had been working on setting up a production facility here in the Ukraine." He paused to see if that would start things off.

The chair squeaked as the man twisted and put his hands behind his head. "Yes. I'm sorry to hear of his death. He was a good man."

"Yes, he was," Jake agreed. "I was hoping we could still work the plan. Is that possible?"

Petrov let out a heavy breath that whistled. "I'm not sure you're in a position to do that, Mr. Adams."

Wait a minute. How would this guy know what he was capable of? "Excuse me?"

"I'm just saying...Mr. MacCarty said you were working security for him."

"When did he tell you that?"

"At the dinner party the first night."

"You were there?" Jake asked.

"Yes."

"You saw Yuri Tvchenko's death?"

"I'm afraid not," he explained. "I had stepped out to make a call. When I returned, he was lying at your feet."

It was strange that Jake didn't recognize the man from the party, but there had been a lot of people there. And after Tvchenko collapsed, things became hectic. "I was working security for MacCarty, but I had also planned on helping him set up a production facility."

Petrov's brows rose. "Is that so? He hadn't mentioned that to me."

They stared at each other for a moment.

Jake wasn't sure how to proceed now. He didn't like this smug bastard. If he asked for specifics on the deal, then he'd know Jake knew next to nothing about the plan. Yet, if Jake acted as though he knew everything, then there would have been no reason to ask for more information. Maybe it was time for a little bluff.

"I looked over the agreement in principle," Jake started. "In fact, I sent a copy to Max's son in Portland yesterday. Andy will be taking over the operation, and I'm sure he'll want to proceed with his father's plan."

Petrov's complexion seemed to change from ivory to a milky white.

Actually, Andy was a skinny fourteen-year-old who was worrying more about his acne problem and voice change than an international contract. Bio-tech Chemical was a privately held company, but it would take months in probate to figure out who was in charge. Jake's early guess would be MacCarty's wife, who had stayed active in the marketing and human resources departments over the years.

Petrov was considering what Jake had told him. Finally, he leaned forward on his desk and said, "I'm sorry, Mr. Adams. But I'm afraid we'll have to proceed in another direction. It's my understanding of international law that an agreement in principle can be broken by either party any time before a contractual commitment is reached. Our government needs to move forward in a new direction."

So that was it, Jake thought. "So, you have another deal?"

Petrov shifted in his chair. "I'm afraid so."

That was awfully quick. MacCarty and Swanson's bodies had not even been released for shipment back to Oregon. "I see. May I ask which company?"

The Ukrainian smiled. "I'm afraid that's confidential."

This was going nowhere fast. Jake knew he'd get nothing more out of Petrov. He rose from his chair and reached across the desk to shake hands. "Thank you for your time, Mr. Petrov."

Jake left the office, said goodbye to the receptionist, and went out into the stark marble corridor. His steps echoed back from the high ceiling, and he stopped for a moment to gaze at a painting on the wall. It was a bloody scene of Cossacks on horseback stabbing foot soldiers with long swords. He felt a little like those men on the ground. Only he was dodging bullets. He thought about MacCarty and the tentative deal he had reached. It was amazing that the Ukrainians had been able to come up with a new deal so quickly. Maybe more than just a coincidence.

34

HOUSTON, TEXAS

It was a bright, clear morning closing in on noon. Not a cloud in the Texas sky. It was the kind of day that would stagnate quickly and suffocate anyone stepping outside after lunch.

Yet, it was also a perfect day for flying. Baskale kept the twin engine Beechcraft at three hundred feet, following a quarter mile south of Interstate 10, heading east, just a half hour out of Houston.

He peered over his shoulder at his best man, the strong one. He was huddled over the metal box and had just removed the cover. Inside, the cluster bomb had been opened, exposing the bomblets for the first time. Baskale had come to trust this man he had met only a few weeks ago. He rarely became familiar with associates. Too many had died for the cause, even though Baskale knew they were all far better off.

Baskale smiled as he turned and checked the map again. It would be an easy drop. Follow the interstate until it crossed with 610, the ring around Houston, and then swoop in over Memorial Park until he found his target. He had a detailed map of the golf course and knew his target would be on the first five holes. What could go wrong?

Steve Nelsen and Ricardo Garcia sat back in the Army Black Hawk helicopter they had been loaned from Fort Hood. They were on the outer edge of a shopping center parking lot, with an Army Apache helicopter sitting on the pavement next to them. They all had headsets on and were listening to central air traffic control out of Houston International. ATC had queried a plane thirty minutes ago, got no answer, and then had lost the blip from their screen. Minutes ago a small plane had magically appeared on radar alongside Interstate 10, heading right for the city.

"Any flight plan drawn?" Nelsen asked the controller.

"Negative."

Nelsen looked forward at the chopper pilot, who was waiting for directions. "Do you have the target on your screen?" he asked.

"Yes, sir. I suggest we get airborne."

"Let's do it then."

The Black Hawk pilot swiveled around, and he and his co-pilot started clicking switches. The rotors started turning slowly, picking up speed. Across from them, the Apache followed suit.

Nelsen checked his gun under his arm and tapped his partner. "This is it, Ricardo. It has to be them."

Garcia wasn't sure. In one sense he hoped Nelsen was right, but if he was, he knew it would be difficult, if not impossible, to stop the men from dropping the nerve gas. They could shoot the plane down, but the crash and burn would probably release the gas. They had thought of near-

ly every scenario, and come up with the only plan with a
chance for success. He only hoped everything would go as
planned.

In a few minutes the helicopters were airborne and
heading southeast just above the trees.

The Apache was an impressive aircraft, loaded to the
hilt with air-to-air and air-to-ground missiles. The nose
gun alone could drop any small plane with one burst. One
craft would be overkill, but Nelsen was leaving nothing to
chance. There was another Apache taking off from Hobby
Airport south of Houston, and a third from the parking lot
of a mall in the southwest off of highway 59. Two others
were on standby at Houston International. On the ground
over a hundred officers were standing by for directions.
Houston police, Agency officers, and army chemical and
biological weapons units in full Chem Warfare uniforms.

Behind Nelsen was an Agency sharpshooter in a black
jumpsuit, his face streaked with camouflage paint. The
shooter cradled his rifle with the large scope like a baby.
To him it was.

"I've got 'em," the pilot blared over the radio.

Nelsen made his way forward. "Are you positive?"

"It's the same vector H.I. gave us. It seems to be following the interstate in."

"Fine. Head straight for it."

The pilot responded and the Black Hawk surged forward toward the southeast on an intercept course out and
away from most of the major housing units. That had been
Nelsen's main concern. He suspected the terrorists would
try for the former president in his home town of Houston,
but he had no idea which direction they would come from.
And he suspected they would use a plane, since it was the

best dispersal method available to them. Besides, the terrorists had already proven they could fly.

At the Memorial Park Golf Course, special agents from the Agency's internal security department, which had taken over the responsibilities normally associated with the secret service, were monitoring the radio traffic as they watched former president George Bush tee up on the fourth hole.

Bush had refused to change his plans for the golf outing. His foursome included the Houston mayor, a state senator, and a Texas congressman. Bush's son, the Texas governor, couldn't make it, and was home in Austin. Bush wasn't afraid of some splinter terrorists trying to make a name for themselves. Besides, he had survived World War II, unpublished assassination attempts while he was president, and the botched attempt on his life while on his trip to the middle east years ago. What could four men do?

The Agency officer in charge, Lee Burns, was on the ground fifty yards from the fourth tee. He was nervous. He had enough gas masks handy in case the terrorists got through, but in the wide open spaces of a golf course on such a quiet day with no wind, anything could go wrong. And if anything could go wrong, it probably would. Besides, there wasn't a lot they could do against an airborne nerve gas attack, except wait for the wind to disperse and dilute it. They did have the newest truck-mounted carbon units that would blow carbon gas into the nerve gas cloud absorbing much of its deadly effects. But he had been with Nelsen in Mexico, seen what the men were capable of. Burns knew that these men would die for their cause if needed. Happily die.

Burns had heard that a plane was on its way. He had tried to whisk the former president to his limo and back to his apartment, but he wasn't buying it. Bush was determined to play a full eighteen holes. Nothing would stop him.

Stationed discreetly behind trees in the woods, were four Agency sharpshooters in full combat dress and chemical warfare shells. They even had the newest helmets with masks that allowed the best shooting profile available anywhere in the world. They were ready.

Burns trained his eyes toward the west, and hoped his men would not be needed.

Baskale first saw the helicopters as flashes against the green trees along a small creek. They were ahead of him some three miles on a direct course to intercept. He smiled at their ignorance. He had expected just that. He had expected even more than that. The Americans had to be smarter than this, he was sure.

He had two minutes before they were on him.

He yelled back to his man to stand by for what they had discussed. The man nodded.

Banking to the left until he was over Interstate 10, he then turned back to the right, flying just over the eastbound lane. Traffic below was light. It was between the morning rush hour and the noon rush. A steady stream of vans and trucks and cars.

The plane swooped lower until it was right over the top of an old Ford pickup truck.

Behind Baskale, the large man pulled out a bomblet, gave it a quick kiss, and then dropped it into the back of the truck below.

Down on the freeway there was a puff of smoke as the bomblet burst open, dispersing the deadly gas into the air.

The large man screamed with pleasure.

On the freeway, the car behind the truck swerved and crashed into the guard rail. The driver was already dead. Two other cars swerved around the crash and stopped to help. As the drivers stepped out, they dropped immediately to the ground.

The plane continued on. The helicopters were now vectoring toward them.

"What the hell was that?" Nelsen yelled over the radio.

The Black Hawk pilot had banked around and was now just behind the airplane. The Apache was off to its right.

"Shit!" Garcia said. "I think they dropped one of the bomblets onto that truck below."

"Radio one of the chem units to get here pronto," Nelsen yelled.

"Yes, sir," the co-pilot answered.

Nelsen knew it was a waste of time. By the time the decontamination units reached the cite, the gas would be gone into nowhere.

The truck below continued on. The driver was swerving, uncertain what to do, and what it was in the bed behind him.

"What do we do?" the Black Hawk pilot asked.

Nelsen was thinking. If they fire on him, drop the little plane out of the sky, the bomblets would go off, killing far too many people to think about. And in seconds they would be in the thick of the western suburbs. What could they do? "Let me talk with them?" Nelsen said.

The pilot switched frequencies.

"Pilot of Beechcraft 3975. Do you hear me?"

No response.

"We will shoot you down if you do not respond."

"Fuck you," came a garbled response.

"We know who you are and where you're heading," Nelsen said. "Turn your plane to heading One...Five...Zero and proceed five miles to a small landing strip."

"And then you will kill us?" The man's accent was in broken English. "It's a beautiful day to die."

That's not what Nelsen wanted to hear. Think. Think. "It's a fine day. I'm not arguing that. It's the location I'm concerned about. Tell us what you want. Innocent people shouldn't have to die here today."

Baskale laughed. "There are no innocent people."

It was too late. By now they were over the suburbs. Nelsen clicked off the mic and slammed his hand against the bulkhead. "Goddammit." He gazed off to the Apache. It would be easy to simply give the fire order. But where would the plane crash? His luck it would hit a school yard.

"Now what?" Garcia asked.

Of course. "I've got it." He told the pilot to maneuver alongside the plane. In a second, they were just off to the right of the plane and the Apache had moved in behind it. "Hal, scope 'em and see how many, other than the pilot, in that Beechcraft."

The sharpshooter zoomed the scope onto the plane, fore and aft, and then settled on the large man in the rear of the aircraft. "Looks like just one."

"Take him out," Nelsen ordered.

Two seconds after he said it, the sharpshooter fired and the window in the back of the plane exploded. "One down. Pilot to go."

In the Beechcraft Baskale heard only a slight cracking sound from behind. When he turned to see what it was, his best man lay across the bomb case with a hole where his nose used to be.

He screamed a shrill call, his chest heaving. Then he quickly calmed down and prayed for a moment for his lost man. He was going to a better place. Was already there.

Now the plan would have to shift into the second phase. It was their fault. Baskale had anticipated this. It could still work. He powered up to the max, pulled back on the stick, and then banked toward the south over the houses. There were rows and rows of colorful houses along white, cement streets and swirling culdesacs. They all had beautiful aqua-marine swimming pools. The grass seemed so green in the yards. He had never seen such tranquility.

His mind flashed back to the airplane's dials. He would remain just over the top of the houses, for even the Americans would not be stupid enough to shoot him down there.

"Now what?" came a voice over the radio. It was the Black Hawk pilot.

"What do you think," Nelsen screamed. "Keep after them. And switch frequencies to our secure line."

The other helicopters were airborne flying slowly toward their position.

"Helos five and six lift off and secure objective one," Nelsen said. "Helos three and four, get your asses in gear to our location. Fan out to one mile on either side of us."

There were four affirmatives over the radio.

"Where the hell is he heading?" Nelsen said to no one in particular.

Garcia had his eyes on the Beechcraft. "He's gaining altitude, Steve."

Nelsen moved forward for a better look. "Anything down that way?" As he said it, his eyes answered his own question. Off in the distance, some five or six miles, was the Houston Astrodome.

"He's not crazy enough to crash into that..." The Black Hawk pilot turned to Nelsen.

He was afraid so, and said it with his grave stare. "God help us," Nelsen said. "Get on the horn and find out if anything's going on there today."

"I can answer that," Garcia said. "The Astros play New York in a double header."

"How many in the stands?"

"The place holds almost sixty thousand. But since they're playing the Mets, there's probably twenty thousand in attendance."

"Just fucking great." Nelsen thought fast. If they had let the plane through, perhaps one old, former president would have died. But now... "Twenty thousand. Jesus Christ. Is there any place ahead we can take him out?"

Garcia checked over a detailed map of Houston and the surrounding area. "I don't see one. But even the suburbs would be better than the Astrodome."

"We're not even sure he's heading there," Nelsen said. "Can we get the crazy bastard on the radio again?"

The co-pilot switched frequencies.

They didn't have much time for a decision. The Beechcraft was gaining even more altitude and getting closer to the large white dome.

❧

"Beechcraft pilot...you seem to be heading toward Hobby airport. That's great. We'll get you clearance and you can set her down there. Then we'll have a little talk."

Baskale smiled. "You would like that. Get me alone, perhaps. Say I tried to escape."

"This isn't a game, Baskale."

Baskale jerked with the sound of his name. His given name. The Cypriot must have talked. "So, you think you know who I am?"

"You are a proud Kurd," Nelsen said over the radio. "I understand that. I even understand the need for a free and autonomous Kurdistan. Now please set your plane down so we can talk about it."

Baskale shook his head, as if the man on the radio could see him. "I'm afraid I can't do that. We all must die sometime."

By now the Beechcraft was at a few hundred feet, leveled off, and nearly slowed to a stall.

Nelsen shook his head. "That bastard is nuts. He's not coming down. He's heading straight for the stadium. Can you patch me through to the public address at the Astrodome?"

"Too much time," said the Black Hawk pilot.

"What about shooting him down over the stadium parking lot?" Garcia asked.

Nelsen thought about it. "Well?" he asked the pilot.

The Apache pilot chimed in. "Sir, we could vector and shoot him from the side, but every round that misses would hit houses in the background. Same with using any of our missiles."

Well what in the hell good are they, Nelsen thought. "Fucking A..."

They would be over the parking lot in seconds.

"Hal, can you take him out?" Nelsen yelled.

"Affirmative."

Nelsen tapped the Black Hawk pilot on the shoulder. "Pull up alongside again."

The Black Hawk was parallel to the Beechcraft in seconds.

The sharpshooter trained his scope on the cockpit. "Sir, he's not there."

"What?" Nelsen strained toward the window for a closer look. "Does that thing have automatic pilot?"

"Yes, sir," said the Black Hawk pilot.

"Can you see him in the back, Hal?"

"Negative."

He had to be there. Lying down.

They were over the parking lot heading for the dome. They would be over it in seconds.

Nelsen's mind reeled. "He's not going to crash into it. He's going to drop bomblets. Can we get underneath him?"

"The bomblets will hit our rotor," the pilot screamed. "They'll tear us apart and then burst open anyway."

He was right.

It was too late. The plane was over the dome. Then the first bomblet flew from an opening in the bottom of the Beechcraft. Then another and another. One after the next. The bomblets pierced the lucite panels like a knife through a sheet. In no time at all they were past the edge of the dome and the bomblets stopped.

Then the Beechcraft picked up speed and banked hard to the north. The madman was behind the controls again.

The Black Hawk pilot did his best to stick with the airplane, but it was a shaky ride. The Beechcraft reeled around and around the parking lot. Within minutes, people below were rushing from the Astrodome exits in a mad panic.

"Take him out! Take him out!" Nelsen screamed.

The helicopter was shaking violently. The sharpshooter shot once. Missed. Shot again. Missed. A third time. Missed.

"Goddammit! Hit him."

The sharpshooter burst off three more rounds. Then he stopped.

"You get him?" Nelsen asked.

"I don't know. I don't see him."

In a second they all knew why. A body flew from the opposite side of the Beechcraft, and a bright blue and white parachute opened immediately. The man drifted toward the parking lot and the crowd below.

The Black Hawk was still with the plane.

"Circle around," Nelsen yelled. "Let's get the bastard."

"But, sir. The plane."

The Beechcraft was losing altitude fast, heading for the outer edge of the parking lot. Within seconds, the plane crashed into a small swampy area.

"Excellent!" Nelsen yelled. "The water will help hold the gas in place. Now get Baskale."

The Black Hawk pilot immediately dove and banked to the right.

But below the parachute and pilot had already reached the ground. It was a chaotic mess in the parking lot. The

Black Hawk hovered over one side, and the three Apaches searched for the man throughout the large parking complex. But none of them even knew what the man had been wearing or what he looked like. From up there they all appeared as desperate crazy people. People whose eyes were burning, guts wrenching, heads swirling. Some had fallen to the pavement clutching themselves. Some were throwing up. The blue and white parachute swirled around covering people. But the pilot, Baskale, was surely gone.

Nelsen covered his face with his hands. He had lost. Had failed. It was the worst possible outcome. Far worse than an assassination. He glared toward the ground sternly. Somehow, somewhere, he'd get that bastard. No matter what it took.

35

ODESSA, UKRAINE

Three hours had passed since Jake had talked with Victor Petrov, the Ukrainian Agricultural Minister. Time enough to form a theory about what was going on.

Jake called Tully's office and was given his location by a reluctant associate, only after saying who he was and that it was urgent.

Standing back behind some bushes, Jake watched Tully O'Neill and Quinn Armstrong sitting in wrought iron chairs at an outdoor cafe near the Privoz Market. The two men had just been brought their dinner, and were about to dig in.

Walking quickly to the table, Jake startled the two men as he swiftly pulled up a chair to join them.

"Jesus Christ," Tully said. "Where in the hell have you been?"

Jake tried to smile, but other than his early morning encounter with Chavva, he had found nothing amusing about the past few days.

"I've been around." He glared at Quinn for a moment,

still uncertain if he had somehow given up Jake's position while watching Petra and Helena.

There was an uncomfortable lull as Tully and Quinn watched their cooling food. Quinn looked somber, picking at his food like a child who wanted to prove a point to his parents.

"Go ahead and eat," Jake said. "I've already eaten." That was a lie. Jake had eaten nothing since a scant lunch on the street and the fruit Chavva had fed him for breakfast. Yet, he was so tense that food was the last thing on his mind right now.

Each of the men had a meat and potatoes platter in front of him, and Tully started eating as though he had never tasted food. Quinn slowly picked away at his.

"We were afraid you were taken last night," Tully said, while chewing a piece of meat. "What in the hell happened at the apartment?"

Jake leaned back in his chair and looked around. There was an older couple a few tables away, and a table with three younger women even farther away. No one who could hear.

"I was almost killed," he said, shifting his eyes from Tully to Quinn. "As you probably know, I got one of them. But he's not talking. There must have been at least two more. A shooter and a driver. What I want to know is how in the hell they found us? I selected the place. The only people who knew where we were are sitting at this table."

"What in the fuck's that supposed to mean?" Quinn screeched.

"Quiet!" Tully ordered. "Christ almighty. Would you two quit your petty arguing? Remember, there were two other people in that apartment. What about Petra? She could have called someone. Or Helena."

Jake had already thought about that. Why would Petra set herself up? Or her best friend, Helena?

"He's right," Quinn said. "And what about the Brit?"

"Fuck you! Tuck would never sell out. And there was no phone in the apartment," Jake added.

Quinn raised his brows, as if he had just remembered that fact himself. "There was one outside the room," he said slowly. "At the end of the hall. I called Tully from there myself."

Tully stuffed another piece of meet into his cheek. "That's right."

"But I was with them," Jake reminded Quinn. Then he thought hard. "Shit...except for when I went down to the kiosk for a newspaper."

"That's right. And I was in the bathroom."

Tully chimed in. "So one of them makes a phone call, says where they are, and the shooters show up. It's possible."

"That's assuming a lot," Jake said sarcastically. He was still in no mood for conciliation. "That's saying, perhaps, that Petra had more to do with Tvchenko's research than she was saying. And I don't think that's true. Not after talking with her."

Tully glanced up from his meal. "What did she say?"

He had their attention now, their eyes focused on him. "She was working for Tvchenko still. Tvchenko was dealing with some other men. From Petra's description I'd say the Kurds. Tvchenko had come up with a breakthrough in his research. All Petra knew is that it would be very important to the agriculture industry. She knew somewhat how the compound worked, and even suspected there could be other uses for it. But she thought that Tvchenko was serious about its commercial potential. That's all. She did hear Tvchenko arguing with the men, and that was out of character for Yuri."

"So why would anyone want Petra dead?" Tully asked, as he put the last piece of food into his mouth.

Quinn looked at Jake.

"She knew how to mix the compound," Jake said. "Maybe someone wanted exclusive rights."

Tully dropped his fork and knife, and then lit a cigarette. "That's possible. Kill off anyone who knows anything about the new agent, or who might be able to link Tvchenko's work to a certain group."

"Exactly!" Jake pointed a finger at Tully. "Lets say a terrorist group uses the new agent. Authorities would likely find a trace of the compound and eventually link it back to Tvchenko's research. That is, if Tvchenko is still alive. Or Petra. But now the link is broken. Shit!" Jake slammed his fist on the table. He thought about his conversations with Petrov and Chavva earlier.

Jake started to leave, but Tully pulled him back by the arm. "Wait, Jake. I haven't told you everything. Some things have happened that might be related. The cluster bomb that was stolen from Johnston Atoll. It was used just hours ago in Houston."

Jake settled down into his chair slowly. "How?"

Tully glanced sideways at Quinn and then back at Jake. "There was an assassination attempt on former president Bush while he was golfing. Our guys cut the terrorists off, but they apparently turned their airplane toward the Astrodome and dropped a number of bomblets through the roof onto the playing field. A few hit the stands."

Quinn added, "The Astros were playing the Mets at the time."

"God. How many dead?"

"Twenty-five so far," Tully said. "But that'll rise into the hundreds possibly. Some were trampled while trying to escape. One of the Mets outfielders died within seconds. It could have been much worse, but a technician turned off the fans, giving people a chance to escape. Also, we had a few decon units in the area. The carbon units."

"What about the plane?"

"It crashed in a little pond a short distance from the parking lot."

"That was lucky," Jake said. "Probably helped dilute the nerve gas."

"Right," Tully said, exhaling a puff of smoke. "You do know your chemical agents."

"So the pilot was killed?"

Tully shook his head. "No. He bailed out and drifted into the panicking crowd."

"Damn. I hope the Agency is hot on the trail."

"Yeah, from what I hear the officer in charge, Steve Nelsen, is blaming himself. He's totally pissed. A man obsessed."

"Nelsen?"

"You know him?"

"We had a run in a few years back," Jake said. That was putting it lightly. Words had actually turned to full-fist blows. When they were finished, each had lost enough blood for a transfusion. "He's a very determined individual. He likes doing things his way, or not at all."

"That's what happened in Houston," Quinn added. "It was his plan. Right or wrong. Some want to hang his ass out to dry, from what I've heard."

"The MEO wouldn't have it, though," Tully said. "In fact, Nelsen is on his way to this region. Turkey actually. Which brings us full circle back to you, Jake."

"What do you mean?"

"You understand these nerve gas agents better than any one of us," Tully said. "Hell, you even smelled the chemicals at Tvchenko's apartment, just before we were almost blown to bits. You've also spent a great deal of time in Turkey, and Kurdistan in particular."

"But—"

"Let me finish. That friend of yours. The Brit. Sinclair Tucker. He was sent to Kurdistan by his government this morning, after the death of MI-6 director, Sir Geoffrey Baines."

"Baines is dead? How?"

"Murdered in his home last night. Along with his housekeeper."

"I was wondering why Sinclair wasn't around today," Jake said. "That's good. Tuck knows the area as well as anyone. In fact we used to work there together on the verification team."

Tully lit another cigarette from the first, took in a long drag, and then let out a deep breath of smoke.

"What's wrong?"

The station chief hesitated, searching for words. "Tucker's helicopter was shot down by Kurdish guerrillas."

Blood rushed to Jake's head. "Tucker? Is he—"

"The Brits aren't sure," Tully answered. "The pilot was

left at the scene dead. But the co-pilot and Tucker are list-
ed as missing. That's all they know."

Jake knew Tucker was a survivor. If there was a way,
any way for him to be alive, then he was. "I think you
were setting me up for a Turkish vacation before Tucker
came up. What exactly did you have in mind for me?"

"Well—"

"And remember. I'm a private citizen now. I do have a
business, however precarious, to get back to in Portland."

Quinn was watching his boss with great interest, as if
studying how he would someday maneuver as a station
chief.

Tully drew a letter from inside his jacket. It was folded
in thirds. He handed it to Jake.

The letter was actually a plain paper fax from the
Agency headquarters in Langley, Virginia, on Director of
Operations letterhead. It was a formal request that Jake
Adams be reinstated as an Agency officer. Signed by Kurt
Jenkins himself.

When he was done reading, Jake folded the letter and
handed it back to Tully. "How can I be reinstated to something I had never been part of? Remember, I worked for
the old Agency."

"A technicality."

"What does Jenkins want me to do?" Jake was skepti-
cal, and probably for good reason. He didn't want to be
hung out to dry in Turkey. He'd end up in some Draconian
prison as a play toy for sadists.

"You'd be fully sanctioned."

"That's not what I asked, but its nice to know. What will
I do there?"

Tully hesitated again. "Meet up with Nelsen. That's all

they've told me. It's need to know only."

"Great." Jake leaned back contemplating his options as if he really had any. Another unofficial jaunt into the frontiers. "And if I'm picked up by anyone who gives a shit?"

"Like I said. Fully sanctioned."

Jake was a little concerned. He had no diplomatic passport, no official papers saying he worked for the U.S. government. Perhaps that was their intention. If things got harry, which they usually did, then the government could deny any involvement. He had to admit he was beyond pissed off. Somewhere closer to a hit below the belt. He was sick of being shot at, but that seemed to follow him wherever he went. And there was the point of Sinclair Tucker. He hoped that Tucker would come looking for him if his chopper went down in a guerrilla enclave. He'd like to think he would.

"What's in it for me?"

"The satisfaction of a job well done." Tully smiled.

"Right. I don't put my life on the line for nothing. Not anymore." Jake knew he was bullshitting himself. He had already done that watching Petra. But he justified that by knowing he was still under the retainer MacCarty had given him. It was a loose association, but something to ease an already tainted conscience.

Tully brought the tip of his cigarette to a bright red. His left eye was closed, keeping the smoke away. "The owners of the New York Mets and the Houston Astrodome have put up a hundred thousand bucks as a reward for the capture of the terrorist who dropped the nerve gas."

"A hundred thousand?"

Tully grinned. "Government agents can't collect on that."

"What about pseudo government agents?"

"That's different, I'm sure."

Well, the incentive was there. Besides, he had run out of ideas in Odessa. Tvchenko was dead. Petra was dead. Petrov had closed any possible deal with MacCarty's company. And, strangely enough, the GRU and Ukrainian intelligence had been non-existent. He had a feeling that the Kurds had only stuck around in Odessa long enough to tie up loose ends, and were probably long gone. That's what he would have done. The money would be nice, but it wasn't really needed. Jake would have gone to Turkey after his old friend anyway, or even to vindicate his former boss's death. There was also the issue of some undesirable elements with a deadly nerve gas formula that could easily be put together now by a half-assed chemist. He had nothing against the Kurds. In fact, he thought they should have a free and independent Kurdistan, but not at the expense of innocent people.

"All right," Jake said. He started to leave.

"One more thing," Tully said.

Jake glared back at Tully.

"There was a German killed the other day in Berlin. Gerhard Kreuzberg."

"The former foreign minister?"

"Yes. And witnesses said a few Turks had been at the scene. By the time Jenkins sent us the fax asking for your help, the Kurds had finally made a move. They called in responsibility for the German's murder. The same with the MI-6 director. The Brits got a call minutes after his death. The Kurds say they want the United Nations to step in on their behalf to negotiate an autonomous Kurdistan."

"Or?"

Tully hesitated. "Or they'll show the world how power-ful they really are."

"Which means?"

"They were pretty specific about using the most deadly nerve gas ever conceived," Tully said solemnly. "They didn't say where they'd use it, but they did say it would be soon."

"Shit!" If the Kurds were involved at Johnston Atoll, in Odessa, in Germany, in England, then they had come together in a unified effort. Over twenty million strong. It was only a matter of time before they would take no more pushing and shoving. Now they were bargaining from a position of strength. Jake was partly impressed that they had come so far so soon, but he knew that their resolve was never really in question. It was never if, but only when and how.

Jake left Tully and Quinn at the cafe. He had some thinking to do before his flight to Turkey. Walking off through the Privoz Market, Jake could hear thunder off in the distance heading toward Odessa. It reminded him of artillery fire and bombs dropping on dark, obscure night targets.

36

AL-HAMADI AIR BASE
Near Kirkuk, Iraq

It was a hot, dry evening. Clouds obscured the entire compound, which was mostly at rest after a long day of preparedness drills. The front gate was maned by four men in uniform. Three had machine guns strapped over their shoulders, and the fourth had a 9mm sidearm.

Things had been extremely quiet for the past month. The planes that they so vigilantly guarded had taken off on only routine reconnaissance missions, nothing like the bombing raids to the north just six months ago.

Two of the men relaxed inside the guard shack, their outer shirts off, and sweat still showing through their undershirts.

The other two, as ordered, were outside the building, hoping their shift would end soon, but realizing it had just begun a few hours ago. They were the graveyard shift. Nothing ever happened at night.

When the sergeant of the watch first saw the headlights winding down the road, he checked his watch. It was probably just the crew of men who had left earlier to search for two men who had been reported missing while picking up supplies that morning. The timing was right. The base commander suspected the two men had deserted, and would do everything within his power to get them back and make an example of them. All the sergeant knew was he had never seen the commander so angry. Not since the war with the infidels.

As the headlights got closer, the sergeant could hear the engine roaring. It was coming too fast, he thought. And it wasn't the truck that had left earlier, but something far bigger. Maybe the missing supply truck and the two men. He got angry thinking of them. Unlike the commander, he didn't think his men had run off. They should have called and said what had gone wrong, though.

The lights bounced and flickered as the truck hit holes in the road. Yet it continued to gain speed as the driver shifted gears. It was now two hundred meters out, and nowhere near coming to a halt.

The sergeant got nervous. He grabbed his man by the shirt and pointed at the truck. "Shoot it!" he screamed.

The young man didn't know if he was serious.

The sergeant drew his hand gun, leveled it on the advancing truck, and opened fire.

The truck was at a hundred meters. Bullets planked into the hood.

Now the young man knew to open fire, and the other two inside the guard shack had responded, their weapons ready.

Fifty meters and closing. Bullets smashed through the windshield.

And the other three opened fire at full automatic. Hot

shells flew from the breech. Flames cut through the darkness.

Out of rounds, the sergeant scurried toward the shack. Just as he dove inside, the truck hit the outer metal barrier, sending it flying toward the wooden shack. It continued on and crashed through the metal gate, flipping it to both sides like it was liquid.

One of the guards was killed instantly by a metal bar crushing his skull. The other two were on the ground, emptying their magazines. The sergeant had sounded an alarm. It was all he could do.

The truck continued toward the row of barracks. As it did, two men in the back in full chemical warfare suits with gas masks twisted the valve on 55-gallon drums. Liquid flowed through tubes into a compressor that was turning rapidly from a small engine. In seconds, the liquid was turned to a gaseous state and drifted off behind the truck.

Keeping the truck moving between the barracks, the driver twisted and turned the wheel frantically.

By now men were making their way outside, pulling pants up, disoriented.

Perfect!

The truck swept by, and within seconds soldiers were dropping to their knees, dying instantly. Others within the barracks were rubbing their eyes, holding their chests.

Twisted bodies lay twitching in the dirt, their faces grimacing with unknowing wonder. None of them had a chance. They had no weapons, no masks or protective clothing.

Inside the truck, the driver started pulling at his mask

with one hand. Something was wrong. The filters were not working. He screamed into his radio that the filters were useless, but got no response.

Looking over his shoulder, he saw his two men lying next to the metal drums. Dead.

He panicked. He let his hand off the wheel and the truck careened into one of the barracks, smashing through rows of bunks, and settling against an oil heater.

A second later, the truck burst into flames and exploded the entire building, disbursing the remaining gas high into the air across the entire barracks compound.

37

CIA HEADQUARTERS
Langley, Virginia

Although he didn't know it, most of the details of Steve Nelsen's trip to Turkey had been worked out for him prior to his arrival in Washington. He would fly by C-5 from Dover Air Force Base to Incirlik Air Base, Turkey. From there he would meet up with a special forces unit on loan to the Agency. In the meantime, Agency officers would be watching every airport in Turkey for the pilot of that Beechcraft. Baskale.

All Nelsen knew as he paced nervously in the DO's office, was he had been called to CIA headquarters. He had not been back to Langley since the commissioning ceremony for the new organization over six months ago. And this was the first time he had been called to the Director of Operation's office. He had known Kurt Jenkins from the old Agency days, having crossed paths as Jenkins rose higher in the organization, while he seemed to stagnate as a field officer. A good field officer, though. One who got results. Until now. Now, he had

failed miserably. It was true he had guessed the terrorist's
target correctly, and taken appropriate measures, but he
had failed to consider an alternate target. He had even
come up with the right mode of dispersing the nerve gas.
After all, that's how he would have done it. He had
thought like a terrorist and it had paid off. But the leader,
Baskale, had gotten away. And they had only recovered
one of the four terrorists. Dead. All of Nelsen's colleagues
thought the three terrorists would try again, for they had
failed and would never be able to return to their bosses
under those circumstances. Nelsen knew better. The nerve
gas was gone. Had they really failed? Instead of killing
one former president that most of the world had already
forgotten about, they had killed over a hundred, and the
count was rising. Every major news source had picked up
on the story and was milking it for all it was worth.
Newspapers, Network News, CNN, National Public
Radio, the BBC. Everyone. Someone high up in government had leaked that the attack was carried out by Kurdish
terrorists, and the media had linked the bombing of the
Astrodome to other attacks in Germany and England. The
process had started. Now Nelsen knew that he had very
little time to act before every step he took would be mirrored by some news hound out to make a name for himself.

The door opened and slammed quickly behind Jenkins,
who had a sour look on his face as he plopped down
behind his chair. His suit looked rumpled, as if he had
slept in it. He set his briefcase on the desk top. "Have a
seat, Steve."

Nelsen sunk into a leather chair.

The MEO opened the briefcase and pulled out a thin

file. "Good work down in Texas."

He had to be joking. "You're not serious?"

"I'm dead serious," Jenkins said, adjusting his tiny round glasses higher on his nose. "You had the chemical warfare units on cite in Houston at the time of the attack. If we had had to pull them from their normal bases after the fact, it would have taken hours. And who knows how many lives it would have meant? The president is very pleased. So is the CIA director. Malone is preparing a citation for you. You should be proud."

He felt far from it. He had been so close. "Thank you, sir. But I should have caught the bastards, or at least realized they had an alternate target in mind. My failure is inexcusable."

"That was far from failure, Steve. What if they had dropped the bomb on downtown Dallas, or New York, or here in D.C.? How many would have died then? If they had struck the New York City subway system at rush hour, like those religious lunnies in Tokyo, who knows how many would have died. You were right on their tail through Mexico, figured out why they were in Texas, and even planned, as well as anyone could have, to stop them. That's all anyone can ask of you."

Nelsen shrugged. He had to hand it to Jenkins. He was slick with people.

"You get the point, Steve. The terrorists killed a few baseball players and some fans. It could have been far worse." He paused for a moment, as if he had laid out a set of decoys on a pond, was watching a flock of ducks set their wings, about to land, before pow—he raises his gun and starts blasting. But the fire storm didn't come. "You're gonna go out there and catch that bastard,

Baskale, for us. And that's not all...."

Nelsen sat and listened for nearly an hour as the MEO laid out the plan for him. Nelsen interjected with comments only a few times, as he came up with additional ideas that might help the mission.

When Jenkins was done, he could tell that Nelsen was pleased with the MEO's confidence in him. After all, Nelsen had gone to Washington thinking he'd be on the carpet for his fuck up in Houston. Instead, he was leading an international search for Baskale. Nelsen couldn't have been more happy.

"When do I leave?" Nelsen asked.

"One hour. Baskale could have left the country by now on his way across the Atlantic with his two buddies."

Nelsen rose and reached across the desk to Jenkins, grasping his hand tightly and pumping it. "Thank you, sir. I won't let you down. I promise."

After Nelsen had gone, Jenkins leaned back in his chair and wondered if what he had just done was the right thing. Steve Nelsen may get results, but at what cost? He had always been a hot-head. Brutal some would say. Yet maybe that's what it would take to bring down a fanatical terrorist group. He wanted someone tough, who was willing to stick his ass on the line for the Agency. With that in mind, there was no one better.

38

NEAR LAKE VAN, TURKISH KURDISTAN

The dirt roads had been burned by the sun and were cracked and crumbling along the edges.

The village was chosen because it was only fifty percent Kurdish. Those who were not Kurds, were nearly so in their belief that a free Kurdistan was inevitable. Most didn't want the borders to be drawn as far as Lake Van, including them in the embattled enclave, but they also knew that the central Turkish government considered them Mountain Turks as well. And others had tried to come to these mountains. Romans, Byzantines, Ottomans. Tried to include them in their empires, only to be turned back, beaten back by a united front of Turks and Kurds and even Armenians. It was now time for change.

Having traveled steadily since the bombing in America, and his hasty retreat from the falling plane, Baskale was tired on his feet. His black slacks were wrinkled. His khaki shirt, buttoned down in the front, the sleeves rolled up, hung freely over his belt, and the warm air swept up from the valley and tickled his hairy, growling belly. He was hungry. Had not eaten in twelve hours. He wouldn't now until after he talked with the leaders.

After jumping from the plane and mixing with the panicking crowd in Houston, Baskale had been picked up by his two men, who were standing by between the two targets, waiting for his call saying which direction to go. From there they had driven to Galveston, flown a commuter to New Orleans, another to Atlanta, and then split up, taking different flights to various European cities. One had flown to London, the other to Paris, and Baskale to Rome. From there Baskale had gone to Istanbul and then Ankara, picking up a car from there and driving straight through. He had traveled non-stop for nearly forty-eight hours, and it showed in his tired eyes.

He had driven into the tiny village for the first time in nearly a month, when he had taken on the assignment and gotten the names of the three men who would help him. It had seemed so long ago. He had traveled so far.

Baskale left the car in front of the graveyard, as he had been told, and shuffled up the mountain toward the mosque.

The leaders had not wanted any vehicles near the mosque. Nothing to bring suspicion.

He was at home. The sun warmed him thoroughly, like a sauna without the sweat. Like the hot Syrian Desert.

As he reached the outer wall of the great mosque on top of the hill, an older man stepped out from behind the crumbling stone entrance. He seemed like nothing, really, in his baggy pants and shirt, his brown boots with holes in the toes. But Baskale knew that looks weren't always right.

Baskale was cautious. He checked his watch. "I've

come for the noon prayer," he said in Kurdish.

The old man smiled, half his teeth missing. "You are too late."

"But I have a lot to pray for. Allah will understand."

The man backed away.

Baskale started up through the gates when he was poked in the back by a firm object. Was it a gun? He turned his head slowly and saw another old man with a pistol on him.

"Go," the man said.

Baskale did.

Before they entered the mosque itself, the man following him stopped.

Turning to face him, Baskale noticed the pistol was an old Makarov that may or may not actually fire. Regardless, he knew the leaders were being cautious. The Turkish government had been trying for years to plant someone into the organization. At least five had died trying. But this man had met him on his last visit, when he had gotten his orders. Was the caution due to him missing his primary target?

The old man swished his head for Baskale to enter.

Baskale removed his hot shoes and socks, placed them on a mat inside, and then stepped softly on the cool brick into the darkened hall. Instead of entering the mosque area, he made his way around to the old chambers that were carved into the side of the mountain. It was said that the chambers led to a labyrinth of catacombs, where graves of great Kurdish leaders were buried. The mosque was chosen as the headquarters because the leaders didn't think the Turkish government would call in air strikes on a sacred building. Time would tell if they were right.

At the end of the hall, lit only by a natural hole through stone that viewed the valley and Lake Van off in the distance, two men sat in wooden chairs, M-16s on their laps. One had a radio. There was an enormous wooden door with chips taken out of it as if someone had beaten it with an ax. The largest of the two rose and turned Baskale toward the stone wall, and then frisked him up and down. Satisfied, he backed up and leveled his gun on his stomach.

Had he done something wrong?

The one with the radio whispered into it. In a moment there was noise on the other side of the door, and then it slowly swung in.

Baskale cautiously stepped inside, and he could hear the two men laughing through the door after it slammed shut. Sure, laugh when you have the guns, Baskale thought.

The room was bright and clean, like a hospital laboratory. It was unlike anything Baskale had seen since driving long and hard from Ankara to Turkish Kurdistan. There was a computer, a fax machine, a television with CNN broadcasting from a satellite dish pointed out through an enlarged hole in the wall. There were other communications equipment that Baskale had not seen since his days with the Turkish army. And even more that he could only speculate on their function.

Back in the corner, Mesut Carzani leaned back in his chair, reading a faxed report that had just come in from an Iraqi Kurdish leader. Carzani's great plan was coming together. His intense eyes, which had not found complete rest in weeks, swished back and forth across the page. When he was done, he looked up at Baskale, who was scanning the place to memory.

"It seems," Carzani said, "that the secondary target was even better than the primary."

Baskale breathed easy. "Yes, sir. I lost only one man."

Carzani thought for a moment. "The American press have called this the most despicable crime against humanity in decades. What do you think?"

Baskale had heard the reports also. From the airport televisions. He was lucky his papers were in order. But he had taken a chance traveling so quickly after the attack. He normally liked to wait. Let things settle down. "Everything went as planned. The Americans had helicopter gunships waiting for us, protecting president Bush. I couldn't take out both targets. I am sorry." He lowered his head to his chest.

Carzani got up and went to the taller, younger man. "You are considered a hero of Kurdistan." He lifted Baskale's head and kissed him on both cheeks. "Your name will be remembered when we have our own history books. For now your great feat will be told again and again, from father to son." Carzani moved toward the T.V.

"But—"

"You wonder how the Americans will know it was us?"

Baskale already knew the American agent had called him by name. "But how will they know it was Kurds who did this?"

Carzani tapped the side of the fax phone. "I called in responsibility. Not from here. Not from this phone. But I sent a fax directly to the vice president. E-mail too. I wanted to be sure they got it." He laughed out loud. "When we become a country, we must come out of the darkness. Think like a civilized culture, not a bunch of goat farmers. Sure we need ties to our past, but we must forge forward. There's so much to do. We have to decide on a capital. That won't be easy, considering the other leaders. We'll have to fight for Mediterranean access. Without that, we'd end up like Nepal. A beautiful country. Don't get me wrong. I've been to Katmandu. But inferior. We need the ocean link. Even if it's just a thin strip of land."

Baskale was confused. Why was this great leader telling him this?

"We have a problem," Carzani continued. "The Americans have vowed to bring the terrorists who dropped the nerve gas on their baseball field to justice." He was pacing now, waving his arms in the air. Settling himself, he sat on the edge of a large wooden table. "They will stop at nothing, Baskale. We'll have to give up someone..." He tried to smile, the tight lines of his dark face coming together.

Now Baskale was concerned. Had he traveled all this way only to have his own people turn him away? Turn him over to the Americans? "What are you saying?"

Carzani noticed his uncertainty. "Relax. You have nothing to fear from all this. You will be protected. We still need great warriors more than martyrs. Now the others..." He trailed off, shrugging.

Baskale thought of the other two men. They had been told to go to London and Paris and finally meet in Brussels. That had bothered Baskale all along. Why Brussels?

Carzani changed the subject. "Look at this." He handed Baskale the fax from the desk.

It was from a number within Iraq. Probably a number with no address. Baskale read it. When he was done, he handed it back to the Kurdish leader. "Is that how it was supposed to go?"

"Of course not." Carzani threw the papers aside. "It means the nerve gas is more powerful than we were told. Now we'll have to be more careful handling it."

The Kurdish leader thought for a minute. Even though his men had died on the raid of the Iraqi air base, their masks slowly letting in the new nerve gas, the attack had been a complete success. At least a hundred men had died. Men who had bombed their villages in the past. Perhaps even some of the same men who had dropped nerve gas on Halabja. Yes, it had been a fine raid, even though the Iraqis weren't talking about it. He would. In fact, he had, sending faxes and making calls to various news agencies. He looked around the chamber cluttered with communications equipment, and realized it was these new things that would distinguish him from all his predecessors. He who could embrace this new technology could rule from anywhere. Even Kurdistan.

Carzani wasn't sure how much to confide in this man. It wasn't that he didn't trust him. After all, Baskale was a great Gazi, or warrior, and the most efficient and brutal Kurdish terrorist in all of Kurdistan, with the exception of perhaps one, whose loyalty was still in question. Yet, Carzani was feeling good about the events of the past week. Finally, the world leaders would have to deal with the Kurds. And there was the problem of the two British spies. His guests. What would he do with them?

Carzani smiled and put his arm around Baskale's neck. "I have something for you. This is what is happening as we speak..."

39

ODESSA, UKRAINE

Victor Petrov, the Ukrainian Agricultural Minister, swirled around defensively with the sound of the warehouse door creaking open and closed, and then there were two sets of footsteps approaching.

Petrov was a huge man and was sweating profusely, even though the room was cold and damp. He had become a bit paranoid following all the deaths. He had called the meeting with the Israeli more to allay his concerns than for any other necessity.

The warehouse on the harbor was a dark and dingy place. Even in the afternoon. Petrov suspected rats lurked in the shadows.

Around the corner came Omri Sherut and his body-guard, the enormous man who had bothered Petrov at each meeting. The three of them stood in near darkness with shadows across their faces. With one nod from Sherut, his bodyguard moved a few steps back, and only his silhouette was visible.

"What's so important, Victor?" Sherut said, somewhat

put off by being summoned so soon to his departure. He was packed and ready to go to the airport when he got the call.

A chill came over Petrov as he stared at the Israeli. He knew he would never be able to trust the man implicitly, but business of this nature required some risk. The benefits far outweighed the prospect of danger. "I'm worried about our deal. The American come by my office today."

Sherut looked surprised. "Jake Adams?"

"Yes. Yes. He said that Bio-Tech was still willing to work a deal in the Ukraine. I don't understand. I thought you said there would be no problem?"

Now Sherut's expression turned to a rare true smile. "Adams was bluffing. He has no power to do anything. He was merely working security for the company."

Petrov tried to breathe easier. "That's what I thought."

Crouching back behind a large wall of crates, Quinn Armstrong listened carefully to the two men. From his vantage point he couldn't make out the faces of the men any more, since they had slipped out of the light somewhat. He had been watching Petrov, followed him to the warehouse, and was certain that Jake Adams had been right about the man. Somehow Petrov was involved with the death of the two American businessmen. How that related to Tvchenko's death, and Petra's, still remained a mystery.

In a moment there was a flash of movement near the corner of the room, back in the darkest recesses of the warehouse.

"I was wondering if you would show," Sherut said,

looking off into what seemed like nowhere.

"We still have some unfinished business," the man said. "I didn't want you leaving without remembering that."

Petrov became more uneasy with this man here. "Is it true that Adams was bluffing?"

The man shuffled his feet against the dirty cement floor. "Adams is a good liar. Listen to what Sherut tells you."

So they were unified in this, Petrov thought. They had both confirmed this individually to him, but he had not been sure. Until now.

The man lit a cigarette and drew in a deep breath, bringing an orange glow to his face.

Sherut laughed. "Is Adams gone yet?"

Letting out a puff of smoke, the man said, "He will be. He's on his way to Kurdistan."

"He thinks he's so smart," Sherut said. "I guess time will tell for sure. I assume he had no problem rushing to the aide of his friend. How noble. He should get a medal of some sort."

The man in the shadows seemed to shuffle nervously. "He thinks he's doing the right thing. It's a pity, really. Some people have this strange sense of duty, without regard for their own safety. It's ludicrous. I think he's a bit touched in the head, myself. But you can't misjudge his dedication, however misguided."

"I won't underestimate the man," Sherut said. "I know what he's capable of. But this time his luck has run out. He's in the middle of something far bigger than even he can get himself out of. I'm quite certain of that." Sherut laughed boisterously.

Quinn waited for a half hour after the four men had

departed before he budged a muscle. He was in shock. He
hadn't actually seen the man through the darkness, but he
didn't need to. The voice had been enough. Now he was-
n't sure how to react. Jake Adams was in trouble and he
was the only one who could tell him that. Had Jake
already left for Turkey?

40

ISTANBUL, TURKEY

Jake was lost in the sounds and chaos of the Istanbul International Airport. He was sitting in one of those cheap vinyl chairs that stick to your pants on a hot day as you try to get up. It was one of those hot days and the terminal air conditioning wasn't doing the job. Hoards of people swept by as they deplaned. He had a half hour left of a two-hour layover on his flight from Odessa to Adana. He couldn't wait to see the airplane they'd use for that final flight. It seemed that not many people were traveling to Adana on that day.

It was late Friday afternoon. Jake had spent the layover wondering what had happened to Helena. He had given her clear instructions to go to Yalta, check into the Summit Hotel, and wait there for him to pick her up in four days. If everything went as he wanted, he'd be in Yalta on Sunday as promised. But he had called the Summit Hotel, and no one matching Helena's description had checked in. Had she gotten to Yalta safely? His mind was flipping back and forth on what could have happened to her. He had been certain nobody had followed him to Nikolaev, where he put her on the train to Yalta.

Jake looked up from gazing at a magazine and saw a woman down the corridor stroll through the crowd. Standing up quickly for a better look, he lost her in the distant crowd. Yet he was certain it was Chavva. It wouldn't have been that much of a coincidence, since they had first met in Istanbul. But it was curious, since he thought she had left Odessa the day before on her way back to Tel Aviv. He smiled thinking of his encounter with her, as he turned to sit down.

Standing just behind him was Sherut, Chavva's boss. He had that smirk on his face, like he was superior and he thought everyone should know it. They stared for an uncomfortable moment.

Finally Jake said, "I thought you went back to Tel Aviv?"

Sherut had his hands in the pockets of a long overcoat that seemed far too warm, considering the temperature. "I was delayed in Odessa, I'm afraid. Business. And you? What brings you to Turkey?"

Jake thought for a moment. He didn't have to tell this man shit, but what the hell. "An old friend of mine. I used to work in Turkey. I thought I'd look him up before heading back to the States." That was really the truth. He was looking for Sinclair Tucker.

Sherut smiled. "I'm just on a layover myself." He pointed to a large flight schedule on the wall. It showed a flight leaving for Tel Aviv in one hour.

"Is Chavva traveling with you?"

He raised his brows, as if Jake had caught him at something. "I'm afraid not. Why do you ask?"

"Just wondering. I thought she worked for you. So naturally you'd be traveling together."

He shook his head and then turned and nodded toward a man sitting across the waiting area. It was the large bodyguard dressed in nice slacks with a black leather coat. He looked like the driver Jake had seen pulling up during his late-night visit with Sherut at the Odessa train station. He was reading a newspaper, but keeping an eye trained in their direction. "Just my associate. Chavva left yesterday, I believe."

There was no arguing. Jake was tired, but sure he had seen her crossing the corridor. It didn't matter one way or the other, really. Jake said goodbye to Sherut and decided to head out and walk until his flight. He hated being cooped up on planes. He went in the direction he thought he had seen Chavva. Nothing. Continuing on, he stopped at a magazine stand and looked behind him. Nobody was following him.

Jake rubbed his left arm against his chest, where his 9mm normally hung. He had left it in the hotel safe, but wasn't sure why. Tully had told him he'd get plenty of firepower once he reached Incirlik. He hoped so, because he felt somewhat naked without it.

He checked his watch. Time to head to the plane.

41

BRUSSELS, BELGIUM

The two Agency officers nervously awaited coordinated backup at the row house apartments four blocks from the north train station. Neither man was familiar with Brussels. They had simply followed their target there on a flight from Rome, taken the train from the National Airport, and walked the four blocks. Only minutes ago the man entered the building, and then the junior officer, Max Noble, had hurried back to a phone, called in their position, and found out the horrible truth. Max was back now, had just given the news to his boss, Allen Gregory, and they stood back in the shadows, waiting for the place to explode with Agency and Belgian officers.

Gregory was a tall man. Blond hair, thinning on top, but never visible since he was rarely without his leather seaman's hat.

Max was the opposite. Short, stocky, with a full head of dark hair that was a touch longer than his boss liked to admit. But Max just assumed Gregory was jealous.

The casual observer seeing them in the park together like that, would think nothing of them. They were dressed in casual clothes, nothing obtrusive. Nice slacks. Neutral dress shirts without ties. And waist-length jackets that were a bit baggy on each, making it easy to conceal their 9mm automatics.

Max hated to wait. Gregory said he would gain patience with age. At thirty-five, Gregory was nine years older than Max. Perhaps a lifetime in this business.

Gregory was an assistant to the Berlin station chief. Had been since it was the old CIA. Two years. He thought back about the last twenty-four hours. How they had been watching the Kurd they suspected killed Gerhard Kreuzberg, the former foreign minister killed by a tiny Ricin pellet. The man had worked sporadically in Berlin under a number of different names. The most recent one, Hosap. When the man suddenly took off by train, the Agency officers were right on his tail. Had they spooked him? Gregory didn't think so. They had stopped in Munich briefly, long enough to call in their position to Berlin, and then continued on with a night train to Rome.

That's when things turned strange. Hosap went directly from the train station to the airport and bought a one-way ticket to Brussels under a different name. Baskale. Just before the flight, Gregory had called in again and report-ed what he knew. He was told to stick with their man. They were sure he was up to no good.

And there they were. The place hinting toward darkness from heavy clouds. A city neither had been to more than once, and that was for a brief meeting a year ago. When Max had returned from calling in, he was clearly dis-turbed. Something wasn't right with the tone of the local

Agency officers. He was sure of it. They were to not proceed without them. That was an order. An order. Max hadn't heard someone say that since he was a marine lieutenant about to blow the shit out of an Iraqi bunker in Kuwait. He had known the men inside were simply pawns not willing to give them much of a fight. But he had followed orders like a good marine does, killing everyone inside. Thirty-five men huddled inside, emaciated from weeks without supplies. Max had felt like such an asshole that day. Orders. Follow them blindly. He looked up at the building and wondered if this was another one of those situations.

After twenty minutes of waiting, finally a car pulled up a few blocks away and a man stepped out, lit a cigarette, and proceeded down the sidewalk toward them. That was the signal.

Another car pulled up from the other direction, a block away. It looked like two or three men in that one.

Max and Gregory moved toward the man with the cigarette. All three met at the corner under a street lamp that wouldn't turn on for hours. It was late afternoon, but the sidewalks were nearly empty. Down a block and a half was a woman with a baby stroller heading toward a park. Farther down, an old man waited at a corner bus stop.

The man with the cigarette had broad shoulders and was somewhere in height between the other two. Perhaps six feet. He wore a long coat that was open in front. Gregory knew he must have had a little extra firepower inside.

"Which one of you did I talk with?" the man asked.

"Me," Max said.

"Great. I called Berlin and told them about our situation. We've got the place covered. Our Belgian friends are

moving in behind the building as we speak. They agree
this is ours. What I couldn't say over the phone is that we
got an anonymous tip about two men at this location. Did
you hear about Houston?"

They both nodded.

"The two inside were supposedly involved."

Max looked confused.

"We only followed one here," Gregory said.

"I know. It doesn't mean there aren't more inside. Our
orders from Langley are to try to take these two alive. Or
three. You told Berlin the man you were following flew
under the name Baskale?"

"That's right."

"Well that's the name of the pilot who dropped the
nerve gas on the Astrodome."

Gregory thought about that. It didn't sound right.
Something was screwed up with the timing, but there was
no time to argue the point. "So how in the hell should we
proceed. For all we know, these guys could have nerve gas
in there."

Max shuddered with the thought. He had spent far too
many hours in chemical warfare suits, until his skin had
turned black from all the charcoal, to even think about
nerve gas. Give him lead any day. Bullets. That's how to
kill someone. Blow a hole in them.

The Brussels officer shrugged. "We don't have time to
round up chem gear. Let's go. You can't live forever."

The three of them headed off toward the apartment
house. As they did, two other men got out of the car
behind them, and three from the car ahead. There was no
way to hide their approach. They had to hope no one was
looking outside. Once they got inside, Belgian police

would show up outside, blocking any exit.

Inside, the men quietly made their way to the second floor and took up positions. Everyone knew the drill. Surprise was the key.

The Brussels man pulled a Mac 10 automatic from inside his coat and nodded his head to Max and Gregory, who were straddling him on each side of the door.

With one quick motion, the Brussels officer kicked in the door, screamed out orders in French, flying into the room.

Two men inside scurried for weapons lying on a coffee table.

Brussels sprayed a blast of bullets against a wall, and the men froze.

By now, Max and Gregory were inside, their guns pointing the way around the room.

Behind them came a wave of others.

Max grabbed one of the men and threw him to the ground, placing his gun at the man's head. "Where's the other?" He asked in German.

The man didn't say a word.

"Where's Baskale?" He tried in English.

Still no answer.

Gregory turned over the man he had been holding to one of the other Brussels officers, and Max did the same. Together they quickly scanned the room and noticed the bedroom door closed.

Just as they were about to crash through the door, bullets started exploding from the wood. They each dove to the side, their weapons aimed at the door.

Behind them, one of the Brussels officers and a Kurd were hit by the spray of bullets and collapsed to the floor.

"Hosap!" Max yelled. "Stop shooting. Nobody has to die here today," he continued in German. He glanced back at the two men hit on the floor. The Brussels officer had taken a round in the shoulder, but he was pulling the Kurd away toward the outer door. The Kurd took a shot in the stomach, but he'd probably live.

"*Shade! Eine Kriger sterben auf Schlacht.*"

"This isn't a battle," Max yelled back.

Before the Kurd could answer, there were two separate guns firing within the room.

"All clear," came a call in French from within the room. The Belgians must have come up the back stairs and fired through the window.

Seconds later, the bedroom door opened and two Belgians dressed in black clothing came out, followed by a cloud of gun smoke.

"Damn it!" Gregory said, as he noticed the man he had followed from Germany lay riddled with bullet holes on the floor against the bed. "We needed him alive."

The Belgians shrugged.

42

ADANA, TURKEY

Jake's flight from Istanbul to Adana had been less than impressive. He flew in one of those old sputtering-engined behemoths that seemed like only a miracle would keep it in the air. His only solace had been a splendid view of Ankara, and he had smiled thinking of some of the times he and Sinclair Tucker had roamed the streets at night, searching for those unknown places that the average tourist would never see. If there was an average tourist in the Turkish capital.

Having packed light for the trip, carrying a single bag aboard with him, Jake stood now in the arrivals area of Adana airport, wondering about his friend, Sinclair. He knew Tuck was still alive. And if Jake was right, Tucker would be doing everything in his power to escape and find out if the Kurds were producing Tvchenko's new weapon.

Jake noticed a large young man scanning the crowd near the exit. He looked like a U.S. Marine, with tight cropped hair, a chiseled jaw, muscles that dwarfed the people around him, and perfect posture. The man was wearing jeans and a sweaty Khaki shirt that bulged with each movement. Jake suspected the man was an Air Force security police sergeant in his early twenties.

Moving to within a few feet, Jake reached his hand out to the man. "Jake Adams," he said.

The man startled. "I'm sorry, sir. I didn't have a photo of you." He shook Jake's hand. "I'm Sergeant Maki."

Tully had told Jake a man would meet him at the airport and drive him to Incirlik Air Base, but that was all. "That's all right." Jake thought for a moment. "You were expecting someone a little different?"

"Well—"

"Let me guess. Your boss, a security police captain, told you to show up here and pick up some spook. So naturally you assumed I'd be some huge sonofabitch with teeth like a lion. Am I right?" Jake started toward the door.

The airman didn't know what to say. He looked embarrassed.

"It doesn't matter," Jake said over his shoulder. "Let's go."

Outside, there was a circular drive lined with taxis double parked. Two drivers at the front of the pack were arguing over who should get the next fare. Jake looked around for his ride, and then headed toward a newer Volkswagen Eurovan with Turkish plates. By the time Jake reached the van's passenger door, the airman had caught up with him.

"You have a key to this boat?" Jake asked, smiling.

The airman quickly opened the door for him, helped Jake put his bag in the side, and then they both climbed in.

The airman was about to crank over the engine when he glanced sideways at Jake. "Sir? How did you know which vehicle?"

"Sergeant Maki. You're a Yooper. Probably from Marquette, Michigan. You joined the Air Force at age seventeen because you couldn't play hockey and you didn't want to cut pulpwood for the rest of your life. But you wanted to be a soldier without being a Marine or Army grunt. So you chose security police, where you could still be a real man. Stop me whenever I miss something."

The sergeant was dumfounded. Finally he shook his head, smiled, and turned over the engine. He put it in gear and headed off. "It wasn't Marquette. It was Houghton."

The sergeant drove toward Incirlik, winding the van through cluttered streets where cars sat abandoned along the side, their hoods popped up and frustrated drivers leaning in to fix them. Horns blared and sirens sounded all around. Not much had changed since the last time Jake had been there. He could still smell the familiar kabobs wafting ubiquitously. He loved the kabobs. Jake and Sinclair had spent a week at Incirlik being briefed by day on what was happening across the border in Iraq. By night they had tried to put a dent in the local beer supply. He remembered how hot and humid the place had been. It was sweltering now, and he slid his leather coat off and threw it in the back. As he did, his ribs twisted wrong, bringing extreme pain. He had almost forgotten about the bruised ribs. They were healing, but wouldn't be back to a hundred percent for weeks.

Sergeant Maki entered the north gate of Incirlik Air Base without fanfare and proceeded along a tree-lined boulevard, pulling up to a small one-story earth tone building that resembled a shabby house with a flat top. There was no sign out front, unlike all the other buildings on base, so Jake immediately assumed it was the Air

Force Office of Special Investigations, or OSI. While a captain in Air Force intelligence, Jake had worked closely with OSI special agents during one of those well-intentioned president's war on drugs.

"Sir, you can leave your bag here with me," Sergeant Maki said. "They want you in there for a briefing."

Jake looked up and down the street. The building was completely isolated, with no cars sitting out front to indicate anyone was even inside. "Thanks. Where will I find my bag when this is over?"

The sergeant hesitated. "I was told to bring it to the Visiting Officers' Quarters."

"Where someone will dig through it with a fine-toothed comb, no doubt," Jake said. "I can save you guys the effort. There's nothing in there but dirty clothes mingling with clean clothes."

The sergeant smiled. "I just follow orders, sir."

That's the problem, Jake thought. It's one of the reasons he'd left the Air Force and the CIA. Too many people following orders. Jake retrieved his leather coat, got out and shut the door behind him, and then leaned through the window. "You tell those bastards I'm gonna count my skivvies when I get my bag back."

Sergeant Maki laughed and then drove off.

Jake wiped the sweat from his brow with the back of his hand. He wasn't used to the heat anymore. It was difficult to breathe. He wished he'd have some time to acclimate, but knew time was important. It was nearly dinner time, and he guessed he'd be briefed and on a helicopter by dark.

He knocked on the heavy door, saw a camera above and to the left in a corner, heard a buzz, so he pushed the door inward. Inside was a narrow passageway with another door at the end. A large man quickly came out the door. He was wearing a green T-shirt, tight to his skin, with a 9mm Beretta strapped under his left arm.

Without saying a word, the man checked Jake for weapons and used a hand scanner to sanitize him for bugs.

"Can I see your passport?" the man finally asked.

Jake slipped his passport from the inside pocket of his jacket and handed it to the man.

The man gave it a once-over without a single facial variance and then handed it back and nodded for him to enter the other door.

"Thanks, sergeant," Jake said. He knew OSI agents hated being called by a rank. It somehow made them feel less important, less mysterious.

Inside the other door was a conference table with six men gathered, all dressed in dark battle fatigues, looking over papers spread out in front of them.

Standing behind the table was two other men. Jake immediately recognized the largest of the men at the table as Steve Nelsen.

Nelsen looked up. His eyes were red from no sleep. It looked as if he'd been crying. He took a long sip on a mug of coffee, keeping an eye trained on Jake the whole time. When he was done, he moved out from behind the desk and met Jake at the door.

"How the fuck did you ever get involved with this thing?" Nelsen asked, his hands on his hips.

"Nice to see you too," Jake said.

Nelsen pointed a finger at Jake's chest. "I want one thing clear right from the start. I run this operation. Civilians better stay clear."

"If you want to keep that finger, get it away from me." Nelsen glared into Jake's eyes.

"I don't take orders from you, Nelsen," Jake said. "I was told I run the operation."

"You're a fuckin' civilian."

"So is your boss. So is the president. Besides, when did you join the military?"

Nelsen looked like he'd explode, when another man came between them and reached out his hand to Jake. "So you're Jake Adams," he said. "I'm Ricardo Garcia. Steve's associate. It'll be great working with you. I've heard so much about you, I feel I know you already."

Jake shook the man's hand and smiled. "I hope you got a better briefing than Steve would have given you."

Garcia laughed. "I'm still learning what's bullshit or not with him."

Nelsen glanced sideways at Garcia and mumbled something under his breath. Then he said, "Let's cut the fucking pleasantries and get to work. We've got terrorists on the loose. Ricardo, make sure these guys know exactly what we want of them. And get the damn pilot over here pronto."

Garcia smiled and took a seat at the table with the soldiers.

Nelsen pulled Jake aside and escorted him to a back room, a soundproof interrogation room. He took a seat at a wooden table and motioned for Jake to do the same. Then he opened a folder and spread out six satellite photographs.

Jake sat down and reached for the photos.

"Not so fast," Nelsen said, slamming his hand onto the photos. "I want to know how in the hell you got involved with all this?"

Jake smiled. "It bothers you, doesn't it. Just a regular guy helping the Agency track down terrorists."

Nelsen saw where Jake was heading, and decided not to bite. "Bother me? Yeah, it bothers me. You quit the old Agency. Some said you were fired. I wouldn't have doubted that for a minute. You were one insolent bastard all along."

"Respect should be earned," Jake shot back. "Some people think it comes with their position."

"See what I mean. It does come with the position, asshole."

"Listen. If we keep this up, the bad guys will die of old age. And I'm sure you'd rather help them along with a little lead poisoning. That is your specialty."

"There you go again," Nelsen said. "You think I'm some fucking Rambo. Shoot first and then make up answers from a dead corpse."

"Now that you mention it."

They stared at each other for an uncomfortable moment, each waiting for the other to blink.

Finally, Jake reached across for the photos again, and Nelsen let him have them. The first two were close up shots of helicopter wreckage, still smoldering. The next two showed a wider view of a mountain village, and Jake wasn't sure what he was looking for in them. And the last two were closer views of an old mosque.

"Do you have an eyepiece," Jake asked.

Nelsen reluctantly handed a small optic that photo analysts and nearly every serious photographer would own.

Jake took a closer look at each photo. In a moment he slipped the photos to the center of the table. "Interesting."

"What do you think?"

"I think the helicopter was shot down with 50 caliber machine guns. It hit the ground pretty hard, but probably didn't kill everyone. It looked like it hit the skids first and then the rotors torqued it onto its nose."

"Right. That's what I thought. What about the others?"

"What am I supposed to see? I saw the dog taking a shit, if that's what you mean."

Nelsen laughed. "That was a nice touch, wasn't it? These photos don't tell you much about the village. They're more for orientation. We shifted a few satellites to cover Kurdistan ever since we suspected the Kurds were involved. It's a big area, as you know. The PKK guerrillas have backed off in the past few months. It's almost as if they were holding off for something big. Not wanting to make waves. The Turkish government is confused, even though they haven't been overly active in squashing the PKK in the last six months anyway. The Turks are simply counting their blessings. The Agency feels differently."

Jake shrugged. "Makes sense to me. If you're planning something big, don't bring attention to yourself. The Kurds were most certainly involved in Odessa."

"And in Houston, on Johnston Atoll, in Brighton, Berlin, and even Brussels. Not to mention the attack in Kirkuk, Iraq yesterday."

"I know about everything but Brussels and Kirkuk," Jake said.

Nelsen explained what happened in Brussels, how they had captured two of the terrorists from the Houston attack, and possibly one of the men who had assassinated the German. "And in Kirkuk," Nelsen continued. "A small group of Kurds crashed a truck though the air base gates and spread nerve gas throughout the barracks area. At least a hundred died, including the terrorists. It seems their masks and suits didn't work."

Jake had been staring off at the photos, but he looked up quickly. "What type of masks and filters."

"I'm not entirely sure. We got a report from Mossad. They said the equipment was first rate."

"My God."

"What?"

Jake thought for a long minute. Was that Tvchenko's newest weapon? Made in Odessa, tested in Iraq by the Kurds? "That means we have no way of combating the compound. We can't even protect ourselves or our troops. The new agent must be able to penetrate standard chem and biological equipment."

That had completely slipped Nelsen's thoughts. "The Kurds have the perfect poor man's nuke."

"We've got to stop them," Jake said. "Before they produce the stuff in mass quantities."

The problem was, under ideal conditions the U.S. would have simply sanctioned air strikes to destroy production facilities. In Kurdistan that would be nearly impossible, with the mountainous terrain and the prospect of collateral damage to civilian populations. Jake knew all of this. He also knew that if the Kurds were even close to producing vast quantities of this new nerve gas, then the Kurds were in a great position of strength. They could demand respect and damn sure get it.

"Why are the Turks so willing to let us handle the situation?" Jake asked.

"Our government told them we could handle the matter discreetly. That we had chemical and biological experts willing to go in first to sanitize the area. We have forty-eight hours before the Turks hit the entire region with air strikes, followed by massive troops."

"Experts?"

"That would be you."

"I know what sanitize means," Jake protested. "Nobody said shit about that."

Nelsen nodded his head toward the other room, indicating the special forces troops.

"Great. Let's hope the Turks can tell time."

43

TURKISH KURDISTAN

The boat ride from Yalta to the port in Batumi, Georgia had been rough across a stormy Black Sea. She wasn't used to traveling by boat, and had puked her guts out three times to the sound of a laughing crew of pirates. If she had had her way, she would have killed them all and left them floating on their rust bucket.

From Batumi she had picked up a small Fiat, a beat up piece of junk held together by dirt and wire, crossed the Turkish border, and traveled the hinterlands along the base of Mount Ararat.

She had dumped the car ten kilometers after passing through the city of Van, just before dark, and now she was trudging along an old dirt road dressed in dark, Muslim clothing from head to toe, her newly black hair tucked discreetly under her scarf.

When she had made her way along the winding road, and had climbed high above Lake Van, she slipped off into the low bushes and extracted a small instrument from a pack. She turned on the global positioning device and took a reading. She was only ten kilometers from her target. She could take her time in the darkness, rest for a while to regain her strength, and still be to the tiny village before dawn. She was right on schedule.

Farther up the road in the Kurdish village, there was a small stone building that looked like a barn. In fact it had been a barn until four months ago, and the smell of sheep and goats still permeated the air.

But now the barn was a laboratory.

Two men in white lab coats stood before a stainless steel table, one looking into an electron microscope, and the other held a petri dish and watched his boss.

"Has it mutated?" the man with the dish asked.

"Just a moment."

The man at the microscope had picked up his degree, a master's in biochemistry, at Johns Hopkins University the previous May. His assistant had nearly finished himself, before they were both called back to Kurdistan. They were needed far more here.

Finally the man at the microscope removed his eyes from the optics and looked at his assistant. "It's no wonder the masks didn't work in Kirkuk," he said. "As the compound turns to gas, it splits and shrinks but maintains its total structure."

"Is that possible?"

"I've read of such things, but I've never seen anything like this. It will be too dangerous to handle. Suicide."

"Does it matter?"

The head chemist thought about that for a moment. Would his boss care how unstable the compound was? Even for them to mix it? Probably not. Results...that's what counted.

"It's even more deadly than the Ukrainian said. He must have known. Why didn't he tell us?"

His associate shrugged. "Maybe he didn't have time to. But we have all of his notes translated. Does he talk about controlling the molecular structure or guarding against inadvertent exposure?"

The head chemist stared off into nowhere. He was sure he had read through every last piece of data. Yet there was nothing definitive about collateral exposure. Perhaps the Ukrainian had died too soon. Maybe Carzani should have brought him to Kurdistan until they had produced all the nerve gas they needed. Now, the question was, who should know what they had found?

He glanced off to the storage tank that held over 50 gallons of the nerve gas in liquid form. They were about to go into full production and then ship off the product to storage cites across Kurdistan in villages similar to this one. No government would be able to find all the nerve gas after that.

"What have we done?" the chemist said.

Less than a kilometer up the road, in the darkest confines of the mosque, Sinclair Tucker lay on a bed of straw, his lower leg aching where the fibula nearly protruded from the skin. He had managed to block most of the pain from his mind by thinking of times he had been worse off. Like when he was shot in the stomach in Bucharest by the overzealous security agent. Or when he broke his shoulder from the thirty-foot fall from the building in Sofia while chasing a double agent who had just given up his cover. But in the end, the swelling and piercing pain came back. He had ripped his undershirt into thin strips and tied off rolled cardboard around his calf in a makeshift splint. If nothing else, he no longer had to look at the bone and the disjointed leg.

Not that he could see anything at this hour. Since they had taken his watch after the crash, he wasn't entirely sure of the time. The last call to prayer was hours ago just after sunset, and the chiming bells had even ceased at ten. He guessed it was nearly midnight. Maybe even one. But he couldn't sleep. The co-pilot lay four feet away on a small straw mattress, something maybe large enough for a small child. Tucker had insisted the co-pilot take the softer bed. He was in much worse shape, slipping fast into delirium. Tucker could find no real visible signs of injury, except for bruises on his chest and abdomen. And he knew that was a bad sign. He suspected the co-pilot had broken ribs and maybe even ruptured his spleen. He had a fever now and would mumble incoherently. Death was trying to lift the man from pain.

Tucker felt bad for the man. It was his fault he was here. Sure he was a soldier and had known he could die for the queen when asked, but it was Tucker who had gathered them to this rendezvous. The chopper pilot had already given everything. The worst part of all is he didn't even know the man's full name. Since they had been on a special operation, the pilot and co-pilot had not worn name tags. But Tucker had caught the pilot slip up once on the helo flight from Diyarbakir. He had called the co-pilot, Jet. A nickname probably. All flyers had them, as if they had been issued one with their wings.

He only wished he had told Jake Adams what he was up to.

Tucker shifted and tried to find a more comfortable position. But there was none.

Suddenly there were footsteps on the bricks outside, and they stopped outside the large wooden door.

Jet stirred and mumbled something, then went quiet.

The door opened and a bright light shone in, blinding Tucker.

He could hear feet shuffling closer, with the light shaking slightly, and then whispering.

"So, Mr. Sinclair Tucker," came a sharp accented voice. "It seems your government doesn't want you back. They say they have no idea what you were doing in Kurdistan. Perhaps you can explain it to me?"

Tucker leaned up on his elbows, squinting his eyes away from the light. This was a new man, not the same one who had beaten him after each bogus answer he gave for the first twelve hours after his capture. Not the man who had discovered he had a broken leg, and would kick it just for the hell of it. Who was this one?

"I told your friend. I work for the foreign ministry in Ankara. We were looking for a British tourist who has been missing for five days."

The man with the light laughed boisterously. "You're sticking with that story?"

Tucker tried to shift his stiff leg, but he couldn't even budge it. It was if the leg had a mind of its own, and wouldn't let this new man know it was broken. "I cannot tell you any more than that. That's what my government sent me out of the office for. I didn't want to come here."

The light shook as the man moved closer. "You have a problem with Kurdistan?"

"No, no. Not at all. I just feel that tourists have become

a pain in the royal ass. We've told them to stay out of the area, and they defy our requests. They should suffer the consequences."

"If this was the case," the man said, "then why didn't your government simply call our leaders and ask us if we had seen the man."

Tucker had thought of this himself. A lie should be iron-clad. "We didn't want to offend your leaders by suggesting they had had something to do with the tourist's disappearance. For all we knew, the person had simply run his rental car off the side of a mountain."

There was whispering again.

Tucker didn't see it coming, but a foot swung and smashed directly into the broken bone. Without even a scream, Tucker passed out immediately.

44

TEL AVIV, ISRAEL

Sitting back in his comfortable leather chair in his
lavish apartment overlooking the night lights of Tel
Aviv, Mikhael Chagall, the director of Israeli Intelligence,
was somewhat disturbed being awakened at such an hour
by his assistant, Yosef.

His assistant had poured himself a drink and was working up the courage to speak freely.

"Well, Yosef," the Mossad director said. "What's so
important?"

"When we had not heard from Omri in the past few
days, I started asking questions through other sources.
The Kurds have cleaned house in Odessa."

"That's what we figured they would do," the director
said, put off by the obvious.

"True." Yosef took another sip of cognac. "But the
Americans are on the move. Jake Adams is heading
toward Kurdistan."

Chagall knew not to ask how his assistant knew this, but
he wanted to. He also knew that information was power,

and the more he had of one, the more he'd have of the other. "One man. How much damage could he do? What about Chavva? Have you heard from her?"

The assistant shrugged. "She could be in place already."

"She's one of our best. She must be protected when this is all over."

"I understand," Yosef said. "But what if she is..." He wasn't sure how far he could go with the director, even though they had been friends and allies for years.

"She will do what is right, Yosef." Chagall thought for a moment. "And I only hope Omri has completed the equation and is there for her. He better hope so."

ODESSA, UKRAINE

Quinn Armstrong was on hold. He had been for the past ten minutes, waiting for the Director of Central Intelligence himself to pick up.

Checking his watch again, Quinn realized it was closing in on seven p.m. in Washington. The Director would be in his evening security briefing, discussing what the Agency would brief the president on the next day, baring events of the evening. Pulling him from that meeting would be nearly impossible, yet he had tried nonetheless.

He glanced down at the phone. He had wanted to call secure from the office, but that would have been out of the question. He didn't know who to trust, so he decided to go straight to the top.

In a moment there was a click on the other end.

"What can I do for you?"

Who was that? "I'm sorry," Quinn said. "I was holding for the Director."

"Who is this?"

He hesitated. "This is Quinn Armstrong. Deputy station chief in Odessa. I must speak with the Director on an important matter."

"This is Kurt Jenkins. I'm sure you've heard of that name. You can speak freely."

That means he was being recorded by the CIA Director of Operations himself. "Sorry, sir. I didn't recognize your voice. But I'm not calling secure."

"I know that. What do you have?"

Quinn quickly laid out what he knew for sure and what he suspected he had stumbled across. When he was done, he asked, "What should I do?"

"You can go to Turkey."

"But—"

"Go to our office in Ankara. I'll leave orders for you there. Be careful."

Quinn was about to ask another question, when the line went blank. He slowly set the phone back in its crevice, slid back on the sofa, and ran his fingers through his hair. How in the hell had he gotten himself into this mess?

He was about to get up, when the front door burst open. The first round hit him in the forehead before he even saw the flash. The second and third rounds from the silenced gun hit him in the shoulder and the stomach. Rounds four and five went into his thigh and ankle. Three more rounds hit the wall behind him and the sofa next to his flaccid body. For the average investigator it would look like a gang hit with random fire. However, the first shot would have been enough.

The door slowly swung shut, and the shooter walked off down the hall.

45

ADANA, TURKEY

Jake knew there was more to the story than what Agency Special Agent Steve Nelsen had briefed him on. The military had been like that, hiding behind the obliquely defined "need to know." The old Agency had even been more obscure in its definition of who should know what when. Jake even understood that Nelsen had probably wanted to tell him more about the mission prior to their departure, but he didn't like it one bit. He wasn't even sure what their intended objective was.

Sitting back in an old chair in the operations building on the first floor of the Incirlik Air Base air traffic control tower, Jake gazed across at the rest of the men. The six commandos were nearly identical in size and shape, dressed in dark camo, and currently spreading make-up on their faces like supermodels. None of them had any insignia on their uniforms that indicated which service they represented, or which country as far as that went. Yet anyone could tell that they were trained killers willing to die for any cause. Just following orders. They were good at it. They could have been Navy Seals, Army Special Forces, or even Air Force Special Ops. It was more likely that they were former military, Agency-trained commandos.

Off to one side of the commandos stood Steve Nelsen and Ricardo Garcia. They were dressed in civilian clothes. Garcia could have passed for a Turk, but Nelsen looked more like a middle linebacker at a church social. He seemed out of place in Turkey, even though he had worked there for so long and was fluent in the language. His eyes were intense. His jaw locked tightly. And then Jake thought of his own appearance. He too could have passed for a Turk, he thought. From a distance.

Jake looked out the window. It was completely dark outside. Only the red and blue ramp lights flickered like stars off a sea of concrete. It was overcast, with clouds and a light mist coming down. Either that, or the humidity, which was smothering, had escaped like tears from the clouds.

In a few minutes a helicopter's familiar whapping of air sounded in the distance.

Nelsen came over to Jake. "Are you ready?" he asked.

"I'd be more ready if I knew more."

Nelsen moved uncomfortably close, contemplating Jake's words. "Listen," he whispered. "The three of us," he nodded toward Garcia. "We're gonna take Baskale. The terrorist. They want him back in Washington to stand trial."

The helicopter swooped down and rocked to a halt fifty yards from the building.

"Just like that? What about Sinclair Tucker?"

Nelsen sighed and looked away. Then he turned back

toward Jake. "The Brits are trying to work a deal. They got caught with their pants down, and they're back peddling."

"I've got to find him, Steve. You know we're good friends."

"That's personal. If we've got time, we'll look for him."

Jake knew that's all he could hope for. He didn't like it much though. "What else is going on here, Steve?"

Nelsen motioned for the commandos to head out to the chopper, and they quickly picked up their gear and were out the door.

"Their mission is to secure the weapons."

"You mean to destroy the entire village," Jake said.

Nelsen reeled around, pointing a finger at Jake's chest. "God dammit. I'm not going to talk philosophy with you. They're trained for a mission. Let them do their job. You of all people should understand. You saw Halabja. You know what chemical and biological weapons can do to a human body."

There was a strange look on Nelsen's face. Something Jake hadn't seen before in the man. A caring perhaps. Caring for something more than simple ideology. Perhaps Nelsen was human, and not the carnivorous asshole Jake had always thought he was.

"Let's go then," Jake said without conviction.

Jake and Nelsen and Garcia hurried out onto the ramp and ducked under the slowly moving rotors. When they were aboard, Jake and Steve were handed headphones by a crew member.

On the way to the helicopter, Jake had noticed something interesting. The chopper was an Italian-made Augusta-Bell Huey, and had the symbol of the Turkish agricultural ministry on its side. The Turkish Army had purchased a bunch of the old choppers that dated back to Vietnam. They were a good old bird, especially in remote terrain. The outside might have been conventional, other than the bogus agricultural symbol, but the inside was completely different. There was high tech equipment everywhere.

"The headphones are for internal communications only," Nelsen said. "You can talk to the pilot and co-pilot and the crew chief...or me." He smiled.

"Great."

Jake heard the final clearance from the air traffic controllers.

"That's the last we'll hear from the outside," Nelsen explained.

In a moment they started to lift off. Jake looked down to the tarmac and noticed a master sergeant in air force blues trying desperately to get someone's attention. He was waving a piece of paper at them, as if they had forgotten something. Nelsen saw the man and said nothing.

"What was that all about?" Jake asked.

"I don't know," Nelsen said. "We're running silent now. Nothing can stop us."

They had lifted off at three a.m. and had flown for over an hour through the darkness toward the east. Jake had checked his watch periodically and imagined where they were. They were flying just above the tree lines. They had caught the Euphrates River and followed it for a while. Not long ago he had made out the lights of Diyarbakir to the north, so the river below was the Tigris. The plan, as Nelsen had explained it, was to follow the Tigris until it was joined by the Batman. Then they would head north up the Batman River Valley. Just south of Lake Van, they would head east again, skirt around the lower foothills and head to the mountains above the city of Van. Nelsen had never even mentioned the name of the village they were heading toward. But Jake had been to Kurdistan many times, and he knew there were numerous villages that weren't even on maps. It was the Turkish government's denial of their existence.

Jake hated flying in helicopters. He had done it in the past reluctantly. He wished they had simply piled into rental cars in a caravan to Van, but knew they would have never made it through Kurdistan at night without being stopped and questioned. Flying was the only solution.

Nelsen had opened up somewhat to Jake. He had his eyes closed, and Jake wondered how he could sleep with all the shaking and pitching. Garcia looked like he had seen a ghost. His face was pale, and he seemed airsick. The commandos were all sprawled over each other, snoozing like puppies snuggling for warmth.

The pilots started giving brief comments about their location, the weather ahead, and estimated time of arrival. They were a little over an hour away. Crossing into Kurdistan now. Jake felt under his left arm the new 9mm Glock Nelsen had given him, fully loaded, with three extra magazines. He had stuffed the magazines to the inside pockets of his leather jacket. Buried into a secret pocket of the lining, was his only identification. A visa card. He could get anywhere in the world with that. Everything else, including his wallet and passport, he was forced to leave in the briefing room at Incirlik. The wonderful world of black ops.

46

KURDISTAN

Sneaking through the darkness of the small Kurdish village, Chavva paused for a moment behind a stone wall that lead to the mosque butted against the mountain. She was tired, but wouldn't think of sleeping. It was far more important for her to have that shaky edge. That feeling of pure energy that most would associate with hunger and fatigue, but what she had always felt as an inner power. Something like a wolf that hadn't killed in a week.

It had been a long journey from Odessa. After seeing Jake Adams at the Istanbul airport, she had taken the flight to Diyarbakir, acquired the truck, and rode the bumpy dirt tracks into the heart of Kurdistan. All the while she had thought of Jake, wondered what he was doing at the airport. Hoping he was still safe. She couldn't get him out of her mind.

She pressed her shoulder against the stone wall and listened carefully to voices from her past. There were screams of horror and wonder. How could this be happening? Tears rolled down her cheeks and she sobbed with pain. A pain that would end only with her last breath.

Deep within the catacombs of the mosque, Mesut Carzani, the new Kurdish sultan, set the phone down and smiled. He turned to Baskale, his trusted *Gazi*.

"Everything is working as planned," Carzani said. "The Americans are on their way. The same man who had chased you across Texas."

Baskale looked surprised. "They sent that man after me?"

Carzani nodded.

It was more than Baskale had dreamed for. A chance to meet up with the American again. "How do you know?"

"Let's say...we have friends in interesting places."

Sitting back in the shadows of the dimly lit room, the man finally rose from the chair and approached the two Kurds. "What about the other American from Odessa? Jake Adams? Is he with them?"

Carzani smiled. "Of course, Omri. He's the last one to...take care of from there."

Omri Sherut gazed at the two men for a moment. He knew there was another, but he didn't want to mention that person's name. He would take care of that one on his own.

Carzani put his hand on Baskale's shoulder. "Go to the men and let them know the Americans are on their way."

"Yes, sir."

"Allah is with you."

On the outskirts of the village a lone woman in a long peasant's dress, with a scarf covering her hair, made her way along the dirt road. She had kept to the side of the road since dropping off the Fiat, but her feet were sore and she couldn't help feeling tired. She was traveling on adrenalin and nothing else. Her mission was too important to let a little pain stop her.

Suddenly a man stepped out of the bushes and trained his M-16 on her. "What are you doing here old woman?" the man asked in Kurdish.

She didn't understand him, but she slowly stepped toward him.

He pulled the bolt back and let a bullet slam into the chamber.

She was now just inches from the muzzle.

He asked her to move along, shifting the muzzle with a nod of his head. He was young. Shaking. Scared.

As the barrel turned, she caught the end with her left hand, and straight kicked the man in the crotch. He sunk to his knees in pain, dropping the rifle into her hands. She jammed the gun butt into his skull and he immediately crashed to the ground. She dragged him back into the bushes and checked his pulse. He was alive. She thought about letting him live, but changed her mind. She couldn't let anyone know she was there. She pulled the man's knife from the sheath on his hip, and with one quick jab, penetrated his chest and drove the blade into his heart.

He wiggled for a moment, and then went limp.

47

CROSSING KURDISTAN

The Huey chopper swooped low across the mountains. Jake looked out the window and could see the first glimmer of morning in the silhouette of the mountains to the north. They were crossing Kurdistan now. He could barely make out the snow on the caps of the volcanoes. He had been here before. They were close now.

The commandos were checking their weapons, slapping loaded magazines into them.

The pilot came over the radio. "Hang on folks. We're going a little lower."

Shit, Jake thought. How could they get much lower?

"Five minutes for the first drop."

"First drop?" Jake asked Nelsen.

"That's us."

Jake thought they would be together. All nine of them.

"I'll explain on the ground," Nelsen said.

The chopper dipped down and seemed like it would surely crash into the side of the mountain, but at the last second the nose popped up and they were slipping along the tree tops, with a rocky ledge to their right.

"The Brits were shot down a mile ahead," Nelsen said. "They came in too high and too far to the west."

In a few seconds the chopper lurched to the left.

"Shit!" The pilot yelled. "We're taking ground fire."

The windscreen had shattered with two holes, and the fifty caliber rounds had sunk into the bulkhead above the cockpit.

The helicopter zipped forward and down quickly. Jake held his breath, thinking they were crashing. Then the pilot pulled back and brought the chopper to a halt, and they slowly sunk into a clearing below.

Nelsen and one of the commandos slid the door open.

"We can't set down here," the pilot yelled over the radio. "It's too rocky. You'll have to jump."

"What about a rope?" Jake asked.

Nelsen shook his head. "No time. We have to hit the ground and move out before the PKK get us. Drop down to the skid, hang, and drop. Try to miss the boulders." Nelsen ripped his headset off and slung a backpack over his shoulder. He moved toward the opening.

Nelsen went first. In a moment, he was swallowed up by the black abyss below.

The chopper rocked violently.

Jake was next. He held onto the side of the door for a second and looked down. It could have been three feet or three hundred. He had no way of telling. He stepped out to the skid, swung his hands down to the metal rails like a gymnast on a high bar, and then dropped his feet and body downward, catching himself with a lurch. He looked down, saw nothing, and dropped. In a split second his feet hit the ground, his legs collapsed, and he fell to his right, smashing into a huge rock and rolling onto his side. He lay in pain, having hit his bruised ribs. A hand grasped his collar and dragged him a few feet to one side.

The helicopter hovered above, the rotor wash kicking up dirt. Jake could see the chopper as a backdrop to the sky, which seemed brighter from the ground.

Garcia stepped onto the rail above, reached down for the bar, and then seemed to float headfirst toward the ground in slow motion.

When Garcia hit the ground, his head smashed into a large rock before his hands could stop his descent. He was dead before Jake and Nelsen reached him.

The chopper started rising up toward the treetops.

Nelsen crouched down next to Garcia, checking his pulse. He shook his head.

Jake had his gun out and watched the edge of the woods, which were starting to become more visible, and let his eyes settle on the bundle of a man a few feet away. "Is he?"

"He's dead. Broken neck. God dammit!"

"We've got to get out of here, Steve. What's the plan."

The helicopter had reached the treetops and started down along the edge of the mountains. It had gone just half a mile when the shooting star seemed to come from nowhere and explode into its side. Then the entire chopper blew up into nothing in a huge ball of flames, followed immediately by a secondary blast.

Nelsen turned quickly and stared in wonder. Jake had seen the whole thing, but couldn't believe what had just happened.

Jake heard the bullet pass by his head before he heard the shots being fired from the woods above them. He returned fire with one quick burst. "Let's go!" he screamed, grabbing Nelsen by the arm and hauling him down the side of the mountain.

The woods below were fifty yards away. Bullets echoed down the mountain, hitting the dirt, hitting the trees in front of them, and probably missing them both by inches.

They reached the woods and pulled up behind a large clump of trees.

"What in the hell is going on?" Nelsen said. "Those fuckers had to know we were coming."

"I don't have time to argue with you there. Now tell me what in the hell is going on?"

"We needed the commandos," Nelsen said. "We can't pull this off without them. We're screwed."

Jake looked into Nelsen's eyes. It was the first time he had seen that face on him. It was fear. Nelsen had always been this tough sonofabitch who everyone thought would screw his mother if given the chance. And now he was breathing heavily, sweating from every pore on his body, and shaking. He was scared.

There were flashes from the woods above, followed by the crackling of gunfire. Jake thought of returning fire, but knew the men were beyond his effective range. And the muzzle flashes would highlight their position.

"We're screwed if we stay put," Jake said. "Let's go. We've gotta get the hell out of here."

Listening carefully, Jake could hear the distinct sound of twigs cracking. The shooters were coming around the south side of the clearing. Perfect. They had made their first mistake. Jake remembered the satellite photos, and knew they must head north to reach the Kurdish village. He started running through the thick forest. Nelsen was right on his heels.

They were running laterally along the steep grade of the mountainside. It was starting to get a little lighter, making it somewhat easier to see the ground unfold in front of them. Brush slapped across their faces, Nelsen tripped over a dead fall, crashing to the ground. Jake stopped and helped him up. They were both breathing heavily. It must have been the elevation, Jake thought. At least eight thousand feet. Jake looked behind them and listened. He could hear nothing. Nobody following them. He wondered now if the men had forced them to head in that direction. It they were herding them, much like they would heard their sheep, toward others who were waiting to ambush them ahead.

Nelsen pulled at Jake this time. "We have to move," he said.

"Wait a minute," Jake whispered. "Maybe that's what they want us to do. If they sent a small group to the south making noise, and another group to the north quietly, they could be just ahead waiting for us."

Nelsen thought it over. "All right. What do you suggest?"

"I say we head straight up the mountain for high ground. Once we reach the rock massif, we head north again. They'll never guess we'd head uphill. Then we can keep them below us all the way to the village."

"I thought you were in the Air Force. Not the Army."

"It's the same way I hunt deer in the Rockies. Mountain Lions do the same thing."

"Great."

Jake crept slowly up the mountain, listening for any movement. After about a thousand feet, they reached a rock cliff that stretched all the way around the mountain for a mile in both directions. The satellite photos had shown Sinclair Tucker's helicopter had gone down a half a mile ahead. They had the high ground now, and they paused for a moment to catch their breath.

Nelsen had a confused expression.

"What's the matter?" Jake asked.

"I think you just saved our lives, and I don't like it one bit."

"Afraid you might have to do the same for me some-day?"

Nelsen didn't answer.

"Listen," Jake said. "If you want me to help you any more, you'll tell me the entire mission. You don't want Garcia's death to go for nothing. And those six commandos, the two pilots..."

Nelsen sat down in the dewy grass, looking out over Lake Van to the northwest, which was sparkling green with the first light of day.

"The government could give a shit about Baskale," he whispered. "Sure it would have been nice to capture him and bring him to justice in the states, but that's not our main concern."

"I didn't think so."

"Number one priority is to take out the laboratory. Three of the commandos were set to do that. The other three were heading for a mosque in the village. They were to take out a man named Carzani. Mesut Carzani."

"That name sounds familiar," Jake said.

"It should. He's a Kurdish tribal leader. The one who helped the Iraqi Kurds after the Gulf War. He took over the PKK a few years back, and now he's formed an alliance with Kurdish tribes in Iran, Iraq and Syria. He even controls the vast Kurdish radicals in places like Germany and England."

"So he ordered the deaths there?"

"Right."

"How do we know all this?"

Nelsen hesitated. "Human intel. Some from Mossad, I understand. I don't have details. Nobody ever gives us the details. You know that."

Jake was well aware of that fact. Another of the many reasons he quit. "And what were we supposed to do?"

Nelsen turned away and looked toward the north.

Wait a minute, Jake thought. What else was there? Tvchenko is dead. His assistant, the only other person who knew what he was up to, dead. Only the Kurds had the formula. Tvchenko's secret. Of course.

"That's it then," Jake said. "You're here to take the formula back to the Agency. So only the U.S. has it."

Nelsen swished his head back toward Jake. "What did you expect? You think we can let a bunch of goat herders have the most deadly nerve agent in the world?"

Jake had never even considered the fact that his government would want Tvchenko's agent. But of course they would. He had been such a fool in Odessa. All along he had played right into the government's little game again.

"I suppose there's no reward for the terrorist?"

"Is that how the station chief in Odessa lured you here?" Nelsen gave his first human smile.

"That fucker, Tully." Jake shook his head. It wasn't like Jake wouldn't have come to Kurdistan anyway, considering Sinclair Tucker was still missing. But the money would have been nice to at least cover expenses. Or maybe hospital bills. "So, they know we're here," Jake said. "What can we expect to accomplish now?"

Flipping the backpack from his shoulders, Nelsen opened the top and pulled out a package.

"C-4? You've got bullets flying at you, and you've got plastique strapped to your back?"

"Everybody has to die sometime."

Jake thought about the men who had just died. Had they gone for a righteous cause? Only time would tell.

"That's enough C-4 to take out half the village. We could destroy the lab and still find Sinclair Tucker."

"We take out the lab, and then get the hell out of Dodge. We don't even know where the Brit is being held."

"If Carzani is in the mosque, my guess is Tucker isn't far away. You take out the lab, I'll find Tuck."

Nelsen didn't like it, but he wasn't in any position to argue. "We go everywhere together. But first the lab."

48

Mesut Carzani swiveled back in his chair and swung around toward Omri Sherut. He was talking to Baskale on the radio.

"I know that," Carzani said, smiling. "I saw the helicopter crash from here. Were there any survivors?"

"I'm afraid so," came a muffled response.

"How many?"

"Two."

Sherut looked a bit concerned. "Does he know which men survived?"

There was no response.

"It doesn't matter, Omri," the Kurd said. "There are only two of them. We can handle that. Besides, they would be crazy to try anything. Only two men?"

Omri Sherut wasn't so sure. If one of them was Jake Adams, then crazy was the best way to describe him. He should have killed Adams in Odessa when he had the chance. He would have if it had been his choice.

"I don't think we should take these two men for granted," Sherut said. "They just might be crazy enough to try something."

❧

The woman crouched in the woods above the old barn, watching people come and go from the front door, yet still able to see the back, where goats and sheep had just been fed and watered by a teenaged boy. The barn looked like every other barn in the village, but she knew this one was different. Her people had found out about the large shipment of isopropyl alcohol to the barn, and she even knew about the two men who had been studying bio-chemistry in America, who she suspected were in there now mixing the compounds. She had learned all of this from her contact in Georgia. She knew she had only one choice, and that was to get what should have been hers in the first place.

The morning had broken. Villagers had started setting up a market on the street. A Saturday ritual. Women carried baskets on their heads. Young girls followed them with buckets. To the casual observer, it seemed like any other Turkish village. But this one was different. All the men were scattered about in small patrols. She had watched them form up an hour ago. Some headed down the mountain in trucks and set up a road block. Others had taken off on foot toward the crash site, searching the helicopter wreckage. She was still not certain of the nationality of that helicopter. The Kurds had been so quiet in the past month, not wanting to make waves, she suspected. Downing the helicopter would surely bring a retaliatory strike. Especially from the Turkish government. How much time would she have?

She sunk lower to the ground and covered herself with leaves and grass. Wait a minute, she thought. The Kurds must have known they could shoot down the chopper without fear of reprisal. Of course.

Jake and Steve Nelsen had managed to stay away from all the patrols, keeping as close to the rock cliff as possible. They sat now overlooking the Kurdish village.

Watching the morning activity in the village through binoculars, Jake couldn't help drawing similarities to his trips to the safe havens. The people had been so poor, yet they had this spirit and pride within them that all the money in the world couldn't buy. They could have been starving to death, but still made sure the children were fed and drank enough water. Halabja had been different, of course. Jake had been there secretly, much like now, but by the time he reached the Iraqi village, almost five thousand people had died. He had held the fifteen year old girl in his arms, trying to give her strength and courage to survive. She had lost everything. Her mother. Her father. All of her brothers and sisters. And why? Because she had gone alone to the neighboring village to buy a goat for the family. She had seen the jets fly in. Jets had been flying by for over eight years. It was all she could remember. Jake had learned all of this from her in the three days when she refused to leave his side.

Jake scanned the village from one side to the next. He saw the mosque. He saw the laboratory barn. He noticed where each sentry stood. How vigilant they were, or were not.

"What do you think?" Nelsen asked.

Jake lowered the binoculars to his chest. "I think we're nuts. The place looks like a military fort."

"What do you mean? All the men have gone off in other

directions."

"Looking for us. No doubt."

"True."

"Where were you planning on dropping the commandos?"

Nelsen pointed down the dirt road below the village. "We would have come in under darkness, though."

"Hardly. Who in the hell set up the timing? You, me and Garcia would have gotten here after the shooting started. In full daylight. We should have gotten here at midnight with night vision goggles...the works."

"I didn't plan this one," Nelsen said, his jaw clenched. "This one was Langley all the way."

"I had a feeling," he muttered. Jake looked out through the binoculars again. "The new Agency is just as fucked up as the old Agency."

"You got a better plan?"

Jake gazed back at Nelsen. "You got that right." He laid out what he thought they should do. When he was done, Nelsen let out a deep sigh and agreed. They would hold tight until dark.

Sinclair Tucker had heard about the American helicopter being shot down by a guard who had brought him his breakfast. It had been the arrogant young man in his early twenties. Tucker wondered now if his friend Jake Adams had been in the chopper. He knew that Jake was crazy enough to come after him. He smiled now, his first smile since he himself had crashed.

He tried to eat the mushy grain covered in goat's milk, but he couldn't force himself this time. His leg was feeling a little better. The swelling was down slightly.

Looking over at the co-pilot, he slid off of his makeshift bed and scooted over to the man in the flight suit. Tucker touched the man's hand, and quickly pulled his hand away. He was cold and clammy. He moved closer and checked for a carotid pulse. Nothing. He was dead.

Tucker flung the bowl of food against the stone wall. Now he was alone. His survival depended on keeping his mind fresh and nursing his leg. Heated anger flushed through his body. If he got a chance now, he would try to go after the guard.

Chavva was in a small cafe in the village, the only restaurant in town. She was drinking coffee and eating eggs with a slice of lamb.

She was wearing a black skirt that rested on her ankles, a tan blouse covered by a long leather jacket, and heel-less leather shoes. She could have fit into any Turkish village, and her Kurdish while ordering her food, had been perfect. Some things were never forgotten. The owner, an older woman, had mentioned she had not seen her in town before, and she had said she was visiting an old friend. Chavva knew the woman would never ask for a name. That was a trait of prying westerners.

She would walk the streets throughout the day, freely. And wait for her time. The night.

49

Darkness was complete across Kurdistan. Heavy clouds had moved in from the west, making it impossible to see more than a few feet in any direction. And that's exactly how Jake wanted it. He and Steve Nelsen had slowly crept down the side of the mountain, starting at ten. It was now almost midnight. Just eight hours before the Turkish Air Force was scheduled to bomb the area back to the stone age.

Jake and Steve were above the barn converted into a laboratory. They would enter from the back, one at a time. Jake agreed to go first.

He was outside the old wooden door that would normally be used to usher goats and sheep out of the elements, but was now locked tight with a padlock. He checked the strength of the wood. It was solid. He would never pick this lock.

He moved to his left where a window was covered with wood. It too was solid. Then he had a thought. The place was old. Many times there was space between the outside pens and the inside stalls. He climbed over the fence among the sleeping sheep. A few stirred as if a wolf was among the fold. He got to his knees and dug with his hands at the base of the building. First there was hay and sheep dung mixed, and then he felt a space. About six to eight inches. He stopped and listened. Nothing. Then he found a rock and started scraping away the loose dirt until he had more than a foot to crawl through.

In a second he was inside. He had only a small flashlight, but a dim red light shone from across the room, so he could make his way without stumbling and save the light. Other than the smell, the place was nothing like a barn. There were stainless steel benches, microscopes, refrigerators; all the equipment for a modern lab.

Jake wasn't sure what he was looking for. He hoped to find a folder or a file with the magical words "formula" sprawled across the front, but that wasn't likely. In the obscurity of near darkness, he started rummaging through a file cabinet. It was nearly empty. One drawer contained chemistry text books. Another had papers, copies of articles from prominent American and British medical journals. There was nothing here, Jake was sure.

He started closing the last drawer when he first heard the noise. It could have been a mouse or a rat, but it was more likely footsteps. Jake quickly ducked behind the metal cabinet and drew his pistol. He had to be careful, because Steve Nelsen was supposed to follow him there with the C-4.

In a moment a dark figure slid from the same direction he had come, probably the same hole. The person was too small for Nelsen. The movements were like that of a ballerina. Precise, quiet, and with perfect direction.

As a silhouette, Jake could see a gun in the person's right hand.

Now the figure was within arm's reach. Jake swung his foot up, knocking the gun from the hand and catching the person in the hip. Then he swept with his left foot and thrust with the butt of his gun at the person's chest, knocking the person to the ground. In a split second, he was on top of the body, his gun propped under a small chin.

The body struggled beneath him. Jake flicked the light on the person's face. For a moment Jake couldn't believe his eyes, and then the body seemed to settle down, as if it too understood something new. The hair was dark now instead of blonde.

"Helena," Jake said. "What in the hell are you doing here?"

Her jaw tried to move away from Jake's gun. "Could you put that away," she said softly. "It could go off."

He moved his hand to her shoulder, keeping her down on the cold cement floor. "Well?"

"You're smart. What do you think?"

Jake wondered for a moment. The last time he had seen her, he had just put her on a train for Yalta and told her to stay put for her own safety. He remembered her sad eyes. How she had not wanted to go. And just prior to all that, he had killed the man who had killed Petra, her best friend. He had questioned how the men knew they were at the place. How they had been discovered. Had she given them up?

"You tell me? I thought I sent you to Yalta."

She had an incredulous look across her beautiful face, as if she were playing her violin and a note she had never heard had escaped. "You don't understand, do you?"

That was an understatement. "Let me guess. You were working with Tvchenko."

She smiled. "Close."

"You were trying to get his formula for your government?"

"Better."

Jake thought again. Helena had traveled extensively while a musician under the old Soviet government. Of course, she had worked for them all along. "Okay. Either the old KGB, or the GRU. I'm betting on the GRU, since that's who Tvchenko had worked for."

"You are smart, Mr. Adams."

"And you've come for Tvchenko's formula. But it's not here."

"Are you sure?"

"About the formula?"

"About everything."

"You mean about you setting us up in Odessa? Why did you have Petra killed?"

Her expression turned grave. "I loved Petra. It wasn't me. If it had been, I would have done it myself. But she was my best friend. I thought you set us up."

"Me? Why?"

"It was too easy. You try to get what you want from her, when you find out she has nothing to tell, you have her killed. I hated you for it. My tears on the train were for you. Because I knew I would have to kill you, and I didn't like that one bit."

"I had nothing to do with it," Jake pleaded. "I was doing the Agency a favor. I told them I'd help out. They were short handed. Why in the hell would I kill Petra?"

"Well I knew it wasn't Quinn Armstrong. They were lovers."

"I thought so."

"Can you let me up? This floor is cold."

"You said you wanted to kill me."

"Then. Later my contacts told me who had given up Petra."

Jake put the light on her eyes. She tried to turn away. "Who?"

"I can't say."

"Can't, or won't?"

"There are some things that must remain secrets, even though our governments are no longer real enemies."

Jake couldn't argue with that. He didn't totally trust her, but wasn't certain what else to do. So he let her up. "Where do we go from here?"

She found her gun and put it back in its holster under her arm. "I have to have the formula. It was mine from the beginning. Tvchenko double crossed us. He was trying to set himself up for retirement. Working as many deals as possible."

"Do you know who killed him?"

"I thought you did."

Jake shook his head. "I was an innocent bystander at the conference."

Since the two of them had been talking, Steve Nelsen had no problem sneaking up on them.

"Who the hell is this," Nelsen asked.

Helena startled and reached for her gun.

"I wouldn't," Nelsen said, pointing his gun at her.

Jake gave Nelsen the quick version of who she was and what she was doing there. When he was done, Nelsen was shaking his head.

"This case is getting stranger by the minute," Nelsen said. "Anyone else you haven't told me about, Jake?"

Jake was about to answer, when there was a rattling at the front door only twenty feet away. Jake cut his light. The three of them breathed quietly in the darkness for five minutes.

Finally, Jake said, "Must have been a watch checking the locks. I say we get the hell out of here and head to the mosque." Jake's eyes had adjusted to the red light completely now, and he could see Helena's face. Nelsen was back in the shadows.

"You think Carzani has the formula?" she asked.

"It makes sense to me. You've got the most deadly nerve agent ever produced, you keep the formula close to home. Besides, I'm sure that's where they're keeping my friend, Sinclair Tucker."

Helena's eyes seemed to grow, as if the sound of Tucker's name would kill anyone who heard it. "Who is that?" she finally asked.

"A friend. I'd like to get him the hell out of here."

"Let me help," she said.

Nelsen moved forward quickly. "Wait a minute. I'm not letting some broad with GRU come along for the ride."

"What are you going to do, Steve. Kill her?"

Nelsen thought about that. "Maybe."

Jake gave a slight laugh. "Let's go. We've got work to do."

50

The mosque was a dark shape nestled against the side of the mountain. There was a dim light at the front gate and two more along a stone path that wound around to an outer entrance. That had bothered Jake all day as he watched the place through binoculars from high above. He had timed when people entered the front door to pray after the call to prayer from the minaret. Occasionally a suspicious few would divert around to the side. From satellite photographs, or even from a casual observer, the place appeared to be a simple village mosque. But it wasn't.

Jake had also timed how long each person stood watch at the front gate and at the side door. They were on for exactly four hours. He'd try to take advantage of that. It was half past midnight, a half hour away from watch change, and the guards might be tired.

Having just scaled the stone wall at its farthest point from the gate, Jake and Helena were sitting among a clump of bushes at the base of a huge oak, waiting for Steve Nelsen to make his move.

❧

Nelsen had scaled the wall on the opposite side of the gate, and made his way to behind the guard posted on a bench under a tree covered by a canvas awning.

The ground was damp with dew, so he could walk quietly. He crept closer. He could see the man now, an old Makarov cradled across his lap. He was an old man. Nelsen thought about that for a moment. Should he kill him? Or simply take him out?

Nelsen ducked under the tent awning. He was only a few feet from the old man now, yet he still wasn't sure what he would do. He reached down swiftly with his right arm, pulled the man off the bench by his neck. The Makarov dropped to the ground. With his massive power, Nelsen lifted the man high in the air and twisted to throw him over his shoulder, when the neck snapped. The old man's body went limp and crumpled to the ground at Nelsen's feet. Damn it! Nelsen hurried from under the tent, which faced the gate, and searching the outer perimeter, he made his way toward Jake and Helena.

"First one's down," Nelsen whispered.

Jake pointed toward the side door, and all three of them took off quietly.

In thirty seconds they were in place to take out the next guard. There was no good approach to this man without being spotted. So Jake would be a decoy drawing the man out, while Nelsen caught him from the side.

This guard was big, almost as large as Nelsen. And he had an M-16 with a standard 30-round magazine. He might not go quietly.

Jake came out of the bushes and strolled up the brick

walkway. He hoped the man wouldn't shoot first and ask questions later.

When Jake was thirty yards away, the man startled and trained his gun on him. Jake thought of diving to the grass, but he held his ground. He knew a few Kurdish phrases. Maybe that would give him time. "I've come to pray to Allah." Sure it was lame, but he had to try.

The man moved closer.

Come on, Jake thought. A few feet more.

As the guard came within range, a leg flew out of nowhere sending the Kurd to the stone path. Then the two men struggled on the ground. Jake hurried forward and moved the guard's gun out of reach. Jake was about to help Nelsen when there was a single silenced shot and the Kurd had a shocked look on his face, along with a bullet hole in his forehead. The Kurd hit the ground as if Nelsen had thrown a sack of grain.

Helena stood a few yards away and slowly lowered her silenced 9mm. "You were making too much noise," she explained.

Nelsen dragged the man into the bushes.

Jake checked the M-16 over to make sure there was a round chambered. They could use the extra firepower.

They went into the open corridor, down the long exposed hallway, with arched brick facing a garden, and stopped outside a large wooden door.

Nelsen pulled Jake back. He checked his watch. "Just a minute." He glanced back toward the edge of the village, where the laboratory barn was.

"When did you set it for?" Jake asked.

"About..." Nelsen checked his watch again.

There was a huge explosion across town, with an instant

fireball rising up through the night air. The orange plume rolled upward as if God were pulling a yo-yo from a tremendous campfire.

"Now!"

Jake could feel the percussion as the ground shook with the force of a great earthquake.

The three of them climbed over the wall, through an arched window, into a garden on the other side. They crouched in bushes.

"Carzani will send some of his best men to check on the explosion," Helena said. "We'll shoot them once they clear the door."

In a few seconds four men came flying out the wooden door and hesitated for a second, looking at the fire ball across town.

Without thinking, Jake leveled the M-16 and sprayed the men on full auto. All four crashed to the stone floor.

"Hurry!" Helena said, jumping the wall.

Jake and Nelsen were right on her tail, locking the door behind them.

Inside was another corridor with another door at the far end. That one was closed. They slipped forward in the darkness, checking in front and behind them with each step. As they neared the door, voices echoed from behind it. Jake couldn't make out what was being said.

Instinctively, the three of them knew what they had to do. But then Jake stopped them with a halting hand. "If we take them alive," he whispered, "we have a much greater chance of finding the formula, and knowing if it's the only copy."

Nelsen and Helena gazed at each other. They nodded.

Jake reached for the handle. With one swift pull, he

flung the door open, and Nelsen and Helena rushed in.

Jake followed with the M-16.

A young man startled and leveled his rifle at the trio. Helena shot him three times in the chest. He crashed backward against a console.

An older man screamed to stop, his hands in the air. They were the only two in the room.

Jake stood at the door, slightly ajar, watching their back.

"Move away from the radio," Nelsen yelled in Turkish, his gun pointed at the man's head.

The older man's eyes pierced through Nelsen, not even blinking.

"Move away!" Nelsen repeated.

Slowly the man shuffled to one side. "What do you want?" the man asked in English.

"Mesut Carzani?"

The man smiled. "So you know my name? What are you doing in Kurdistan? You are in free and autonomous Kurdistan, and you will be tried and shot as spies."

"He's got balls," Nelsen whispered over his shoulder to Jake. "I want Tvchenko's formula."

Carzani laughed out loud. Then his face turned grave. "You will get the business end. You just blew up our lab. The nerve agent is everywhere in the air."

Nelsen looked back at Jake, raising his brows.

"You have a twenty-mile-an-hour wind out of the south," Jake said. "The explosion would have quickly disbursed the compound high into the air, and the wind will push it up the canyon, combining with the downward thermals from the mountains. You might have to replace some sheep and goats. I hope your men have enough sense to stay away for a few hours."

Carzani thought about that for a moment. "Can you at least close the door?"

Jake thought about what he himself had just said. But what if the wind shifted? He slowly closed the door.

"The formula?" Nelsen said.

The Kurd's eyes shifted toward a fire safe along one wall.

"So, it's in there?" Nelsen asked. "Open it!"

Carzani hesitated.

Jake leveled the M-16 on the box.

"Wait!" Carzani yelled. "It's wired. I must disarm it or we will all die." Carzani went to the safe, pulled a key from around his neck, slowly opened the box part way, and then disconnected a trip wire inside and brought the top all the way open.

Helena rushed toward the box. As she did, there was a flash from the side and she swiveled toward the floor, returning fire twice.

Before Jake or Nelsen knew what had happened, Carzani was on his stomach, a bullet in his right lung and another in his liver. Near the fire safe, Helena lay on her back holding her left shoulder.

Jake ran to her and set the rifle on the floor. "Let me see it?"

She reluctantly removed her hand.

The bullet had entered her shoulder, but he couldn't find an exit wound.

Her chest was heaving from the pain.

"Can you breathe normally?" Jake asked. "Slow down and try to breathe normally."

She took in a deep breath and let it out slowly.

"Does it hurt to breathe?" Jake asked.

She shook her head.

"Can you talk?"

"Yes," she forced out. "What do you want me to say? It hurts like hell."

She was a tough one, Jake thought.

"What about Carzani?" she asked.

Jake gazed over at Nelsen, who had checked on the Kurdish leader. Nelsen shook his head.

"He's seen better days," Jake said. Then Jake rolled Helena over to her side. There was a growing spot of blood on her shoulder. Jake quickly unbuttoned her top and pulled it down over her shoulder. There was an exit wound on the far side of her scapula. Two more inches and the bullet would have severed her spine. But that was the good news. The bullet had probably missed bone completely. If it had hit anything hard, it could have turned inward toward vital organs. But the bullet had even missed her lungs, since the blood was dark red. Jake ripped a piece of cloth from Helena's shirt and stuffed it over the exit wound. Then he found some wide, heavy duct tape on the console and he patched the wound. He did the same to her shoulder where the bullet had entered.

In a few minutes Helena was sitting up. "What about the formula?" she asked.

Nelsen was busy looking through the safe. Most of the documents were written in Turkish, and probably Kurdish. Finally, he pulled out a package of papers with Slavic writing and chemical diagrams. "Got it."

"I don't think so," came a voice from the inner door, which was wide open now. Jake and Nelsen had been so preoccupied, they hadn't noticed the man enter.

Jake glared at the man, who was holding an automatic

pistol on them. It was Chavva's boss, Omri Sherut. "So, Omar. I see you didn't get on that flight to Tel Aviv."

"Nor did you look up some old friend," Sherut said with a gap-toothed smile.

This was the first time Jake had seen the man without his huge bodyguard, or whatever he was. He had to be somewhere close.

"You can give those papers to me," Sherut said, his hand outstretched toward Nelsen.

"Who the hell is this?" Nelsen asked Jake. "You know this Bozo?"

"We've met. My guess is Mossad."

"Well I'm Agency," Nelsen reminded the room. "Last time I looked, we were on the same side."

Omri Sherut laughed. "When the moon is full on a leap year."

"A fucking comedian," Nelsen said. He had returned his gun to its holster while searching through the papers, and he thought of pulling it now.

Jake was five feet from the M-16. His own 9mm was also in its holster inside his leather jacket. "Put the gun away, Omar. I'm sure our governments will work out some sort of deal. They always do."

"Not this time," Sherut said, his gun still trained on Nelsen. "This one's for me."

Jake considered that. Had Sherut been working for himself all along? Jake didn't get a chance to find out.

There were three shots from the open door that Sherut had entered. The Israeli's gun dropped to the floor. And Omri Sherut, as if in slow motion, sunk to his knees.

Jake pulled his gun.

Nelsen drew his.

Out of the darkness came Chavva. She walked up to Sherut, who was still on his knees in obvious pain. "You fucking pig!" she screamed in Hebrew. Then she switched languages and spouted off in a long recitation, as if she were a teacher lecturing an errant student.

Jake watched her in awe. She was dressed in all black, and it clung to her perfect body. A body he had seen and felt and made love to. He had known she was dangerous, and that had been part of the attraction. Yet, here she was now, having just shot a man. A man Jake had thought she worked for. Something didn't quite add up.

When she was done yelling, she finally regarded Jake with a smile. "I had a feeling you would come," she said.

"You know her too?" Nelsen asked.

"Afraid so. Odessa was a crazy town."

"Who are they, Jake?" Chavva asked, nodding toward Nelsen and Helena.

Jake explained who they were. Nelsen still had his gun out, but Jake had relaxed slightly. Looking at Chavva he finally realized what was going on. He had watched Chavva lecture Sherut, and the little girl in her seemed to leap forward, out and away from that tough exterior. He had suspected all along that there was something special about Chavva, but it took that very moment to confirm his suspicions. She had become the 15-year-old girl in Halabja, tears in her eyes, wondering how anyone could be so inhuman. He returned his gun to his holster and walked toward Chavva.

"You were Halabja," Jake said to her. "Tvchenko was talking about you. You killed him."

"I had to Jake. Nobody should make weapons like that." Chavva still had her gun out, but it was poised on

Sherut. "Jake. How could he do this?"

Omri Sherut let out one last gasp and then dropped to his side, looking up to Chavva with wonder in his eyes.

Jake put his hand on Chavva's shoulder. She turned and settled into his arms. "It's okay, Chavva. It's over."

51

Finding out where the Kurds were keeping Sinclair Tucker wasn't a difficult task. Chavva had come across the primitive cells in the depths of the catacombs while making her way toward Carzani's control center.

She and Jake were now sneaking through the near darkness of the damp passageways, with the only light coming from low-watt bulbs strung like Christmas lights down the center of the arched ceiling.

After a short distance they came upon a crumpled body. Jake shone the flashlight on the huge form. It was Omri Sherut's bodyguard.

"Some of your work, I suppose," Jake whispered to Chavva.

She shrugged. "He got in my way."

They continued on, both with their guns drawn.

When they reached the cell area, they became more cautious. There were six cells in all. Three on each side. Chavva was on one side and Jake on the other. The first two doors were open, so they each slammed inward simultaneously, their guns leading the way.

Nothing.

They were empty.

The middle doors were closed, but the far end doors were open. They slipped past the center ones and smashed through the last two.

Nothing.

There was a passageway on the far wall with a closed door. Jake pointed toward it. She motioned that she had come from that way. She had told Jake earlier in the control room that there was a back entrance from the mountain side.

"Tuck. Are you in here?" Jake asked, breaking the silence.

After a moment. "Jake, is that you?"

"Damn straight."

Jake and Chavva moved to the outside of Tucker's cell.

"How'd you get here? You crazy bastard." Tucker laughed softly to himself.

"Same as you. Helicopter. Only mine blew up after I got out."

"Great. I heard an explosion a while back. Was that you?"

While they were talking, Jake and Chavva were both looking for some way to get in. The wooden door was by no means impenetrable, but there was nothing to even pry at it with. It appeared like an old skeleton lock.

"Stand to the side, Tuck. I'm going to shoot the lock."

Jake shot once and missed the metal throw. The second shot hit metal, but the lock held. After the third and fourth shots, Jake decided to try the strength. He kicked the door and it went inward partially, leaving a one inch gap. The second kick did the trick, the door flung open.

Inside, Sinclair Tucker was crouched low against the

side wall, next to a body covered with a blanket.

Chavva waited at the door, her gun still drawn.

Jake helped Tucker to his feet. "You look like shit, Tuck. You smell too."

"I've been here a while, you bloke. Besides, you don't smell great yourself."

Jake had forgotten about crawling through sheep shit to get into the lab earlier.

"I was meaning to ask you about that," Chavva said.

Jake shrugged and then pointing to the covered man at their feet. "The co-pilot?"

"He died a while back," Tucker said. "They wouldn't remove him. The bastards. I don't know how much longer I could have lasted. Thanks Jake." Then Tucker nodded toward Chavva. "Who's this lovely woman."

"I'll explain later. Right now we've got to get the hell out of here."

Jake propped the Brit's arm over his shoulder and started to work his way toward the door.

Tucker stopped him. "We can't leave him here."

"We don't have a choice." Jake checked his watch. "If we don't get out of here soon, the Turks will level the town. Unless we can convince them not to."

Jake saw the movement behind Chavva's shoulder before he knew precisely what was happening. The door across the corridor was opening. With one sudden and fluid motion, Jake pulled his gun and fired twice, just to the side of Chavva's shoulder.

Chavva jumped and then turned to see what Jake had shot.

A man lay crumpled face down on the cement, an M-16 under his chin.

"That's the prick of a guard who kept kicking my broken leg," Tucker said. "Damn it, Jake. I wish I'd done that myself."

The three of them made their way back down the dark corridor to the control room. Nelsen was on the phone when they arrived. Helena was resting on the floor, sitting up against one wall.

"What's the word?" Jake asked.

Nelsen quieted him with the palm of his hand. "But we're stuck here, sir. The entire area is swarming with Peshmerga Guerrillas." He paused for a moment. "Yes. Yes. I can't leave Garcia. I understand. Yes, I have it." He looked at Jake. "He's with me. I don't think he's aware of that. Yes, sir." Nelsen waited for a moment, and then slammed the phone down. "Son of a bitch."

"What now?" Jake asked.

"They refuse to stop the air strike."

"What?"

"The Turks want to take advantage of the opportunity," Nelsen explained. "Besides, the Agency tends to agree with them. They want to make sure there are no other copies of this formula out there, or anyone who knows anything about it."

"How much time do we have?" Jake asked.

Nelsen checked his watch. "Three hours before they level everything east of Lake Van along this mountain ridge."

"They're not going to bomb the city of Van."

"No!"

Jake saw the troubled look on Chavva's face. She had to be thinking of the Iraqi jets dropping chemical weapons on her city as a child. "We have to leave, Chavva."

"I can't go," she muttered. "I must warn the people. Most of them have done nothing. They just want a home-land. You go. Go now."

Jake gazed around the room, and for the first time, noticed Tucker had gone over to Helena and was sitting next to her. Jake hurried to his friend. "You know each other?" Jake asked Tucker.

"I'll explain later." Tucker said, and then gave Helena a kiss on the cheek.

Nelsen came over with the Tvchenko folder. "This is getting too weird. Now these two know each other?"

"Afraid so." Jake was starting to understand how, with-out Tucker's explanation. Sinclair had said he was run-ning an agent, and now he knew who.

"I can't let you go!" Chavva yelled.

When the four of them turned, they saw Chavva point-ing her gun toward them.

Jake moved away from the others. "What are you doing, Chavva?"

"I'm sorry Jake. I must have the formula."

"For who?"

She hesitated and tears streaked her cheeks. "For me. The formula is for me."

Nelsen had the folder in his hands, and Jake quickly pulled them away from the larger man. "Don't give them over Jake."

Jake moved closer to Chavva with the papers. "You don't want these for your Israeli friends, or for your Kurdish ancestors?"

She shook her head.

Jake pulled out a metal trash can from under the con-sole, dumped out the garbage, and set the papers inside.

"Do the honors, Chavva." Jake backed away.

She squirted lighter fluid on the papers and lit a cigarette lighter.

"No!" Nelsen screamed. "That's the most important weapon developed in decades." He thought about going for his gun.

"Don't you see, Nelsen," Jake said. "She knows this more than any of us. She's been there. Nobody should have this one."

Sinclair and Helena agreed with silence.

Nelsen was alone, yet even he wasn't protesting with any great vigor. He didn't say another word.

Chavva lit a small piece of paper and threw it into the can, which went up in a puff of flames. The room filled with smoke, but within a few minutes, the entire Tvchenko file was nothing but ashes. Chavva dumped the smoldering paper, which was light and fluffy now, onto the cement floor, and then dispersed them into nothing. There was no way to reconstruct the most deadly nerve gas ever conceived. It too was nothing more than thoughts in the air of the dead.

Sinclair Tucker helped Helena to her feet, and they stood together where neither could have probably done so on their own.

"Let's go ladies and gentlemen," Tucker said. "Before we end up like those papers."

Nelsen shook his head with a strange smirk. He realized that maybe thousands of lives would be saved by that one simple act by a courageous woman he didn't even know.

The five of them headed out toward the back door. As they reached the cell area, a flash of gunfire pierced the silence. They all dove to the side.

Jake and Nelsen quickly returned fire.

"Where's it coming from?" Sinclair yelled. He was on the ground with his arms wrapped around Helena.

"The middle cell across from your old home," Jake answered.

Jake, Nelsen and Chavva returned fire.

"Is that you, Mr. Agency man," came a voice from the cell.

Nelsen clenched his jaw. "Baskale!" he yelled.

"A good memory. I like that."

"You know him?" Jake asked.

"The Kurd from Texas," Nelsen said. "I had to know someone here." He smiled. "What do you want?" he barked at Baskale.

There was hesitation. "The formula."

"Too late. It's gone."

"I don't believe you."

Chavva yelled something in Kurdish and there was silence for a moment. The only words Jake understood for sure were Carzani and Halabja.

In a moment there was sobbing from the cell. Then a rifle slid out through the opening.

Nelsen frowned at Jake, and gazed at Chavva with surprise.

Chavva walked up to the cell, opened it, and looked down on Baskale, who was huddled in a ball. By now Jake and Nelsen had reached the cell.

Nelsen reached down and pulled the man to his feet. When his eyes met the large Agency man, Baskale's face turned to anger. He took a wild swing at Nelsen, catching him with a glancing blow to the chin, but barely fazing

Nelsen. Nelsen retaliated with a quick flurry of punches to the stomach and then the face, and he followed up with a straight kick to the man's jaw. Baskale collapsed to the cell floor. Out cold.

Chavva helped them out the back way. She agreed to get them started on the road to Van, but wouldn't leave the village before warning the people. They could have a truck she had stashed on the edge of town. She handed Jake the keys. There was still a few hours before the Turks would sweep in and bomb the place.

Jake pulled Chavva aside. "Come with us," he pleaded. "We still haven't gone out." He tried a smile.

"I can't," she cried. "Besides, I'd rather stay in like last time."

"I'll wait for you in Adana or Istanbul."

She pulled out a Turkish driver's license and handed it to Jake. "Here. I live there in Istanbul. Meet me there." She pulled him to her and they kissed for a long moment. "Two days," she whispered and smiled.

Then she was off into the darkness.

52

ODESSA, UKRAINE

Over thirty hours had passed since the Turks swept down out of the west in their F-16s, came in low over Lake Van, and dropped their 500 pound bombs. The attack had been more of a show than anything, with no casualties reported in all of Kurdistan. In fact, only four jets had dropped bombs.

Jake had said goodbye to Sinclair Tucker and Helena at the Diyarbakir hospital, where they both required medical attention, he with a cast and her with a better bandage. Jake had agreed to call him in London in a week to see how he was doing. He didn't expect to see Helena again. And that was a shame, because she was quite a woman. Tuck explained how she had been working as a double agent with the GRU and him. The two of them had become close, to say the least.

At Incirlik Air Base near Adana, Jake and Steve Nelsen had returned only momentarily to retrieve their bags. Baskale, Nelsen's prisoner, had been out cold for much of the trip. The Agency would take him to America, without regard for international extradition laws. While at Incirlik, Nelsen had briefed Jake on what the Director of Operations for the Agency, Kurt Jenkins, had told him on the phone when they were back in Carzani's operations center. The U.S. Air Force master sergeant who had tried to get their attention while lifting off on the mission had been trying to deliver a message from the DO, who had word that they might have been compromised. Nelsen would have to live with the decision to ignore that man for the rest of his life. Ten men had died, including his partner Ricardo Garcia. That fact had finally hit Nelsen, who had become extremely reticent.

Worse than anything for Jake, perhaps, was the news that Quinn Armstrong had been killed in Odessa just after Jake had departed. Jake had tried to sleep on that fact for a few hours, but it had become useless to even try. He knew what he had to do, and he wasn't going to enjoy it one bit. Somehow it had all clicked in his mind, and the bile rose up to his throat just thinking about it.

He was back in Odessa now. He had gone to the hotel, retrieved his 9mm from the safe, and was leaning against the wall in an apartment complex. He had never been there before, but had gotten the address from the DO before leaving Turkey.

It was just after noon and pouring rain outside. It was the kind of day that drove the solemn to insanity.

Jake was breathing hard. He tried to calm himself, but it was no use. He reached down for the handle on the door and let it sit there a moment. He pulled his Glock, thought of charging in, but then slipped the gun behind his back into his pants.

The door was unlocked. He slowly opened it.

Inside, the room was dark but everything was still in plain view. The man Jake had come to see was slouched back on the sofa, a glass of whiskey in his left hand and a cigarette dangling from the side of his mouth.

"So, Jake. You're back in Odessa," Tully O'Neill said. "Have a seat."

He was slurring his words. Jake could tell he was on his way to a great drunk. If he hadn't already reached there.

"Why?" Jake said.

"So you don't have to stand?" Tully laughed and then coughed until he inhaled on his cigarette.

Sitting on the table in front of Tully was his own 9mm automatic and an extra magazine, fully loaded. Jake assumed the magazine in the butt of the gun was also full.

"You know what I mean, Tully. Why did you sell us all out? Money?"

Tully swished his head from side to side. "You'd never understand. Just go back to your private practice and find some missing person, or save a Goddamned cat from a fucking tree, or whatever it is you do now. I don't need you. I don't need anybody."

Jake didn't like where the conversation was heading. "I could see someone giving the locals special consideration, like you did with Victor Petrov. You figure, 'what the fuck' make a few bucks off the Ukrainian Agriculture Ministry." Jake watched Tully's eyes, then continued on. "Then you decide to work a deal with Omri Sherut, who, I might add, sold you out pal." A little lie never hurt, Jake thought.

"You don't know what the fuck you're talking about."

"I know enough, Tully. You set up the hit on MacCarty

and Swanson, which is the only thing I don't fully understand, since they only wanted to set up a damn fertilizer
and pesticide facility."

"I'm supposed to know that?" Tully mumbled.

"You had them killed for nothing!"

"I didn't do it. I swear. It was Sherut. He thought they
had worked a deal with Tvchenko, since you were the last
to talk with him, and you worked for them."

Jake felt like pulling his gun and shooting the bastard
right through the skull. He was breathing harder now.
"You knew that wasn't true!" Jake yelled.

"Sherut wouldn't listen. He wanted to cut down all the
competition."

Jake shifted his stance, his hands on his hip ready to pull
his gun. "You knew Tvchenko had sold out to the Kurds
before I even got here, and that the Kurds and Sherut were
simply cleaning up all the loose ends. You had overheard
all that from the tapes. You had Quinn bring them to you
so you could hear them exclusively. You also knew that
Petra Kovarik had contacted the GRU and was thinking of
selling what she knew. That's why you sent Sherut's men
to kill her. And me. Or anyone else who got in the way.
The man I shot at the apartment was one of Sherut's men.
I didn't realize it until much later, when Sherut only had
one goon at his side. I connected the dots."

Tully lit another cigarette from the butt of the first, and
then finished his glass of whiskey. "You're a clever young
man, Jake Adams. I could use a guy like you working for
me."

"Yeah, right. Like Quinn Armstrong?"

Tully looked away and then down at his gun on the
table.

"You want to explain Quinn?" Jake asked.

Tully thought for a moment. "I never wanted him to die. He was a good man."

"But?"

"He was too good. He found out about us. He would have blown the whole deal."

"So, you blow his brains out?" Jake slid his right hand farther back on his hip, and fought off the urge to kill Tully.

Tully shook his head and inhaled deeply on the cigarette. Then he picked up the gun and stared at it. "We all die a little every day, Jake. Sometimes it's better to go quickly. Life is more painful."

Jake was about to slide his hand back to his gun, when Tully quickly shoved the barrel into his mouth and pulled the trigger. The shot was muffled, but there was a hole in the back of Tully's head, with blood and brains splattered on the wall behind the sofa. Tully lay slumped awkwardly on the sofa like an old man who had fallen asleep in front of the television.

"Damn it, Tully," Jake muttered. "Why?"

Jake left the apartment and took a cab to the airport. He checked his watch. His flight to Istanbul wouldn't leave for another hour.

During the cab ride, he pulled Chavva's driver's license from his pocket. He smiled looking at her face. She was so beautiful. Maybe she could finally leave her past behind, forget about the horror she had known, that which had become so much a part of her. Maybe he could help her forget with time.

ISTANBUL, TURKEY

It was early evening, a red glow hanging over the tall minuets of the Blue Mosque.

The call to prayer echoed through the narrow streets as Jake walked along a busy market where vendors were selling fruits and vegetables, rugs and clothes, and live poultry.

He checked the address one more time and looked up to the second floor of an apartment building. He smiled and went inside, making his way up the stone steps.

When he reached the second floor, he found the door and stood for a moment wondering if she was even there. He started to knock, when the door slowly opened on him.

Standing inside, her dark hair resting on broad shoulders, Chavva smiled at him. Her large round eyes searched him carefully for any imperfection.

He went inside and she closed the door, turning back toward him.

"Finally," she said. "You keep a date without sneaking into my room and pulling my naked body from my bed."

He took her in his arms and they kissed for a long while.

"I was hoping to find you like that again."

She kissed him quickly. "We have time."

CPSIA information can be obtained at www.ICGtesting.com
Printed in the USA
LVOW13s0120160714

394551LV00013B/252/P

9 781609 770228